ONE WEDDING AND AN EARL

#4 The Duchess Society Series

BY

TRACY SUMNER

WOLF PUBLISHING

One Wedding and an Earl by Tracy Sumner

Published by WOLF Publishing UG

Copyright © 2022 Tracy Sumner
Text by Tracy Sumner
Edited by Chris Hall
Cover Art by Victoria Cooper
Paperback ISBN: 978-3-98536-142-7
Hard Cover ISBN: 978-3-98536-143-4
Ebook ISBN: 978-3-98536-141-0

WOLF Publishing - This is us:

Two sisters, two personalities.. But only one big love!

Diving into a world of dreams..

...Romance, heartfelt emotions, lovable and witty characters, some humor, and some mystery! Because we want it all! Historical Romance at its best!

Visit our website to learn all about us, our authors and books!

Sign up to our mailing list to receive first hand information on new releases, freebies and promotions as well as exclusive giveaways and sneak-peeks!

WWW.WOLF-PUBLISHING.COM

Also by Tracy Sumner

The Duchess Society Series

The DUCHESS SOCIETY is a steamy new Regency-era series. Come along for a scandalous ride with the incorrigible ladies of the Duchess Society as they tame the wicked rogues of London! Second chance, marriage of convenience, enemies to lovers, forbidden love, passion, scandal, ROMANCE.

If you enjoy depraved dukes, erstwhile earls and sexy scoundrels, untamed bluestockings and rebellious society misses, the DUCHESS SOCIETY is the series for you!

#1 The Brazen Bluestocking

#2 The Scandalous Vixen

#3 The Wicked Wallflower

#4 One Wedding and an Earl

#5 Two Scandals and a Scot

Prequel to the series: The Ice Duchess

Christmas novella: The Governess Gamble

ONE WEDDING
AND
AN
&ARL

He's more of myself than I am. Whatever our souls are made of, his and mine are the same.

Emily Bronte

Epiphanies

His

Where a boy learns his father is a very cruel man indeed

Ollie's stomach tilted as the village constable dragged his brother down the winding drive leading from the estate.

Xander Macauley didn't struggle, didn't once glance toward his window. He wasn't going to forgive this transgression, not ever. Ollie had had one chance to have even a sliver of a family, and he'd ruined it. Been too cowardly to speak up, and now it was too late.

When he could no longer see the figures in the setting sun, Ollie swallowed his misery, his heart lodged in his throat. With an oath that shouldn't pass the lips of an eleven-year-old boy, he cracked his forehead against the glass pane. His shoulder ached to the bone, dislocated a week ago, and popped back in place by the sibling he'd come to love this summer.

A young man who thought Ollie had betrayed him.

Oliver. His father preferred Oliver. He would never be Ollie again.

Anger took him on a raging river, emotion he rarely allowed. His elevated position as the future earl hammered into his brain long enough to keep him wary of every move he made. Before he took his next breath, he was striding down the corridor and into his father's study, the glossy walnut door that had kept him out since birth slapping against the wall.

His father glanced up from the ledgers spread across his desk, eyes exactly like his *and* Xander's heating behind wire frames. Their shade was unusual, tarnished silver, nothing else like them in England. In the world, though Ollie hadn't yet seen much of that. Enough resemblance to declare Xander as his father's bastard as incontrovertibly as a brand.

"*Oliver.*" His father snapped his quill to the desk, a move that displayed the impatience his calm tone buried. His face was flushed, his hair unkempt, his clothing rumpled. The room reeked of brandy and sweat. Since his wife's death, the earl did nothing in half measure, including slowly killing himself. "You know not to interrupt when I'm working. The earldom doesn't run itself. I only pray you can pull your weight when the time comes. Not lose what the title stands for, as seems to happen with the younger set."

Ollie advanced until his knees, quivering but concealed by woolen trousers that were also good at concealing bruises from his father's temper, bumped the massive mahogany desk. A family treasure his great-grandfather had won in a horse race with the Duke of Manchester in 1788. He'd often imagined dying slumped atop it, the earldom swallowing him whole. "Xander didn't steal your pocket watch."

The fifth Earl of Stanford bowed his head, his laugh dry and hard, pure contempt for the boy that would be the sixth flowing between them. Wrestling a cheroot from his waistcoat pocket, he took flint to tinder, set flame to tip. "I know that, silly lad. It was that imbecilic footman, Alexander. I only brought him on as a favor to my solicitor. He's known the family since the Dark Ages. Trying to get him off the savage city streets, bring him to the country." He sucked in a breath and released a rank, filmy vapor into the air. It swirled about his head like the mist that enfolded the meadows surrounding the estate. "He's suffering due punishment, then he'll be sent back to London to make his way as best he can. I've been charitable and found him a position as a chimney sweep. You'd better be thankful that half brother of yours has too hulking a frame to be a climbing boy or that's what he would have got, too."

Black dots swirled before Ollie's vision, his eyes pricking with tears. Xander's sentence was worse than this, even. "If you knew he was innocent... then *why*? Why send your son away? Why let him think I betrayed his trust? He'll be returned to the workhouse, my lord, the *workhouse*." Xander had told him tales of the place, haunting, horrible tales of beatings and gruel served with worm-ridden bread. Sickness and despair, such things a child should never see. He'd alleged that Ollie would never make it a month there, what with his feeble lungs and forgiving nature. Ollie wanted to argue, had even started to before shutting up because he feared his brother was right.

Xander Macauley was anything but forgiving. His belligerence was one point in his favor. The tough survived in forbidding worlds, it seemed.

The earl braced his fists on the desk and rose, close enough to strike, a sufficient threat to have Ollie backing up a step. "He's the child of a doxie I made the crude error of associating with in my youth. She was as beautiful as they come, and he has her look about him, I'll admit. That is my only excuse. He's nothing more to either of us, Oliver. Those damned eyes gave me little alternative but to recognize him. You have them, too, curse it. This little gift tossed in my lap, a stolen timepiece, presented a satisfactory solution. No one expects me to house a common thief, a rookery rat, due to a trace of shared blood crawling through our veins." He thumped his fist to the desk. Three defining knocks. "You'd best, and *soon*, my boy, forget him."

Ollie took a breath, a big, stinking-of-smoke one. He kept himself from coughing by sheer will when his lungs were burning from the effort. He waged a fight with himself to steady his voice during these confrontations. To sound steady and sure, like Xander always did, not rasping and feeble.

His lungs *were* weak; he was scrawny. But he was growing. Getting stronger every day. Xander had said he would likely be as tall as he was someday. The moment Ollie could leave, he would. Find his brother. Apologize. Beg if he had to. He could send a note easily from Harrow, take a hack, and meet him in the city. It didn't have to be long; he was returning to school in less than a month.

He'd repair this muddle. Because no boy should grow up without his brother by his side. It was the best plan for both of them.

"I can see the wheels spinning, lad. Christ, if you don't have your mother's impotent tendency to let every emotion show on your face. It's a handsome face, however, so there is that. Spineless *and* unattractive would have been a trial to overcome." He leaned until his fetid breath rushed past Ollie's cheek. Until there was no whisper of sound aside from the wind shrieking against the fogged panes, the tick of a clock on the mantel signaling the end of this childhood. "There'll be no more Harrow. I've let them know you aren't returning and have arranged for a local tutor. Derbyshire's best, I'm told. Where I can keep a close watch on my ailing heir. An heir who crafted foolish notions about his bastard brother this summer and brought this conclusion down on his own head."

Ollie squeezed his eyes shut, blocking out the shimmer of delight rippling across his father's face. He was going to be sick all over this bloody desk that his father loved more than he loved his sons. Sinking into the armchair, he dropped his head to his hands. His lungs would not, at the moment, allow enough air to keep him standing. "You can't. You won't. You don't even like when I'm around. Send me away, let me go."

"Ah, dear lad, you know I can. I will. I *have*. From now on, it's just you and me."

Hers
Where a girl learns the true meaning of the word "alone"

Necessity Byrne flicked the tattered curtain aside and glanced at the squalid lane where she'd spent her entire life. Shoreditch remained unaffected by calamity, while in this neat little abode, the silence was deafening, the air dense with ripples of disease and death.

She bit back a curse—and the urge to smash every chipped dish in the dwelling upon the scuffed plank floor. *Nothing* had changed out there when everything in this cozy nook that had once been her home was altered. The clomp of horse hooves on the pitted dirt path, shouts of vendors hawking fish and baked chestnuts. Carts, children, dogs, and rubbish littered about. The usual chaos in the slums.

She nudged a stray flower petal with the toe of her tatty slipper. The vase on the table held two roses, one for each decade of her parent's marriage. Vibrant crimson last week, now wilted gray. Like her future, unless she came up with a plan.

Holding back tears, Necessity patted her coat pocket and shot a glance at the rucksack at her feet.

She had foodstuff for a week *if* she rationed carefully. Fifty shillings in the leather bag she'd taken from beneath her parent's straw mattress. Her mother's pearl ring, her father's pocket watch. Items she suspected she'd have to sell at some point. It would kill her, but she was a rational girl who understood ugly things must happen to survive. Her sketch book with notes on the herb garden she'd been planning to plant in the spring. A packet of lavender and rosemary seeds purchased at Spitalfields market just two short weeks ago. She was proficient with medicinal properties of plants, a skilled gardener, a talent she hoped to turn into a business someday.

She had plans and a blaze in her belly to accomplish them. Add desperation to the mix, having not a *soul* in the world to count on, and Necessity had no choice but to succeed. She smoothed her hand down her coat, hitched up her trousers. Her brother's clothing. As he'd no longer be needing them.

Pressing her palm to the glass, the chill landed hard in her chest. The scent of her mother's perfume filtered through with her indrawn sigh. The aroma of roasted meat, an extravagance they couldn't often afford but had managed recently to celebrate her brother Tom's birthday, lingered. Raucous laughter lived in this room. The image of Jane sprawled on the armchair by the fire, a book in her hands. Alfie drawing as he'd loved to do, his gap-tooth smile lighting up the space.

These were lifeless remembrances now. Faded and more so every day, like cloth sitting too long in the sun. Cholera had taken her family down like a scythe to wheat. One day standing, the next decimated. For reasons she couldn't understand, leaving only her standing.

She hitched the rucksack on her shoulder and gazed about the tidy, threadbare flat. One last glimpse, then her future beckoned. She had no option but to chase it. Even if she had the blunt to extend their lease another month, maybe two, she couldn't stay. The building's owner, Mr. Santander, had made it quite clear he would "help" her. An adequate room on Anning Street at the bargain price of ten shillings per month. *His opinion*, this adequacy, when she knew the building to be rat-infested and hideous. This filth in exchange for certain carryings-on he was able to describe in enough detail for Necessity to understand she had to run.

Growing up in the rookery, she'd seen things no young girl should have. Shadowy happenings in murky alley corners. Acts in public house corners witnessed when she'd peeked inside as her mother tugged her past. Grunts and moans, lips parted to expel hard, harsh breaths. Clutching hands and bumping bodies. She *knew* what Santander wanted; it was whispered all over the district. He liked young girls. It's why her father had kept his daughters out of sight during his visits to collect rent.

She shivered, squeezing her hand around the rucksack's leather strap. She wanted no part of this bedlam, did not understand why anyone would unless forced.

She closed the door behind her, pressed her brow to the scuffed wooden jamb, and wiped away the misery leaking from her eyes. She would leave the only home she'd ever known and hope that, someday, she'd find the courage to love again. To have a family. To be happy.

<hr />

Theirs
Where an earl and a gardener meet

Oliver Aspinwall, the newly disfigured Earl of Stanford, woke to find someone sitting by his borrowed bed.

A female someone he'd never met.

A domestic in the Duke of Leighton's household, Stanford instantly assessed. Ragged fingernails. A streak of dirt on her chin. Her clothes, the standard service-issue black.

Standard issue *men's* clothing. An overlong coat and trousers, a tattered cord for a belt, and a threadbare hat she'd pulled low to cover part of her brow. However, the gentle curves beneath the layers were anything but masculine. Also, she smelled faintly of nutmeg.

He turned his head to get a better look because, even in the murky candlelight, something was splendid about the scene. He groaned as pain radiated across his cheek. His stitched skin itched like fucking mad. *Christ*, that drunken sot behind his brother's gaming hell had gotten him good.

"It's not as bad as it looks, sir. The sawbones did clean work. Scars make a man, and you're going to have a right flashy one. If you ever wished to appear rough around the edges, it's been granted," she whispered and applied a cool cloth to his cheek.

He lifted his hand to touch, but she stayed the movement.

"Lucky for you, he missed yer eye. My ma was a healer of sorts. A midwife, too. She treated various knifings. Though your attacker used glass, which creates an angrier wound. Jagged. A dirty rotten fighter is what you faced. I soaked this cloth in feverfew tea, you see. I had a wee garden in a ratty spot behind the workhouse, but the patch grew nonetheless because I have the touch. The herb will help heal your skin if you use it. Every day. I'll leave enough for a month. Alas, no addlepated medical man is going to recommend it. Don't even think to ask. I knew they'd toss me out if I suggested it. I saw them bring you in." She shrugged, as if this made perfect sense. "So here I am, sir."

"My lord," he murmured weakly, unsure why he'd think to correct someone coming to his aid.

She was clever, her gaze narrowing. He had trouble looking away. Her eyes were an unusual shade. Amber, like the last drop of whisky at the bottom of a glass. "My high-in-the-instep lord, then," she said and squeezed the rag into the bowl she held. But her touch was tender when it returned to him. She evidently wasn't one to hold a grudge. "Marquess?"

He breathed through the pain. "Earl."

"Why no laudanum, Earl? No bottles by your bedside."

He shook his head as gingerly as he could without jarring his wound. *Can't.*

"Ah." She dipped the rag again, then pressed it gently to his face. "Troubles with the opium dens. Happens to heaps of returning soldiers. Happens to lots, actually, where I come from. Passed out in the alleys, stepping over them like waste. Stumbling out of flash houses. The world is often a depressing place."

He blinked, bringing her into sharp focus. Her face was ethereal. Truly fetching beneath the grime. "How much do you know about me?"

"Everything they print in those naughty broadsheets. We got 'em at the workhouse. Days old, stained and wrinkled from another's use, but serviceable. Latest rumor is you and that hulking bloke are related. The smuggling one who owns half of London. I believe it, you being brothers or cousins, perchance, after spying him pacing the hall outside this chamber for an hour before he upped and left. He has sad eyes, and those eyes don't lie. Not another set like them that I've ever seen outside yours. The jig is up should you have thought it wasn't."

He groaned, imagining Xander seeing him like this.

She waved off his unease, sensing a delicate topic. "Don't worry, my lord earl, I waited until after he left to come in. I know my medicinal intervention wouldn't be appreciated by the upper class. Seeing as I'm assigned to the gardens. That daft majordomo has shot cross stares at me since I arrived."

"Xander Macauley isn't upper class anything," Stanford murmured, wondering vaguely if they'd given him laudanum, although he'd begged them not to. He felt woozy, and this grubby little urchin wasn't clearing up the picture. Though she didn't smell nearly as filthy as she looked. "Who *are* you?" And he'd love to tell her that Leighton's major-domo was likely trying to determine how to tell her that her ruse of dressing as a man wasn't working. At all.

"Necessity Byrne of the Shoreditch Byrnes. It's actually Josephine, but my pa called me his little Necessity, and it stuck. My mother called me Josie. She was educated, even had a governess of sorts when she was a babe. Her father was a cobbler of some import in Beaconsfield.

We could read, and she didn't allow us to talk like we'd crawled from the gutter. Although my accent, however hard I've worked on improving it, is nothing like your fine vowels."

"The Shoreditch Byrnes," Stanford whispered, oddly charmed. Her cockney *was* on the light side. With a little more polish, combined with that beautiful face, she could go far.

"All deceased. Cholera. Leaving me at twelve to manage on my own, hence the workhouse. I survived by my skills with herbs, mostly. Buying and selling from that squalid plot I was telling you about in the stews. I dressed as a lad for those years. I know you're wondering. Protection, if you get my meaning."

"Getting harder now, though, isn't it?"

She glanced at her body with a faintly betrayed expression. "Quite."

She'd rattled off her dismal history with impressive steadiness. Not one flicker of her eyelid or twitch of her hand. Her voice was as steady as if she'd been ordering bread from a shop down the way.

He had a feeling this had taken lots of practice.

She stood, giving him another shock. Tall and slender, coltish. If not for the delicacy of her features, those plump lips, the curve of her breast beneath her linen shirt, she might have been able to pass for a lad.

"I left the feverfew there." She nodded to the bedside table. "I'll be in the garden should you need more. I'll have a lovely herb patch by fall. Use it every day until the wound closes, and the tenderness dissipates."

Stanford lifted to his elbow, staying her. His cheek throbbed in time to his heartbeat, but his curiosity about this chit was weightier than his distress. His desire not to be alone was even greater. "Xander Macauley placed you here? Working in the garden?"

She halted at the door, whipped off her sad excuse for a hat, and spanked it against her thigh. Her hair rolled out like honey, a golden, unbound mass. Arousal swam to his toes and back, filling his chest with a fierce yearning he hadn't experienced in years. "It was the lady he has eyes for who placed another lucky soul and me. Lady Philippa. I seen him look at her earlier, hot as a brand. One second enough to know. She hasn't told anyone the apprentice gardener is a woman, even him. Or her brother, the duke. Leighton. We're waiting to spring it on them until it's too late. I'm fortunate in the green, you understand, anything I touch growing wild, so much promise they won't be able to let me go. My plan, my lord earl, is to become the most famed gardener in England." She twisted her brim into submission with a smile that lit him to his toes. "Next to Capability Brown, of course."

With that ludicrous declaration released to the universe, Necessity Byrne strolled from the Earl of Stanford's borrowed bedchamber with the grace of a rookery queen.

Leaving a scarred earl transfixed.

Chapter One

WHERE A GARDENER LOCATES A GARDEN (AND AN EARL) IN NEED

Derbyshire 1828

S cars make the man.

Necessity Byrne had told him this long ago, when she'd been brimming with youthful conceit. Certain every word rang with her unadorned version of the truth. Under the mistaken assumption that anyone would care to hear a bedraggled orphan's opinion.

Although she'd meant the scars located inside, not out. She wasn't sure this had been clearly communicated.

As she stood on a gentle slope near the bottom of his side garden, a sprawling medieval fortress standing guard at her back, she wondered if he remembered her.

Because she remembered him.

Oliver Aspinwall. Earl of Stanford. Tormented war hero. Ruffian. Outcast. Opium addict. Owner of one of the oldest titles in existence. Half brother to an infamous smuggler. Most eligible man in England despite the scar tarnishing his otherwise handsome visage. Every duke in sight was married or near death, so a young, obtainable earl presented grand promise indeed.

Even one with a troubled past.

Her hand clenched around her folio, the diagram of the earl's ramshackle gardens, incomplete but hopeful. Indeed, how could she forget him? The memory circled her mind... his eyes, a color as rare as a ghost orchid. A spark of vibrancy in an otherwise bland world. An uncommon shade of gray, moonlight striking stone. Ash upon brick. Eyes unlike any she'd ever seen aside from his half brother's, a salient fact she'd recalled about the earl when Xander Macauley arranged for this assignment last month. Because this feature linked them, in society, for *life*. Brothers, no one could argue.

Her services were a gift, Macauley had stated.

A gift the scarred earl likely did not *want*.

Necessity took off her bonnet and leveled her hand over her eyes to better see him. She wasn't one to turn away from a valuable opportunity. She had more guts than that, he would find out.

Lord Stanford crossed the unkempt lawn of his Derbyshire estate, the tails of his shirt smacking his lean hips, arms more muscular than she remembered held rigidly by his side. A long, lanky silhouette moving toward her, features lost to shadow. The gray stone turrets of his home rising behind him, imposing and enchanting at once. His posture projected annoyance, his clothing indicated hard labor. Although she couldn't quite see his expression or those wondrous eyes, she visualized suitably, a sketch in her mind. A vision that had never, frankly, left her.

Masculine frustration she'd expected and was prepared to confront. Experienced at confronting it. No one appreciated meddling older brothers or stubborn horticulturists with formidable opinions. Her being sent to Aspinwall House to restore grounds in extreme disorder was fraternal intrusion and nothing but. Necessity had recognized this right off, even if she didn't understand the reasoning behind it. Family issues were the most complicated under the sun, and she didn't wish to insert herself into that conflict.

Although if Xander Macauley was going to hire someone to assist his half brother in restoring what had once been the finest gardens in Derbyshire, she was the best landscape architect in England. She *was*.

And no one could change her mind about believing this.

During her brief conversation with the earl three years ago, she'd been dressed as a lad—a bogus presentation Lord Stanford had immediately rejected. Her curves unfurling like a rose in bloom, betraying her as only nature could.

She'd finally secured the position of her dreams as a gardener in training, working in the Duke of Leighton's household, her gift with herbs bringing her to the injured earl's bedside her first week in residence. His grievous wound obtained in a scuffle behind his brother's gaming hell, a drunken baron slicing his cheek with a shard of glass over funds lost that night. She'd gone to Lord Stanford's sick chamber, without asking, because few appreciated the power of medicinal herbs. When feverfew was a known curative, after all.

The Duke of Leighton and his progressive duchess had surprised her, keeping her on once her fraudulent ploy was revealed, and she moved into wearing ragged gowns. She'd stayed there for two years before saving enough to open Byrne Cultivation and Design. Stayed long enough for the generous proprietors of the Duchess Society, of which the Duchess of Leighton was one, to better prepare her to manage a business that would involve dealing with society.

Fancy teacups and engraved forks no longer sent a bolt of terror through her. She now knew how to use them. They'd also managed to erase cockney from her accent like a hand dusted across a chalkboard. Clothing from the top affordable modiste in London, bonnets and the like, proper posture and coiffure, and in the end, she looked like one of them.

When she was nothing like them and never would be.

The desperate girl orphaned at twelve after a horrid bout of cholera tore through her household was still inside her. Every shilling stuffed beneath her plump feather mattress proof that Necessity Byrne of the Shoreditch Byrnes wasn't going to leave the slums behind. That life trailed after her like mist and always would.

Moreover, she could tell the earl, because the anger radiating from him as he approached was starting to heat *her* up like a burst of undesired sunlight, that she presently counted the Duke of Leighton, two

viscounts, Tobias Streeter—a bastard son of a viscount himself—
Marquess Elderberry, *and* the Dowager Countess of Crumwall as
clients. So many new projects had arrived in the past six months that
she'd had to hire five additional gardeners to assist her. Making for a
total of nine on her payroll. *Her* payroll. *Her* business. She'd essentially
taken this job in the wilds of Derbyshire—and the earl's gardens were
in poor enough condition for it to be called wild—because Xander
Macauley had cajoled her into it with a slick smile and a smooth bit of
finessing she wasn't capable of disputing. Everyone said he could sell a
king a crown he didn't need, then be invited to stay, and dine off royal
dinnerware.

And they were right.

She hadn't even wanted to venture to the country. The streets of
London were her domain. She understood them, and they understood
her. The varied sights and sounds filling her up like rainwater filled a
trough. The filth, the grime, the chaos made sense to her. Although,
she surmised with a glance around her, the mist hanging over the
meadows, the high, green grasses hitting her ankle *were* appealing. Air
that smelled of woodsmoke and florals beat out the rank stench of coal
smoke and roasting meat, she'd admit. This morning, she'd found wild
honeysuckle winding up a sugar maple that had to be a hundred years
old. Mysteries she hadn't anticipated because she hadn't known to
anticipate them. She'd never in her life left the environs of London.

She turned from her perusal of his estate to the man. Unfortunately, he complemented his gorgeous surroundings.

When Lord Stanford got close enough, the scent of his shaving
soap drifted along on a lazy spring breeze. His gaze caught hers,
sunlight darkening his eyes to the color of ash. There they were, just as
she'd remembered. She waited patiently while he stared, blinking once
to bring himself out of it. His appreciation was belated, begrudging,
stifled even—but it was there. In the subtle flare of his pupils and his
nostrils, his throat lengthening in a tight pull.

There was power in beauty.

Although she cared more for her mind, her knowledge of flowers
and herbs and soil, her cat, Delilah, her neat little flat above a shop on

Bond, or the fresh malt loaf she purchased each morning on Bridle Lane, she'd taken steady note of the advantages that lay behind possessing an attractive veneer. She used hers when it benefited, as anyone would. For a girl born with absolutely no advantages aside from a passion for plants and a pleasant appearance, who could blame her?

"Did he send you? Arrange for restoration of my estate without thinking to tell me?" The Earl of Stanford was slightly out of breath, the utter picture of a menacing aristocrat suffering through his stay in the country. No coat, tousled hair, a fine sheen of sweat on his brow, forearms exposed by sleeves hastily rolled to his elbow, dark bristle covering his jaw. His words were precise, potent, assertive. The scar cutting across his left cheek, giving his appearance a battered elegance he'd more than earned—if not in an alley behind a gaming hell, then in India where it was said he'd valiantly fought for England's glory and almost died.

He had society in his titled pocket, his future neatly laid out amidst the four-hundred-year-old stone and metalwork at her back. He could do as he chose, take them or leave them in the end. Rules and conduct would not make or break him unless he let them.

Men were so damned lucky, she thought with a shiver of resentment. They could act and *do* without reservation.

Then they turned around and expected everything, anyway.

Necessity jammed her bonnet on her head and, wedging her folio under her arm, tied the ribbons in a loose knot beneath her chin. She'd given him enough of her for now. "I don't know who you're referring to, my lord. So rudely, I might add. You could be wrong about me altogether. What if I'm here to repair your drapes?"

His broad chest rose on a breath, his jaw muscle ticking in time to his fevered reasoning. The sunlight played over his ink-black strands, threads of silver shooting to the forefront. Quite a picture he presented standing there, the handsome, aggrieved king of the castle. Perhaps surprising them both, he reached, a caress as light as gossamer, dusting his finger along a streak of dirt on her hand. "I think I've pegged the situation correctly."

She exhaled softly, determined to start over without her pride in the way this time. "Xander Macauley hired me, Lord Stanford. With notes about where I should start restoration, should you be too busy to guide me. A situation I'm sorry I'm forced to relay to you. I'm not happy he *left* for me to relay it to you. I can't say why that is. I manage plants, not familial relationships."

"Hell's teeth, he can't stop for even one bloody second," he muttered and spun on his heel, heading down a gravel path that needed urgent re-graveling. She made a mental list as she trailed behind him. Order stones from McKinsey. Tulip bulbs from Archibald and Sons. Sage. Iris. Lilies. Gain measurement for the windows in the conservatory. Draw a diagram for the patch of land on the western edge she felt would make a fine vegetable garden. Check the soil around the ailing elm tree on the front lawn.

She could see his renovated grounds unfolding beautifully in her mind. Trim, green lawns. Flowering shrubs, the scent of them mixing with the hint of splendor already present.

So, this is what's become of the Wicked Earl, she concluded, keeping her gaze on the overgrown ryegrass and unkempt azaleas—and off his muscular bum. Athletic like a dockworker's, nothing soft about it. Most toffs she knew spent the day sitting about on theirs, so they had to be cushy, didn't they? The earl had put on at least two stone since she'd last seen him, lying injured in a duke's guest bedchamber, his face a grievous mess, his pain unaided because he'd made the unsound choice to abuse substances upon his return from India. He had the body of a rookery bruiser now. The speculation about his laboring to rebuild his estate, something unheard of in the *ton*, must be true. His brawn shouted *work*.

My, she thought, struck a shade breathless by his unexpectedly strong physique. Keeping her mind on business was proving to be a battle as tough as getting Lord Stanford to let her transform his estate. Because she didn't want to give up the job, or the garden, now that she'd gotten a look at it. And the man? Well, he'd be nice to observe, no real effort there. As long as she didn't *touch*. She knew the boundaries. Rookery girls and titled peers were never to meet.

Challenges all. Nevertheless, dear God, did she love them.

She threw out what accounted to a dare in her book. "You're going to reject the gift of my services when your brother is paying the bill? Could do anything you'd like, at his expense. I have citrus trees that are dear in cost coming in from Spain next week. They'd look lovely in that tatty conservatory of yours. With a little work on the structure, too, of course." She'd bring up the windows she wanted to install, the granite flagstones, in another conversation.

His shoulders lifted on a sigh. Then with a foul oath she clearly heard, he halted in the middle of the path, causing her to almost run into him.

Instead, she circled round front, opening her folio to present her diagrams. Knowing this moment of indecision on his part could secure the campaign. Pointing to the rough sketch of his side garden, she tapped the foolscap sheet. "My plan is to surround the sundial with hydrangea. Place a mix of gardenia, boxwood, blue holly, and juniper at the eastern edge. Lay new stone around the borders. I saw broken urns in the conservatory that I believe came from this area, and upon repair, we can reinstall. I have three assistants, my most talented gardeners, arriving in two days. We can start there, then move to the larger sections to the west. All told, I think my team can put things in order in one month."

His gaze swept her drawing with little interest. That would have raised her temper, but for the lost, helpless cast to his features that tugged somewhere near her heart. "Sounds expensive to maintain. My nosy brother on the hook for that, too?"

She hummed, impressed by how quickly the earl got to the heart of the matter. Few thought about the expense to sustain after repair. "We'll have to discuss upkeep. I wasn't paid for future visits."

He grunted, his breath escaping through a decidedly patrician nose. However, he was listening. Shifting in his scuffed boots like he wanted to flee... but listening.

Avoiding the power of his liquid silver gaze, she continued, "I would like to be given access to your library to research any notes left by the previous gardeners. For instance, the chestnut tree in the back meadow—"

"Planted in the mid-1700s by the third earl. There were five originally but only one survived the winter of 1807." He flicked his hand blithely as if his answer meant nothing when she could see that it did. She could see that he was entrenched deeper than he wished to be in this place. Territorial, like he was discussing a horse he owned. This was an interesting deduction she hadn't counted on. *He loves this place and has put his heart, what he has, into it.*

"The third earl," she repeated to keep the conversation going when it seemed he'd decided not to say more.

He dragged his hand across his neck, wiping away a drop of sweat she'd been watching roll past his jaw. *He has a callous on his thumb*, she noticed in amazement. She'd never met a toff with such. "He was very fond of the outdoors and worked with Capability Smith, I think it was. You'll find the ledgers on the bottom bookshelf in the library, the one near the back window. Left side. Cracked black leather covers. I think the invoices are there as well. I haven't looked at them for years, but I know they're there."

In her excitement, Necessity forgot her training with the Duchess Society, the reminders about polite decorum and proper behavior, and tugged on his sleeve. A common action from a common girl. Touched his wrist with her ungloved hand, which she realized in retrospect was a mistake. His skin was warm, his blood pulsing beneath her knuckle. The hair on his arm soft and dark. Curiosity about the man blossomed, and her cheeks lit. Of all the unfortunate happenings of the day, this was the worst. But what he'd told her was incredible. "Capability *Brown* worked on these gardens?"

In a move so subtle it was hardly apparent and certainly not discourteous, he shifted out of reach. Removed himself as he'd seemingly been doing with everyone since his accident. "Vines are overtaking the fruit trees. The conservatory windows are shattered. The lawns and shrubs and the like haven't seen significant care since my father left this world in 1820. The place looks like it's bloody haunted, and the gardens are the best introduction to the disorder. Why you'd care to leave London for this, even for a fortnight, I can't imagine. Doesn't Tobias Streeter have you working on his terraces in Islington? Enough to keep one busy, isn't it?"

Surprised he knew anything about her, although the broadsheets mentioned her now and again, Necessity turned in a gradual circle, taking in the lush meadows and verdant hills, the sweet scent of spring riding the air. Rhododendrons sparse of bloom because they'd not been pruned in years. Yew that had been allowed to grow high above her head. Blades of grass tickling her ankle, bald spots showing the peat-brown earth beneath. Healthy soil in need of kindness. The manor behind her, yet to be explored, equally distressed but glorious from what she'd seen. When she'd never had a castle to explore. In the far distance, she could even see a river shimmering in the sunlight.

But the absolute joy...

Capability Brown had worked on these gardens. She could not *wait* to get her hands on those ledgers. And invoices. *Original* invoices. Perhaps notes, sketches, diagrams! The Earl of Stanford unknowingly possessed a museum collection of horticultural artifacts, and he could not care less.

However, she cared greatly.

"It won't be comfortable for you or your *team*," the earl reminded her when he could tell she wanted the position. "The roof leaks in almost every bedchamber. Wind sneaking through cracks in medieval stone isn't pleasant in the dark of night. My cook is mediocre at best. My staff consists of fewer souls than necessary to maintain proper service, and the ones remaining are not too happy to have been disregarded for years. No tea in the afternoon or crisp silk sheets or anything like that. Not yet, anyway. There are spider webs and loose planks and uneven borders on the carpets. Scents of mold and decay lurking in every corner. Wings you won't want to even *think* of entering. Get lost in them and never come out."

It sounded fascinating as she'd never seen such a place in her life, but she thought it best to keep her mischievous nature to herself. Men didn't appreciate curious women.

As for the condition of the estate, Necessity could remember the first time she slept on silk sheets. The first time, in fact, when she went to bed without hunger gnawing a hole in her belly. October 1823. Those days after her parents died rolled over her like a wave. Need and want and disgust spiraling through her. The disrepair here didn't disturb her. Not like it did him. But then again, in all fairness, she didn't have any idea what his memories held. He was rumored to have had a bleak childhood. "I grew up in the rookery, my lord. If you recall. I can handle a leaking roof and spider webs just fine."

He was silent for a moment. "The Shoreditch Byrnes," he finally murmured, giving up a piece of their time together, however brief it had been.

Their gazes locked as her smile broke free, quite unstoppable. His breath caught with the force of it; she watched it happen. Lips parted, a hint of emotion long contained sweeping his face.

He *remembered* her.

"He's trying to be a good brother," she said to make him feel better, which she desperately wanted to do. A shock in itself as she spent her days reviving *plants*, not people. The problematic relationship between the Earl of Stanford and his half brother was fodder for the gossip rags and not her concern. She wasn't adding that burden to her slim but capable shoulders.

The earl scrubbed his hand over his cheek, the uninjured one, leaving a streak of dirt behind. A bewildered move she found unusually endearing. Little boy lost. "He's sticking his nose in where it isn't wanted. Again and again since India. Now I know why he came," he tossed over his shoulder as he turned toward the house, his gaze shooting to a high window she bet Xander Macauley currently occupied. "Meddlesome cad."

"So, you'll let me review the ledgers, have my team start work in two days? We can meet to discuss each step if you'd like. If there are sketches from the original plans, I'll try to stick to them. Also, the accommodations here are more than acceptable, please don't concern yourself with this aspect of my temporary residence here. Your housekeeper, Mrs. McKinstry, who informed me she's been here since before the French revolution, showed me to a bedchamber that wasn't... horrendous." Cobwebs in the corners and a thick layer of dust slicked over every surface. He was right about everything, but Necessity wasn't afraid of a little hard work being placed unexpectedly before her. She could clean her own room.

Taking another studied review of the brooding man standing before her, it didn't appear he was afraid of hard work, either.

"Do what you want with it. I'm sure this Capability person knew the right of it." He glanced again to the upper window, his jaw, quite a nice one, going hard as stone. "As if I have any choice. Xander and I are doing our best to get along, and I'm the bad brother in this scenario, so I'm left to say yes to every damned thing he places before me."

Although she had no clue what he referred to. She was left only with his boorishness stinging like a lash's bite.

Calling on the composure the Duchess Society had drummed into her, she pressed her lips together, holding back a blistering retort. Remembering her training. *Women, even those in business, even those who are right, must often remain silent.* His wasn't a congenial welcome—but the Earl of Stanford wasn't known to be a congenial man. Besides, he was giving her freedom to design as she wished, instantly increasing her enthusiasm for the project. The enhanced budget unfolded in her mind.

For placing her in this uncomfortable position, she was willing to let Xander Macauley pay.

Finally, but very importantly, Capability Brown, her hero in every sense, her fanciful mentor, had sunk his fingers in the soil right beneath her feet. As she would. A first in her book. A dream. A checkmark for *life*.

"Why are you smiling?" the earl snapped, brushing back a lock of hair the color of coal that had tumbled across his eyes.

Her fingers trembled against the leather spine of her folio. Something about him weakened her knees in an unfamiliar and disturbing way. Maybe it was the boyish charm threading through his haughty authority. Regrettably handsome, enough to melt butter on cold toast as her mother used to say. Despite the dreadful scar marring his left cheek. Broad-shouldered and brooding, impatient and disagreeable, simply reeking of masculine condescension. A proper, regal grump. One who had piqued her interest and then some.

He snapped his fingers, bringing her back to the conversation. "This estate is falling down around me, Miss Byrne. The gardens require talent and blunt. Plenty of both."

She studied him as his gaze scooted away. He didn't want to be coerced into providing insight into his situation. Any more than he'd provided, that is. Which was a bit.

"The challenge," she finally said in reply to his earlier question, meaning the plants not the man. A wee lie, that. "It's not the money. I have clients on a waiting list in London." And Capability Brown's notes. She couldn't forget about those, wouldn't forget.

"Is that it?" He glanced around as if trying to see his estate as she did.

She chewed on the inside of her lip. Well, there was the matter of her slight but perceptible attraction. Possibly more than slight if she examined it closely. He was handsomer than she remembered. Angrier, too. An aura of strength she hadn't recalled radiating from him like heat from a hearth fire. Intelligent, exacting, and heroic in his own cantankerous way.

She liked those traits in a person.

Though she'd never been attracted to a client.

A gust of wind ripped over the meadows, tugging at his hair and shirttails, the force of it pushing them closer together, for a heartbeat, nothing more. He had a tiny freckle above his upper lip in the shape of a star. In a face otherwise set solid as stone, the charming spot brought the impact of his scowl down two notches. She clenched her folio to keep from making a gross error in judgment and touching him again. She couldn't disregard instinct, not when her life depended upon her *own* dependability.

The tense anticipation she typically felt only when competing with a rival for a landscape project mustn't be ignored. Keen awareness flavored with a dash of excitement. Plausibly, an enemy in the making.

Not a friend and *certainly* not a lover.

The moment felt significant in a way she wasn't prepared to define. It also felt inconvenient. Frowning, she watched his displeasure blossom, the downward tilt of his lips making her wish to do things that would make him smile. Laugh. Groan in delight.

Perilous cravings. How dare she imagine them with a man that was well above her class.

The earl shook his head, *no*. Slicing through the shadowy threads of attraction with a destructive stare.

Just that, nothing more. Then he turned on his heel and strode away without another word.

He had to know he left her intrigued beyond measure. Challenged. Curious.

And a curious woman was beyond dangerous.

Chapter Two

WHERE AN EARL GIVES HIS
MEDDLESOME BROTHER A REPRIEVE

I t wasn't the first time a woman had looked at Stanford with a
gaze that could crack stone.

They liked the scar, he'd come to find, when he'd hoped the
mark would keep people at a distance. Making it good for something.
Still, it was the first time in years he'd wanted to drag the hot-eyed
woman to his bedchamber and rip her gown off. An outdated, atrocious scrap of a gown that had looked as gorgeous as a queen's on
Necessity Byrne's luscious body.

Stanford pulled a fast breath through his teeth, willing his body to
ignore his ravenous mind.

How was that going to work for the next month? His cock stiff-
ening every time he got within view of his bloody *gardener*. Couldn't
Xander have hired an old man for the job? Now Stanford had a
gardener he didn't want living under his leaking roof—one with creamy
skin and a golden, unbound mass of hair falling past decidedly plump
breasts.

Although a one-second glance around his estate proved he desperately needed horticultural assistance. While a two-second glance at his
gardener proved... *Fuck*, he thought and cursed. It proved things a man
sometimes wished to hide.

What made him want to put his fist through a wall was the fact that his brother had planned on Necessity Byrne doing more than trimming his hedges. He wasn't missing this salient fact. Or his eager reaction, right on schedule.

When he wasn't lonely.

Xander was a man surrounded by so much newfound love he thought everyone else should dive in headfirst, too.

Another gust off the meadow tugged at the collar of a tattered shirt he wore only for hard labor. His trousers were fit for the ragbag. His hair was overlong, his jaw unshaven. Decidedly unfit for visitors. Although he hadn't known he was receiving any on this fine spring day.

Bothersome. Irritating. Genuinely infuriating. Because his brother's concern, after years trudging along without it, threatened to soften a hardened heart Stanford had gotten used to possessing. A secret he wasn't about to share with Xander or his pack of reprobates the earl had reluctantly made his own. The Dukes Leighton and Markham, Tobias Streeter, Dashiell Campbell. Chance Allerton, Viscount Remington, when he showed up. He had friends where he'd had none before. Stanford kicked a pebble from his path into the overgrown shrubs his newfound gardener was eager to manhandle.

Therefore, he was *not* lonely.

He counted off the number of indecent proposals this month alone with each crack of his bootheel upon gravel. He had to fight women off since the gaming hell mishap. They liked a battered earl better than an untarnished one. Which made him distrust the entire lot. The mystery behind his redesigned visage plus a weighty title allowed early and glowing mention in *Debrett's,* making for a man every society mother felt her daughter could tame. Should tame. *Would* tame.

His earldom, God help him, was practically the oldest in the land. What a carrot to dangle.

Nevertheless, he understood what they wanted. To soothe the scoundrel. Calm the cad. Break the beast. Educate the earl. He'd heard them all. Read them in the broadsheets over bohea tea day after day when he'd done nothing since the tussle behind Xander's gaming establishment to earn their consideration.

Before that, yes, indeed, he'd made a show of things. Stumbling from opium dens at dawn. Membership revoked at White's *and* Boodle's. An overturned phaeton on Bruton. A sunken skiff on the Thames. Leagues of unsuitable women warming his bed. Why, he'd nearly tumbled from his spot in the upper reaches at the opera one boozy evening. One of the dukes grabbing the back of his coat just in time.

But since the knifing incident, naught. As wholesome as a nun.

Or his transgressions executed in secret, in any case.

A well-behaved pupil with a controlling older brother, a growing gaggle of posh and not-so-posh friends. Even a glimmer of a future on the horizon if he squinted hard enough into the distance. That was the biggest change, that he wanted to squint at anything.

Smacking the servant's door open with the heel of his hand, he took the stairs to the upper salon he'd appropriated as his study two at a time.

He'd done nothing to gain attention since the knifing aside from being Xander Macauley's half brother, of course.

The man drew attention without trying, every gaze in every room he entered turning his way. Even if he wished to hide, that light help-lessly struck Stanford. Some people were born with a powerful brand of indescribable charisma. There was no way society's liquid attention wouldn't spill on the lesser brother, too. The crossest brute London had ever seen, tamed like a kitten right before society's eyes was the finest form of entertainment since the antics of mad King George. Lady Philippa, better known as Pippa, sister of the Duke of Leighton, one of Macauley's best friends and now one of Stanford's, bringing the rookery titan to his knees.

It had been a grand show to watch unfold.

Now, out of sheer boredom or some infantile retribution, Xander had placed this eccentric girl in Stanford's path. Woman, rather. All grown up. Quite nicely, in fact. Necessity Byrne, the most lethal chit that could be drawn into his self-imposed Derbyshire dotage.

A scandal who didn't *care* if she was a scandal.

Blind indifference drew the *ton* like flies to jam. A wrecking ball in skirts with a face—and body—one did not easily forget was not what he needed to keep his peace or his sanity.

My plan, my lord earl, is to become the most famed gardener in England.

Because he damn well remembered almost everything about their first meeting, even if she did not. And this little nugget worried the hell out of him.

Stanford halted at the top of the staircase as Necessity's words from years ago sank claws into his memory, his hand circling the oak banister he'd slid down, then been confined to his room for two days without food because of the boorish transgression.

She's bloody well done it, he reasoned. *Gone and made herself almost as infamous as my brother.* Stanford recalled being unduly charmed by a coltish chit dressed in lad's clothing kneeling at his bedside. The curve of a breast straining against cotton his first clue that this was no boy assisting him.

He'd imagined her beauty a feverish dream.

Alas, that was not the case.

Her hair had the wispy hue of the stars he viewed nightly through his telescope. Shot through with gold and darker hints of honey. A vision of it spread like sunlight across his sheets wasn't improving his mood. He didn't need temptation in the form of an audacious landscape artist, or whatever she called herself, mucking up a peaceful existence he'd fought like hell to obtain.

He had a lovely, rather shy but *very* welcoming widow in the village he visited for that sort of thing. When the need arose. Manageable, *civil* need.

Necessity Byrne wasn't shy in the least. Hadn't once cast her gaze to the ground in maidenly decorum. She looked right at a person. *Through* them, rather. Like a bloke. Daring Stanford with eyes the incredible color of Macauley's whisky. The new vintage that lit with a tinge of amber when it hit crystal. She smelled of rain and earth and trouble. Made his scar itch like it did when a storm was approaching.

These were not good things.

He flexed his hand, the spot on his wrist she'd grazed with her ungloved finger hot to the touch.

Necessity Byrne had given him her full attention—and regrettably it made him burn.

He didn't want this distraction. Repairing his relationship with his brother *and* this estate was his only priority. It would take years to restore what his father had let rot in Derbyshire. Years more to allow pleasant memories to override the awful.

That was a key piece, he realized. To wake without nightmares. To be happy. To be *whole*. He wasn't dragging another person into his troubles or his quest for contentment. And to do this, find a measure of stability, he needed to stay away from London. Away from the opium dens, gaming hells, and greedy, grasping mamas.

He'd fought a war in India, and he wasn't fighting another in Mayfair.

Too, love made one vulnerable, and he wasn't up to the challenge. Beyond his brother being in residence at Aspinwall House for only the second time since Stanford had betrayed him fifteen years ago.

And he'd about paid off that debt, he believed.

Stanford sucked in a calming breath when he reached his study door. The faint smell of linseed oil and lemon stung his senses. The sconces were lit, glass sparkling, tossing an unfettered spill across his path. His small staff had finally got to this floor. He was chipping away at the past bit by bit until only the present remained.

Palming his belly, he felt the quiver.

Nerves. This was nerves he was experiencing.

A mountain of bills littered his desk. The weather was improving enough for repair on the stable *and* the conservatory to start. The village vicar had contacted him about assisting with repairs on a building they hoped to use as a schoolhouse next fall. A request, after his father's years of negligence, he could not dismiss. He had guests he was unprepared to host taking up two shabby bedchambers ill-equipped for the task. His cook was annoyed. His footman, the lone soul dancing attendance at Aspinwall House, jaded. The Aspinwall housekeeper of forty years was threatening to take her pension and retire to her sister's home in Gloucestershire.

And the cream on the cupcake? A gorgeous chit with a fiercely intelligent, recklessly careless gaze, hems filthy from her "business" endeavors, would be sleeping five doors down from his room this evening. In what his mother had once called the green bedchamber.

It was the only space available for immediate—and unplanned—placement.

He might not act the part, but Stanford knew every inch of this residence, every loose brick, every medieval inscription, every nick and scratch. Had hidden in the cupboards and under the beds. Behind curtains and in the secret passages. He'd had no choice when his father's rages began to burn brighter than the hearth fires.

He loved the stack of stones, the meadows, and fields. The river running through the western glade. The oak forests and sloping pastures. The scent of woodsmoke and pine that stung his nose and his heart.

And he hated it. Loathed the memories attached to every blade of grass, every buffed dent in the walnut bannisters. His father's presence lingered, but this was diminishing. With time, things passed, as they said. Which he was finding to be true.

His current dilemma was having the patience to determine which emotion would win out.

Stanford hesitated when he found Dashiell Campbell, his brother's wayward protégé, lounging in the doorway of his study like he owned the room. Like he owned the entire damned pile of stones surrounding them.

"I guess you knew she was coming," Stanford said, an edge he couldn't hide crisping his voice. "Her *team*, whatever the hell that means, trotting along behind her in two days' time. When I barely have accommodations for you and Xander, much less London's most notorious horticulturist and whoever Necessity Byrne employs to dig in the dirt for her."

Dash shoved off the jamb, his smile blinding. He was dressed for the country in shirtsleeves and rough cambric trousers. A paisley waistcoat in a shocking shade that matched his cobalt eyes. Polished boots, that were surely Hoby, reflecting an image of abraded planks and faded carpets. He was considered the most handsome man in England; a burden Stanford couldn't imagine carrying. Worse than a bloody title. "Aye, a crafty move, wasn't it? Bound me to secrecy, your brother. Sorry, laddie. I have to follow orders, you see. Don't know if *you* know, but

Miss Byrne does much of the dirt digging herself. Dinna get a good look at her, then? If you did, I can't imagine arguing with that piece hanging around for a week or two, beautifying the place in more ways than one."

"I got a good look." Stanford growled and motioned Dash aside. "Quite enough of a look, thank-you."

With a chuckle, Dash tossed a pair of dice between his hands, his gaze shifting to Stanford in a sly manner the earl didn't miss. Assessing, always assessing his moves. In his youth, Dash had been a card sharp of such renown that he'd sat down a year ago and written a book about ways to con the system. A manuscript ultimately bringing him as much notoriety as his sweet face. To call the volume *popular* was to undercut its popularity.

But Dash was in the midst of his own crisis, though he didn't realize it. Stanford knew those types of transgressions and could spot another's a mile off. Dash had overturned a carriage on St. James last week, hence this trip to the country until things settled in the city. His employer had demanded it.

Dash made a sweeping and unnecessary gesture, inviting the earl into his own domain. "The Byrne chit is known as a genius with flowers and such. Let her have a wee hand with your gloomy gardens, I say. After all, Macauley already laid down the blunt. Canna very well send the viticulture lass back to London when her services are paid for."

"Some gift." Stanford elbowed Dash aside, searching the darkened chamber for his brother. "More like punishment. Also, viticulture is winemaking. You mean horticulture, Campbell."

Dash muffled a laugh in his fist and followed Stanford into the study, closing the door behind them with a soft *snick*. If there was going to be a brawl, a sealed chamber would better hide the ruckus. "Truth be told, that's punishment I'd like. Too many stout opinions but from such a bonnie confection, who cares about a little female pecking? Why do you think Jasper Noble is sniffing after her like a hungry hound? It ain't her remarkable skill with petunias."

Stanford paused, a dart of something he didn't want to feel piercing his chest. "Noble?"

"Nothing noble, actually, about that nob. I heard him talking about the lovely gardener across the faro tables last week. Said she was the comeliest chit in London, loud enough for every bloke in the room to hear. Not respectful that, even if it's true."

"Isn't," Stanford murmured, recalling that Dash had requested they correct him when he fell back into what the Duchess Society called "lazy" speech. He'd been asked to present his book at numerous events, a surprise to anyone who'd met the man as he wasn't an orator. Dash claimed he didn't want to sound like an uneducated Scot, even if that's what he was. He'd improved himself—speech, dress, manners—to the point he could almost, *almost*, pass for the elegant swells he'd once robbed blind. If not for the shifty gaze and wandering hands that even now occasionally slipped into pockets not his own.

Stanford halted by the settee his brother lay stretched upon, Xander's arm tossed over his eyes to block the glow from the hearth. Chest steadily rising and falling, deep sleep for an exhausted father of two. "You should talk. Your face isn't exactly dreadful," Stanford grumbled, wondering at the rudest way to wake a person. Macauley had called him "baby bro" yesterday. He could punch him for that alone.

Dash shrugged and threw himself into a brocade armchair that released a ferocious, dusty puff when his long body hit it. "Can't say I'm not blessed."

Glancing over his shoulder, Stanford leveled out his tone to what he hoped sounded like bland interest. "Jasper Noble, huh? Isn't he the bloke the Duke of Markham planted a facer on at Epsom last year?" Xander had called the man a thug. And it took one to know one. They'd been fighting for business along the Limehouse docks for the past year or more. Not a friendly relationship.

Dash yawned and let his head drop back, his gaze roving the ceiling. He lifted his arm, pointing. "A proper crack there that's going to need attention."

Stanford's jaw tensed. "I'm aware, thank-you. There's at least one in every room."

"It was Leighton that Noble got into the tussle with, you ken. At Ascot. Whispered something improper about Leighton's hellion of a duchess. The duke's fuse runs quick, even if his wife does occupy the outer realm of respectability. Crankiest toff I've ever encountered but a prime opponent with his fists." Dash scrubbed his hand over his jaw. "I've been behind a swing or two of his at Gentleman Jackson's myself. About knocked my clock off."

"Hmm," Stanford returned, wondering at the curious sizzle in his belly. What did he care if Necessity Byrne had men trailing after her? If she, common-born and as free-wheeling as a bloom set loose in a gust, chose to associate with a man of dubious character? Wasn't that an appropriate match? Like for like?

Although he couldn't disagree with Dash's brash assessment.

She *was* a bonnie confection. Someone had to take a bite. It's what men *did*.

"March ahead with your plan for revenge, my lord, tis fine," Dash whispered, lids dropping, voice thickening with slumber. "As your brother's able assistant, you have my permission. Wake him up. Make him pay."

Stanford rolled his shoulders with a sigh. His guests were like two cats, lounging about on every piece of vacant furniture, napping the afternoon away.

Dash pocketed his dice in his waistcoat and kicked one boot atop the other, settling in for his leisure. "Aye, we all know what Macauley's scheming. Matchmaking, though I can hardly believe it. He's gleaned dreadful ideas from those Duchess Society termagants. What happened to the rookery brute what took me in, that he's now so full of affection? Sending the girl who healed your sliced cheek to finish the healing, am I right? Without a stitch of clothing this time if the plan goes according."

Vexed by Dash's correct assessment, Stanford gave the settee's scuffed leg a kick. Which elicited absolutely no response from his drowsing brother. "He's slept practically twenty hours since he arrived. Is he ill?"

"The ragged soul's getting no rest what with the new bairn. On the way here, aren't they, his wee family? He doesn't like to go even a minute without them." Dash yawned again, his words slurring. "Says a lot about his concern for *you*, whether you value the concern or not."

Stanford grimaced, pondering how he was going to house more

visitors. He had a charming medieval dungeon that was the driest spot in the dwelling. Maybe he could send Macauley's family there.

"When are they arriving, *laddie?*" Stanford prodded.

"Tomorrow. Traveling with Tobias Streeter and his. brood. The Duke of Markham and his growing posse. Markham is holding a celebration next week in honor of the end of the spring planting season. For his tenants and such. Streeter's not the kind for that sort of thing, but he's just down the way in Hampton Hall, and his leaseholders are invited as well. I believe the Duke of Leighton is coming, too. The entire Leighton Cluster as the *ton* calls them in one tidy spot while London enjoys the calm."

Calls *us*, Stanford silently corrected. A group he was decidedly—and *happily*—a part of. Although this small secret he kept to himself.

Dash came out of his relaxed stupor, his boots hitting the tattered carpet with a *thump*. "Leighton. Coming. Tomorrow. Here, Derbyshire."

Stanford left his stuttering friend—and his plan to unload his brother to the floor—and crossed to the mahogany sideboard that had been in the Aspinwall family for centuries, wishing for the hundredth time in the span of a week he could pour a drink. A fat one smacking the lip of the tumbler. Gin, if he had his druthers. He'd once gone so low as to purchase a bottle from a vendor selling the brew out of a wheelbarrow in Seven Dials, then disappeared for two days. Or perhaps it was Limehouse. At this point, he couldn't recall.

Nevertheless, gin led to whisky. Whisky occasionally leading to opium.

So, oolong tea it was for now.

"Theo's bringing her fiancé if that's the cause of your heightened apprehension, Dash, old chap. I know you two had a falling out of some kind." Stanford made tea, knocking the spoon against the side of the cup lest his friend think he was pouring something else. "William, I think it is."

"Edward," Dash bit out, shoving to his feet.

Stanford stirred a spot of milk into his tea, finally enjoying this conversation. "Professor or something, isn't he? Cambridge." He tilted his head in practiced indecision, rolling his tongue along his teeth. "Or is it Oxford? Quite respected in his field. I'm sure he's written a book or two as well. Maybe an entire library of them."

Dash yanked his superfine coat off a peg by the door and shoved his arms into the sleeves. "My book is walking oot of bookstores faster than they can print 'em, I'll have you know. I've given literary talks at every bleeding cucumber sandwich and ratafia gala in the city. Selling better than any fookin' text on mathematics, what's the truth."

Stanford laughed, his first sincere pleasure in days. Turning to rest his hip on the sideboard, he watched Dash wrestle a rumpled plaid hat of Scottish origin on his head. "Mathematicians are *very* good with details, Campbell. And a shrewd man can tame a woman quite handily if he lets her get lost in them."

This tenet, after *much* practice, Stanford had learned and learned well.

Dash muttered a crude suggestion and slammed from the study, his footfalls ringing on the stairs as he took them at a mad sprint to the lower level.

"Did you have to go there, mate?" Macauley muttered and bumped in beside him, reaching for a cup and the teapot. Aside from a father they both loathed, he and his brother shared little. He was lean where Macauley was brawn and then some. Stanford often felt footman to his knight, which *was* humbling. "I brought the boy along to keep him from overturning any more carriages or risking his life using a creative approach I've yet to consider. If you get him riled up, he'll go to the village and start a brawl in the first public house he encounters. Talking about Scottish independence or that hideous battle at Culloden, topics known to raise tempers faster than a knife to the back."

"He's not a boy, Xander. He's been successfully managing your gaming hell for three years and has written the most fashionable manuscript to arrive since Austen. Tripping through a flower field of silk skirts and amassing what must be a reasonable fortune while doing it. Purchased a place on Bruton last month, didn't he? From that baron who lost his birthright at your club? Viscount on one side of him, dowager duchess on the other. They must be thrilled to gain Dashiell Campbell as a neighbor. I honestly wish I was there to see him stroll the streets every day."

Sighing when Macauley leaned in, he tipped his teacup in his brother's direction. *See, not drinking.*

Chagrined, Macaulay caught his gaze, Stanford's eyes mirrored in his brother's. If they'd thought to hide their relationship, the distinctive shade of gray exposed the connection. "I find myself unable to drop the protective routine. You once asked me to play the hero. I hated you saying it at the time, but here I am, playing the bloody hero. I know you don't like it. Neither does Pippa... but..." Macauley shrugged a broad shoulder, his cheeks lighting with the faintest hint of pink. His love for Lady Philippa Darlington, the Duke of Leighton's sister, was legendary. Surprising society, but most of all surprising Xander Macauley, who'd sworn to never, *ever* walk the marital plank. "You came back here, facing harsher demons than in London even, Ollie. I suppose I had to make sure you were going to outrun them."

Ollie.

Stanford had only been called Ollie that one joyous summer before his father banished Xander from the estate. He'd tried to forget the nickname, forget that time, but Xander wasn't letting him forget a blessed thing. Not anymore.

Balancing his cup on his palm, Stanford made a convincingly relaxed trek across the room, stopping at his desk to close the journal lying open atop it. When his nightmares were in attendance, he studied the sky for hours through the telescope housed in his library. He didn't want his *protective* older brother to witness evidence of this struggle.

"I'm not lonely," Stanford said without preamble, revealing how close he and Xander had become in the past two years. He never started conversations in the *middle* with anyone else. "And I'm not hiding."

Macauley paused, teacup halfway to his mouth. Rocking back on his heels, he contemplated his response. Stanford watched him prepare. The man was a fierce diplomat, and it wasn't often Stanford threw him a bone. "No one said you were lonely, Ollie. Or hiding."

"There's a widow in the village. Mary Stirling. She's quite accommodating and has no wish to wed again. I've helped her repair things around her manor. Faulty hearth and a door that sticks in the winter.

An uneven stair, a loose stone on the walk. It has worked out well for both parties. We're content with the arrangement."

"Excellent," Macauley murmured, hiding his grin behind his cup. "Glad to hear it. You settle each other's... concerns."

"The earldom is going to my young heir, Bertrand, a distant cousin I don't know well but assume will do a fine job of it upon my demise. No countess arriving, so the ravenous mamas in London can sod off. I have enough funds, just enough, to get this place on its feet. I don't need a pinched-faced, blue-blood's dowry or my future mucking up theirs, what there is of one. I don't wish to perform the *ton's* idea of a lifelong dance. I tossed those constraints out the window along with the opium pipe."

Macauley went back to plotting his strategy, pouring tea he likely didn't want, to keep a gaze Stanford was getting better at reading off the bargaining table.

"You're getting that look, Xander."

Macauley glanced up, scowled, his brow winging high. The rookery boy and the bastard son of an earl merged into one whether he liked it or not.

"Determined hauteur. I recall seeing it on our father's face when he was asked to solve a problem. Forced, rather, as he didn't care to resolve issues, even those he created. You have some of the privileged piece running through you. Against your will, I realize. It's not all Limehouse, *mate*." He dusted his hand over his scarred cheek, then wished he hadn't let that nervous tell pass. "I repeat, as I have since the incident, I'm not your problem."

Macauley smoothed his lip over the rim of the cup, then took a thoughtful drink. "You protected me from a drunken baron, stepping between me and a blade. Only Tobias Streeter has ever done that. Therefore, I can return the sentiment. I wasn't *your* problem. But here we are, connected for life. That's the way with blood, innit? It's not a choice. It simply is. Like love. I'll offer this advice for you since it hasn't hit your hard titled head yet. You don't always *choose*. Sometimes it simply *arrives*."

"It was a shard of glass, not a blade."

Macauley grunted, his frown fearsome. He didn't like to discuss that night. "As dangerous, boy-o. Maybe more so."

Stanford cradled his cup, glancing down into the misty, nut-brown brew. Affection was complicated, love even worse, and he often didn't want any part of it. "Lose the guilt, will you? I don't mind the scar. It shows a trace of what I feel like on the inside. My childhood, the battle with the dens when I returned from India. The unpleasantness of it all. If it frightens anyone, my visage, well, *good*. Let it warn them away. If they could see what's here"—he tapped his chest—"they'd run in the other direction."

Chest lifting with a somber breath, Macauley glanced to the window, the chilled hearth, the line of dour portraits adorning the faded walnut paneling. Anywhere but into his brother's eyes. A direct glance at his long-ago mended injury.

Stanford wondered what it was like for Xander, returning to this estate when he'd been forcibly evicted from it. It had been hard, almost impossible, for Stanford when he was master of the place. Their father hadn't wanted anything to do with a rookery by-blow he'd made the mistake of siring with an Italian opera singer. When it appeared that the boy had stolen a timepiece from the household he'd been invited into upon his mother's death, no one, even his half brother, had stepped forward to say, *he's innocent*.

Which Xander had been, of course. He was the most honorable smuggler Stanford had yet to meet.

Stanford drained his cup and placed it atop a book on constellations that Xander had gifted him at Christmas. "Why did you send her?"

Macauley's lips tilted, enough humor there to spark a fire in Stanford's belly. "Who?"

"You bloody well know *who*. Trim my unkempt hedges, is that it?"

Macauley's gaze shot to his, his laugh arriving like a shot from a pistol. *Cheeky bastard*. His hand went around his belly to hold his mirth in. When he finally had himself under control, he said, "You're wonderful with Kit. With Streeter's brood. Markham's son named his kitten Ollie, for God's sake. They trail after you like your pockets are lined with sweets, mate. A man such as this should be a father."

Stanford dropped into the grubby armchair Dash had vacated, his eyes drifting closed, a headache creeping in. He hadn't slept well the night before. Visions of Raigad plaguing his dreams. Memories of Aspinwall House that lingered like a leaden mist. This place was haunted and not with ghosts. "That doesn't answer my question, *boy-o*."

Although, strangely enough, he *was* good with children. And it did answer the question, in part.

"I should have taken better care of you."

Stanford brushed his wrist across his cheek, grunting out a token response. *Christ.*

"Not then. Behind the gaming hell." The clink of crystal sounded from across the room, a tumbler being filled with what was certainly not tea. Stanford envied the freedom to take a drink and not yearn for the entire bottle. "When we were lads. I understood what I was leaving you with. You accused me of that once, and you were right. I know it was worse here, with that blasted horror of a man, than anything you've told me. I let my hurt get in the way of making the right decision and taking you with me. If that's what I *could* have done. And I'm not sure I could have." He paused, his throat clicking with a hard swallow. "So, in a fruitless effort to make things up to you, because you seemed to show interest in the chit years ago, I arranged for the notorious, utterly lovely Necessity Byrne—a Shoreditch girl, I proudly add—to trim your hedges."

Stanford blinked to find Macauley peering quizzically into his glass as if he'd taken a path he hadn't set out to take. Stanford often imagined the brother bit bewildered Xander as much as it bewildered him. "The ones on the estate, right?"

Macauley's lips slanted, sly and sure. "Any hedges she chooses to trim, mate."

"Don't make it sound frivolous when you're hoping for true love in this thing, Xander. I only asked about her back then because I woke to find her pressing a tea bag to my face. You're a romantic. Fallen as hard as any. Right down the pit. Streeter, Markham, Leighton. Bundles of brawn and shrewd intellect..." He tapped his heart with a pained grimace. "And feelings. *Oh*, the feelings. Almost too many for this battered salon to contain. When we're all together, the Leighton Cluster, for the unencumbered man, it's unbearable."

Macauley cursed, tossing back what remained in his glass. "I bloody well am *not* a romantic."

"When the gardener in question won't want anything to do with a broken-down earl rumored to be a recluse of the highest order."

Macauley snorted and poured another drink. "Go on telling yourself that, brother of mine. Your face isn't that wrecked. You've a grand title, positively celestial, and share my good looks."

It was time to end this drama. Crush his brother's matchmaking fantasy. "Word is, she has Noble on the hook."

Macauley stilled, slanting a hard look over his shoulder. "*Jasper* Noble? The nob I'm trying to outbid for a shipping contract in the West Indies? The crook trying to upstage me as leader of the docks? He's running after that gorgeous hellion of a gardener?" He hummed and took a considerate sip. "Maybe he's got more brains than I gave him credit for if he sees more to Byrne than most, same as I do."

Leader of the docks? Stanford groaned, appalled by this conversation *and* the singular tick pulsing beneath his breastbone.

If he didn't know better, he'd call it jealousy.

After a thready silence, Macauley's scowl smoothed out. Then he saluted Stanford with his glass, his good humor returning. "Well, competition makes a race worth running now, doesn't it? I can't wait to watch you fleece Noble, your first true swindle. My brother at last. What's the saying about rights and beholding? I mean, she's here, under your nose, thanks to me. Let's make our dearly departed devil of a sire proud. Go with a woman you *know* he'd disapprove of."

Stanford rocked forward, his boots striking the floor. "I have an arrangement in the *village*. Necessity Byrne can trim the actual hedges and that's it!"

Of course, that was the moment his landscape architect entered his line of vision, making a hasty sweep past the door Dash hadn't thought to close with his temperamental exit. A three-second, stunning blur in an outdated gown well suited to ditchdigging.

Stanford shoved to his feet. "You bloody arse, I'm going to murder you. After I apologize to Miss Byrne."

When he wasn't good with apologies.

And Miss Byrne doubtless wasn't good at accepting them.

Macauley shrugged—but didn't laugh. Stanford would have leaped over the settee to get to him if he had. He'd put on over two stone in the past year, mostly muscle, and he could give his brother a solid run if it came to it. "At least I forced the introduction, mate. Part of the problem with you, innit, the sober beginning?"

True enough.

Leaving Stanford with nothing to do but give repentant chase for the first time in years.

Chapter Three

WHERE A GARDENER WITH
TREMENDOUS PATIENCE LOSES HERS

Blue-blooded cad. Arrogant bounder. Earl of *nothing* special!
Add to the mix that condescending criminal brother of his.
Necessity strode down the passage, her furious footfalls ringing off medieval stone. Sconces were thankfully lit, unlike the first dark corridor she'd stumbled down, tossing shadow and dim illumination across her path. A *lost* path. She had no idea where her bedchamber was as she'd been investigating the grounds. Green and in the west wing was all she'd been told. Her portmanteau taken up hours ago. Aspinwall's housekeeper had directed her thusly without offering escort. The aged servant had placed her hand on her hip and grimaced as if to say: *I can't help you find your quarters but good luck to you in doing so.*

Moments ago, when Necessity heard the earl's voice sliding like mist down the hallway, a ragged note had held her in place as surely as his fingers wrapped around her wrist. So, she'd lingered outside his study. Snooping, if she was honest with herself.

What had that got her?

Another unflattering summary of what society thought of her.

Halting, she blew out a savage breath. Clenched her fists and willed away the heat scalding her cheeks, although much of his censure was self-directed.

When the gardener in question likely wouldn't want anything to do with a broken-down earl rumored to be a recluse of the highest order.

She wished this statement was true. Could easily pretend it *was* true. She'd never had to hide attraction before, not really, so how hard could it be? Truthfully, the earl had tempted her in some mysterious, niggling way since she'd laid eyes on him. His cheek torn to shreds but his eyes, *oh*, those wondrous eyes, fastening her to him like he held a lock and key.

Nevertheless, despite the spark dancing between them, she'd never imagined that felonious dolt Xander Macauley would imagine her services were anything but scientific and of the horticulture world. She'd worked blasted hard to become a woman who didn't *have* to sell herself. She only sold her knowledge. Her passion. Her body was off-limits and hers alone.

"Men are hounds," she whispered and continued her search for her chamber. Only allowing a curse to fall free when she reached a dead end. *Now what?*

The earl caught her moments later, her eye pressed to a tiny keyhole in the stone wall that let one gaze across the vast woodlands surrounding Aspinwall House. The sun was setting, and the horizon was a burst of crimson and gold bordered by a set of verdant, rolling hills. The scent of pine and woodsmoke lay heavy on the air, the call of a hawk—or owl or a bird she'd never heard in the city anyway—piercing the twilight.

If she weren't so vexed, she would have found it beautiful.

"It's an embrasure," he murmured, coming up swiftly but not silently beside her.

Tossing her hair over her shoulder, she glanced back with a cross look.

Stanford followed the move, his pupils flaring.

Oh, bother, she silently seethed. Men were fascinated by the most mundane bits. A flash of bony ankle, a lock of hair not bound to one's head with pins. She'd restrain her stubborn strands in the tightest chignon she could manage tomorrow. Wear her ugliest dress, although the one she was wearing wasn't set to entice. Let herself get filthy as a dog grubbing in the dirt.

That would show him *and* his silly brother what kind of offer this was, her being here. She was about the plants and nothing more. About that magnificent conservatory in need of attention, the stately line of elms she'd envisioned lining the drive, the herbs and vegetables. The butterflies the new gardens would attract. The birds. The lawns stretching clear to the horizon.

And *almost* most importantly, Capability Brown's notes.

"My lord?" she finally asked, an edge she wasn't about to banish scalding her words.

Gently brushing her aside, he leaned in, pressing his eye to the stone where hers had been. A compelling scent, leather and something spicy, drifted from him. Heat where his shoulder touched hers raced to her toes. His hair was black as ash, overlong, curling about his ears and grazing his scarred cheek. He was taller than she'd recalled. Broader of chest. Rougher than any toff she'd encountered. He radiated a distinctive mix, to her experience, of refinement and ruggedness. When she'd only known men who possessed one trait. Aristocrats or common blokes, never a man who blended both.

"An embrasure," he repeated and stepped back. This time sticking his long finger in the gap, warming her in areas she'd rather not think about. "It was designed to allow arrow fire through the slit at the top and small cannon fire through the circular opening at the bottom. Primitive defense. You'll find them all over the dwelling if you're set to explore." He smiled, an action that didn't seem completely spurious, set to make her forget the ribald comments repeated about her in his study. "Quite remarkable, isn't it?"

She tangled her hands in her skirt, unwilling to soften her stance. So what if he loved this crumbling castle? What business of hers was it? "I'm not exploring, Lord Stanford. I'm lost."

He frowned, a dimple, minuscule and almost bleeding into his ruined cheek, popping up to further aggravate her. "Lost? You're staying in the west wing—"

"Green bedchamber," she interrupted. "Your housekeeper informed me of the location while also letting me know she can't manage climbing stairs." She glanced down the hall and back. "Am I *in* the west wing? How can one tell?"

He shook his head, his gaze glittering in the meager light from the sconce. "No, this is the east. Come, I'll show you."

She followed him down the corridor, taking a left where she'd taken a right, struggling valiantly to lift her gaze above his firm bottom encased in clinging buckskin. The second time today she'd been presented the opportunity. Descending an impressive marble staircase, across a paneled gallery, and up the matching steps on the other side.

She couldn't imagine owning a manor of such magnificence. The sheer breadth was astounding even if the dwelling was in disrepair. The Earl of Stanford had no idea how fortunate he was. Although most in society didn't have funds for upkeep of their inheritances, the financial burdens could kill birthrights faster than Dutch elm disease did a tree.

"What you overheard, my brother, he was jesting," he said, an admission that caused her to stumble over a rough spot on the tattered runner beneath her feet. Instantly, he reached for her, a steadying hand cupped beneath her elbow. "I find myself unable to agree to it most days. His brand of fraternal teasing stings. Xander and I were years apart and are now moving through what I feel is the adolescent phase of bonding. At least you didn't come upon us tossing each other about the room." He sighed out a laugh that rippled across her skin, the vulnerability revealed by the sound digging deep. "It happens. Quite often, actually."

She paused, gently shook free of his hold.

Dangerous, she thought to herself. This man is dangerous. He touched without consequence, and terrifyingly enough, it reminded her of her father. Timothy Byrne had hugged his family often, thought nothing of tipping them beneath the chin. Kisses on the brow had been a common welcome. Tucked them into bed at night. Every night. It scared her that she was reminded of this long-gone affection by the reserved Earl of Stanford.

Most shocking, he'd shared what was a rather startling confession. Unlike any man she'd ever known to say what he was *thinking*.

"My father knew him," she surprised herself by admitting. "Years ago, when Xander Macauley was known to roam the docks with Tobias Streeter by his side. He quite liked him, liked them both, and my father was a difficult man to impress."

"So, I'm to let him pluck my strings because he's a good man?"

Necessity laughed, the sound bouncing off stone and circling them. "Yes, I suppose. I had siblings once, dear to me before they were taken. If you're lucky enough..." She let the sentiment drift away. It didn't help to revisit the past. Cholera had swept through Shoreditch that one summer. That was simply a fact.

The earl's lips parted as he searched for a reply. Flummoxed male beauty highlighted in a shaft of golden candlelight as he sought to provide solace where she'd never had solace before.

She robbed him of the burden, striding around him and down the corridor. "I've never been to Derbyshire," she threw out to direct the conversation as he rushed to catch up. "Never been hired for such an expansive project. Most of my work involves urban gardens which, while charming, are not the size and scope of yours. We don't have such acreage in the city. There's the set of terraces I'm working on with Tobias Streeter. That project is quite something but not starting until September. His wife, Hildegard, is likely why I was given the job. I'm a bit of a pupil of her partner, the Duchess of Markham."

"One of the Duchess Society cases. Brilliant."

Oh, this *man*. "I'm not sure what that means."

"Doesn't matter what it means," the earl said instead of explaining, a note of resignation in his voice.

Her temper flared. He was making no bones about not wanting her here when she was highly qualified to put his gardens in order. "Truthfully, the most important piece on your project is Capability Brown, now that I know he worked here. His notes, if you have them, are more valuable to me than money." She straightened her spine, projecting as much of a threatening stance as she could while having to tilt her head to catch his gaze. His size made her feel positively petite. "But if you've misunderstood my position, or your brother has—"

"We haven't." Stanford's lips tightened, his stride slowing. "I assume you heard what I said while you were skulking outside my study. Xander Macauley is a fool in love. You're a Shoreditch girl, so you can do no wrong in his eyes. It goes to show how far gone he is that he's attempting this matchmaking absurdity with me of all people."

"Because you're unlovable." No mention of the desperate daughters pursuing him. The clinging mothers. The widows, actresses, opera singers. Unable to stop herself, she stared, watching the answer—*yes*—flood his face.

Her jaw set. *I'm not being taken in by this man and his practiced vulnerability.* "Besides, you have an arrangement in the village."

He paused before a door with lime-green trim. The infamous bedchamber. "And you have Jasper Noble."

So that had been discussed as well. Apparently, she'd missed pertinent parts of the conversation. Men and their bloody hypocrisy. They gossiped more than women.

Vibrating with a hundred chilling replies, she instead strolled into the bedchamber, giving it a sweeping glance. It was a delightful mix of hulking mahogany furniture, floor-to-ceiling windows, ovolo molding, and once-vibrant wallpaper. She planned to explore every inch when she could. Open every drawer, peek behind every curtain. She would even go so far as to look under the bed. Even in its shabbiness, it rivaled the loveliest chamber she'd ever stayed in, but she'd be damned if she admitted that to *him*. "Lord Stanford, I don't have anyone—and no one has me."

His lips curved. Her stance was particularly modern for a woman. She wasn't surprised that he didn't believe it. "Then we are on the same page, Miss Byrne."

She grasped the knob, prepared to close the door in his beautiful, scarred face.

But he stayed where he was, lounging like a lion against the jamb, his lashes sweeping low, concealing his thoughts. Challenging her without a word.

She'd rarely felt such a fissure of excitement race through her.

Oh, you foolish girl.

There was a feral quality to the man. More like his rascal of a brother than he realized. Similar to the ruthless types she'd grown up with in the stews. She'd never have guessed Lord Stanford to be an earl if they'd met strolling the docks. A merchant, perhaps. Or a shipping magnate. Not a dandy. A posh nob with an ancient title taking up an entire page in *Debrett's*.

When he continued to stare, she raised a brow. She could dish out the silent treatment, too.

With a crooked smile, appearing to appreciate her response, he straightened from his elegant slump holding up the wall. "I never said thank-you. For your assistance the night of my injury. The doctor said he'd never seen a wound heal as well. Whatever herb it was you used. Fever-something?"

Thank-you? Shocked, she mouthed the words, caught in a slate-gray gaze that never wavered, only drilled in upon her, intense despite its brilliance. The Earl of Stanford was close enough to touch should she think to soothe her startling urge. Close enough to note the lone freckle below his plump lower lip. The smattering of hazel flecks in his eyes. The tantalizing aroma that reached to sting her nose. He had a sun-washed glow to his skin. Was wearing finely tailored but worn clothing that did little to hide the lean play of muscle in his arms and shoulders. While she stared, he frowned slightly, his jaw tensing.

It might not be every woman. It might be only her.

But she found him incredibly appealing.

Finally understanding, Necessity breathed through her attraction, pushing past her wildly beating heart.

This was what had been missing before.

Unlike what most of London believed, she'd only invited one man into her bed. A man who'd touched her tenderly, enthusiastically, properly. When nothing she visualized in her fevered fantasies was *proper*. They'd been like two pieces that fit well enough to form some kind of random puzzle. He'd asked so nicely, been kind and respectful. Hungry for her in his own bookish manner. When she'd been very, very curious. And old enough to take care of herself. No longer a girl and still, astonishingly, untouched.

It had to be someone, that first someone, so why not the attractive bookseller who managed a flourishing store down the block? Although the many things she *thought* one could do hadn't truly happened with her humble lover. Therefore, her curiosity remained.

In any case, it had seemed like a suitable arrangement. Almost a business deal. She and Randall Hawkins were friends, then lovers. And with her decision that it could never be more, back to friends.

Why she continued to buy her horticulture books from him.

"Whatever are you thinking, Miss Byrne? It's turning your eyes a molten amber that..." Shaking his head, he sighed and pinched the bridge of his nose, letting what he was going to say drift into the night.

"I'm thinking of your gardens," she lied. "The apple orchard that receives the morning sunlight and the citrus trees we can house in the conservatory once the windows are repaired. Where I should place hydrangea and azaleas. An herb garden near the kitchens. It was feverfew I used, by the by, for your scar." Testing them both, she pulled her lip between her teeth and watched his pupils do that dance again, his body swaying toward her without his even noticing it.

He wasn't unaffected. She wasn't unaffected, though she hoped she'd hidden it better than he had.

She had a month to examine her attraction to a scoundrel once known for reckless, spirited, *talented*, carnal behavior. Women liked to talk—and they liked to talk about the Earl of Stanford and his antics in bed.

Necessity could be jealous, or she could be resourceful.

On her terms, at her request, should she decide to make Xander Macauley's bet about her a winner, it needn't get in the way of business. If she elected to approach the earl, without threat of marriage, and for a limited time only, maybe he'd say yes.

Stanford scrubbed his hand over his damaged cheek, debating, sensing she was making decisions without him. "I'll allow you to transform my gardens, Sprite. The conservatory. The meadows. It's all yours. Have at it, and *please*, charge my brother twice what you quoted."

"But not you, is that it? Putting those cards on the table in advance of the game. In the event I'd wish to transform a broken-down earl rumored to be a recluse into a new man. An earl who seems little like a recluse and more like an irritable panther roaming his country estate." She shrugged and gave her skirt a neglectful tug, not at all put off by his restraint. "But what do I know?"

He snorted, a ragged burst. "By God, everything you think comes out of that lovely mouth, doesn't it? What damned courage, or foolishness, you possess. I can't determine which. Maybe a clever mixture of both. I was taught since I was in leading strings to hide that."

When she tried to shut the door, finished with his pointed barbs, he wedged his muddy boot inside, keeping it open enough for her to see a wicked grin cross his face. "I don't suppose you're hiding a chaperone of some motley sort in there. Should I wish to continue this conversation. Most *stimulating* I've had in months."

She huffed out a breath. "I'm too old for a chaperone, my lord."

He scratched his chin with his shoulder, playing dumb. "The Duchess Society will agree to that? Seeing as you're now one of their apprentices? Hildy Streeter and Georgie, the Duchess of Markham, are arriving in Derbyshire tomorrow. Streeter has a house down the lane. Didn't anyone inform you? My brother perhaps when he arranged this fiasco? Shouldn't they be informed about the perilous situation you've put yourself in? Alone with a naughty earl in his country manse without sensible protection. Sounds like a situation in need of succor to me."

She gave the door a hard shove, but his strength was resolute. "You *wouldn't*."

"Oh, Sprite, I would. You have no idea what daring me with that whisky gaze for the past half hour has done. I can't imbibe anymore, but I can savor. We're rivals. I recognize it in my gut, but rivals for what, I don't know. But now, you see, I'm plotting, too." He tapped his temple, his smile this side of devilish. "Just as you are."

"I won't have it. Someone watching over me for the first time since my family passed. Since I was twelve years old."

He tilted his head to get a better view of her through the crack in the door. Blinked those gorgeous eyes of his, considering her when it wasn't his place. "It'll be bad for business should this get out. Society has rules and you're mixing with the upper reaches, my darling gardener. Isn't that what the Duchess Society relationship is all about? Learning what's what besides planting daisies and begonias and such. By association, even if only on the marigold side, you have to follow the *ton's* guidelines. I imagine Hildy and Georgie went over this in horrifying detail if you're indeed an understudy of theirs." He laughed, a genuine laugh, nothing false about it, drawing on her last nerve. "You thought to sneak away, avoid policies put in place four hundred years ago. How charmingly naïve. Sweet, actually."

"If I say yes, fine, arrange for a companion I won't speak to for the next month, can I shut this door and be done with you for the night?"

"One more thing before I arrange for your sitter. Have you had dinner?" As if he cared if she ate.

"Your housekeeper sent a tray up." Necessity jacked her thumb over her shoulder, tapping her toe in a furious beat. "Tea, bread, cheese."

The earl's brow rose, his smile growing, damn him. "*Really*? Score one for Miss Byrne."

He placed his hand on the door. She couldn't help but imagine those long, slim fingers tracing the curves of her body. Doing the wicked things that were whispered about him in darkened parlors. "I'll have Mrs. Violet Rothbottom meet you at breakfast. She's served as temporary governess for Tobias Streeter and the Duke of Markham in the past, and I'm fairly sure I can secure her for the next month. Keep her with you, will you please? I have men working on the estate, and frankly, you're a distraction they don't need."

"Sending your friend, I assume. The one you have the arrangement with."

Necessity could have kicked herself once the statement rolled out. What was *wrong* with her? You weren't supposed to talk to a man about his *mistresses*. It was so forbidden there wasn't even a rule about it in that refined conduct, associating-with-the-*ton* book of his.

He turned back—when he'd been leaving, blast it—his eyes glowing in the sconce's gilded light. If she wasn't mistaken, and she usually wasn't, the Earl of Stanford was enjoying this. "I can arrange for her to sit with you if it better suits. Though I think you'll try her patience a little *too* much. And I want to stay on her good side, you see."

Breaking another rule, Necessity growled and slammed an earl's door in an earl's face.

Telling herself jealousy had nothing to do with it.

Chapter Four

WHERE A HEADSTRONG COUPLE
DISCOVER THE ART OF DISCORD

The earl and his gardener stayed out of each other's way for three days.

An early riser, Necessity arrived in the breakfast room after he'd already left. Surprising, as she'd imagined he slept until noon.

She'd heard two scullery maids whispering about him going into the village to assist with repair of a building they planned to use as a school. They'd giggled about the lord of the manor striding about without his coat, shirt buttons undone, the hint of gray in his hair perfectly matching his eyes. And his scar, his roguish, curiously appealing scar. Their cheeks were flushed with delight over their discoveries. She'd been envious. She'd gone years without being delighted by anyone.

When she could tell them the wicked earl was likely staying in the village *after* the repairs to visit his lady friend. There were scandalous arrangements to be made.

Men, as she understood it, didn't like to go long without.

While she'd begun work on his side garden, her assistants having arrived the day before, she spent the nights drafting plans for the larger sections of the estate, hunched over the escritoire in her bedchamber until her bloodshot eyes forced her to retire. She'd ordered citrus from her vendor in the city and a book on designing an orangery that she hoped Randall delivered before the trees arrived. She'd even got around to finding appropriate windows for the conservatory; a costly invoice Xander Macauley had approved for payment without batting an eye.

The Earl of Stanford really was going to make his brother pay.

In her spare moments, she'd begun to explore. The rolling hills and hamlets of Derbyshire were the prettiest she'd ever seen—when she'd not been enthusiastic about traveling to the country. She was a city creature through and through. Rushing rivers, blue-green lakes, and meandering paths snaking through dense forest were wholly unfamiliar to her. Limestone caverns littered with fossils that the Duke of Markham, a close friend of the earl's who'd arrived and was staying with Tobias Streeter, was said to be investigating.

Her chaperone, Mrs. Violet Rothbottom, gamely stuck with her during her pursuits. Knitting in a chair under a towering elm while Necessity dug in the dirt. Striding through the woodlands with silent diligence, holding Necessity's tools while she made notes about plants she couldn't identify. She brought foodstuff each day in a battered leather satchel. Something Necessity often forgot when she was involved with a project.

Necessity had laughed when she'd first seen her companion, fifty years of age if she was a day. Curling gray hair, a surplus of wrinkles about her mouth, and nut-brown eyes that spoke of having seen much. That Necessity had claimed this woman was the earl's lover made her smile. A joke she would have shared with the man had they been on speaking terms.

Somehow, without trying, she amused Mrs. Rothbottom with her enthusiasm. Or her naivete. Necessity wasn't sure which. She could have told her companion that she hadn't traveled beyond London's outskirts, not once in her life. This job was an adventure, and she meant to make the most of it. On someone else's shilling, too, which made it even better.

Icing on the cake, this evening promised to be the most exciting part yet.

Necessity grinned and rubbed her hands together, on her way this very minute to find Capability Brown's documents hidden away in the library. As she traversed the gallery and headed down the corridor the lone footman on the estate had directed her to, Necessity recalled every word the earl had said. *Bottom bookshelf, the one near the back window. Left side. Cracked leather covers.* She planned to cross-reference them against her notes and see how close their visions were. She'd waited until her plans were complete, so it was a true test of talent. She didn't need to be intimidated away from her creativity by the best landscape designer there ever was or would be. But she could learn from him and learn she would.

The Earl of Stanford kisses like a Greek god.

Necessity released a breath through her teeth, not understanding why this bit of nonsense flitted through her mind when she was on a horticultural quest. A silly snatch of gossip she'd overheard years ago when she worked in the Duke of Leighton's household. It wasn't a servant the earl had kissed but a countess. Or a marchioness. Someone high on the social ladder who had blabbed about it after. A frantic soul who'd climbed in Lord Stanford's window to reach him and been welcomed once she got there.

Yet, like a vicious chest cold or a bee sting, something you didn't want but received anyway, it came to mind as she stood frozen in the arched doorway of the library. In the middle, the dead *middle*, of the night. The grandfather clock had struck three, in fact, on her way here.

Everyone was supposed to be sleeping. Except those who couldn't sleep.

Which amounted to an earl and his gardener.

She glanced at her trousers—*bloody hell*—then back at him.

The Earl of Stanford stood before a broad bay window, his eye pressed to a telescope trained on the sky, layers of watery moonlight flowing over him, adding unfair advantage to an already romantic scene. Trousers not so dissimilar from the tattered ones she wore hung low on his hips. Untucked shirt open most of the way down the front, no cravat, no coat. A massive desk situated at a hasty angle by his side, with a journal, quill, and ink atop it. A cup, half a sandwich on a plate.

She stepped inside what was clearly his domain. As wasn't always the case, a library in *use*. Books scattered about. Oil lamps aglow. A hearth fire snapping. The rich scent of tea mixing with the earl's decidedly distinctive fragrance. Bergamot, she guessed. And leather, always the hint of leather. He must ride often, she guessed, adding to her knowledge of him.

This was a space inhabited by a man who didn't sleep as he should. Invaded by a woman who didn't sleep as she should.

Her pulse skipped to imagine they had something, *anything*, in common.

She suspected her fascination could jeopardize her happiness—and her heart. Sleepless nights and restless yearnings couldn't close the gap between an earl with a dilapidated castle and a feisty rookery girl who'd had the choice to become a thief, a light-skirt, or a gardener. And had chosen the dirt.

The Earl of Stanford was too different. Too far *above*. She didn't like reaching for things out of her grasp. As a rational woman, she had never made it a habit to yearn for unattainable pleasures.

"Are you coming in or backing out, Miss Byrne?" he murmured, his eye never leaving the telescope. "I'm waiting with drawn breath for your decision."

Oh, he had to mock her at every turn. Although she *was* lingering like a dithering debutante in the doorway. "In," she announced, then stamped into the room.

He hummed, a sensual gust that curdled desire deep in her belly. "As I thought. Tea is on the sideboard. Cinnamon biscuits, stale but edible, on the plate. I can't offer brandy as, well... you and all London know of my issues." Leaning to the side, his gaze on the sky, he grasped the quill from the desk—left-handed, she observed with another warming jolt of discovery—and jotted notes in his journal, murmuring to himself as she did when she was in the weeds.

Then he grabbed his cup, took a sluggish sip, his gaze finally swinging to her.

And holding.

She swallowed hard and continued her trek to the sideboard, poured tea, pretty as you please. Pretty as the Duchess Society had instructed. A queen couldn't have done better. She wasn't going to apologize for her attire. Not at three in the morning when no one was about.

Too, there was the minute ping of feminine satisfaction zipping through her; she couldn't lie. She didn't mind a man finding her form pleasing, even if she'd kicked decorum in the arse to get the praise.

When she glanced back, the earl's attention was right there, on her bottom as a matter of fact. With scant apology, same as her, he lifted his gaze, enjoying the show on his way up. His expression, for one unguarded second, flared. Hot, aroused male. Eyes glimmering, cheeks lit. His fingers clenched around his dainty teacup as he blinked, once, twice.

Her stomach bottomed out to her knees. Want, *need,* roaring through her. A bit shocking as she'd never felt the like with the bookseller. Which may have been the problem.

They stared, nothing benign about the situation. Something fiery snapping between them like they each held the end of a rope and were yanking it. Conduct unsuitable in London, she supposed. Only, this was Derbyshire. A deserted library and two restless eccentrics.

Who would know? Who would care?

Necessity cared, a little. Not *care* cared. Mild concern. A nagging sense of impending doom. Or better to say *inevitability*.

Groaning into his teacup, the Earl of Stanford shook his head to clear it. "I fear I've been rendered speechless by your presentation."

With a wince, she tossed back a gulp of truly horrific tea, then set the cup aside. Couldn't spit out a chivalrous statement to save his life, could he? "That would be a first."

"Circling back to lad's clothing, is it? I thought we decided by my bedside years ago that those weren't doing the trick."

She swept her hand down her body, signifying her fashion disaster. "Are you going to tell the Duchess Society I'm running around in trousers? Or my chaperone? That would brighten your day. And ruin hers. Mrs. Rothbottom is taking this job very seriously. She actually thinks she's protecting me."

He braced his hip on the edge of the desk, cradling his cup in his palms. His long body held in a negligent posture. There were mysteries shimmering in his silver-splendor eyes. In his beautiful, damaged face. A potent mix she wanted desperately to explore. With her mind, with her hands. With her *mouth*. Her teeth sinking into his skin, her tongue soothing the bite. More immediate desires than she knew how to satisfy with her sparse knowledge. "Are you going to tell Xander I'm here, researching stars in the middle of the night? Which he worries about, God help us both. My lack of sleep. He doesn't know how bad it gets, and I'd rather he didn't." He tilted his head, gesturing with his cup. "My secret for yours."

"Ah," she murmured, hooked. *Damn*. Shrewd play by the nob. He'd revealed a hidden piece of himself, leaving her unable to deny his request. "I will not."

He rubbed his temple, grimacing. "It's a deal." Then sighing, he realized he'd shown his weakness. "Headaches. After the last conflict in Raigad. There was a skirmish, an injury. My final military payment to the crown. Almost my final on this earth. My ears ring occasionally, too, which is almost worse."

Making a mental note to send him chamomile and clove tea, Necessity circled to a bookcase littered with a random assortment of volumes, unwilling to go directly after the Capability Brown records. Jane Austen, Sir Walter Scott, James Fenimore Cooper. Grazing her finger over the worn leather spines, she breathed in the scent of wealth and decay rather than ask about India. Often, she'd found people spoke more when asked *less*. "I'm sorry if I was crosser than the situation called for the other night." She started to shrug, then recalled her Duchess Society lessons and called it back. "I'm better with plants than people."

At his exhalation, she glanced up. Found him staring into his cup, befuddled in a manner he'd also revealed the other night. Charming her without *trying* to charm. Vulnerability wrapped in that brawny, protective shell. The riskiest con alive.

After a lengthy silence, his gaze seized hers, raw sentiment spilling free. "You think I'm *good* with people?"

"Scars make the man," she mumbled, mystified he felt there was a problem. Women climbed in windows to get to him. Had he forgotten the marchioness? His arrangement in the village? The opera singer, the actress. Cousin to the king? Gallons of ink spent on his escapades before he'd tangled with a drunken baron in an alley and decided to abscond.

They hadn't chased him away; he'd run.

Considering, he stroked the back of his wrist across his ruined cheek. "Hmm... yes, you mentioned that once." Inexplicably, a crooked grin tilted his lips, amusement taking hold. At her, at him. She loved that he could swing so quickly from joy to anguish. She wasn't sure what the Earl of Stanford was going to say or do, and it was maddening. Compelling. Frustrating. Captivating. "It's the eyes that saved my face, I suppose. Inherited from my father, unfortunately. But I make the best use of what I've been given. No one can say I don't."

She yanked *Pride and Prejudice* free, wishing to tell him it wasn't merely his eyes. It was everything. A handsome façade. Intellect, wit, and that secret ingredient the lucky few had that drew people like bees to honey. Charisma simply *was*.

With most people, Necessity simply couldn't be bothered.

With the Earl of Stanford, she *wanted* to be bothered.

He nodded to the book in her hand. "The library needs work. My father sold off entire collections to cover his gambling debts. I haven't purchased anything to fill the shelves, rebuild this space. Not yet. Leaking roofs and crumbling beams come first."

A prosperous problem. She'd never had a library of her own. *Someday*, she thought, flipping pages. A few more projects. The completion of the terraces with Tobias Streeter. Then she'd buy the cottage in Islington she had her eye on. It had blue trim windows and a scrumptious, though small, garden out back. There was a parlor she could outfit with bookshelves, perhaps. Some of the best craftsmen in London lived in Shoreditch and had worked with her father. She'd have help the minute she requested it.

Returning to his telescope, he pressed his eye to the eyepiece. "You skinned your knee climbing that ancient oak in the north orchard."

Necessity popped the book back in its slot with a whack. "Mrs. Rothbottom giving updates, I see. The tree is *diseased*. I was checking a lower limb."

"Can I ask that you stay on the ground? Please? Dash dropped a hammer on his foot watching you shimmy down. Thank God, you weren't wearing this ensemble. He would have choked. I'd have had to retrieve my smelling salts." Sliding his fingertips along the telescope's barrel, he adjusted the counterweight. Muscles shifting neatly in his back, his shoulders. Crisp, white sleeves shoved to the elbow, exposing skin covered with hair as dark as that upon his head. "And your assistants..."

Necessity crossed her arms over her chest and tapped her slippered foot in time to her heartbeat. *Here it comes.* Another patronizing decree. A rule. A bloody judgment. "You take issue with female gardeners? Well-trained, intelligent, skilled craftspeople working your estate is offensive merely because they wear skirts and a bonnet?"

He scribbled another note in his ledger, unfazed by her outburst. "I'm a supporter of female empowerment, Miss Byrne. Especially in my bedchamber." Her temper sizzled as this was nothing he'd say to an actual *lady*. "Truthfully, your arrival has improved morale. My lone footman, Driscoll, was set to resign until your team arrived. Now he's happy to wear outdated livery forever if more females with shovels show up."

"That fetching Scottish lad breaking his toe gawking at the help isn't my problem, my lord earl. Nor your miserable staff. Or your maddening brother. Would you care to worry about a disease that can take down a copse of azaleas in a week? Or an unexpected early frost that can lay waste to an entire spring planting? You deal with your difficulties, and I'll deal with mine."

"Stanford. Or Oliver if you'd like to test the limits. Hell, it's the country, so why not test them?" He made another notation on the page, then allowed his gaze, because she knew it was deliberate, to strike hers. "When you say 'my lord earl' in that slicing tone, it reminds me of someone calling after my father, without the earl part, which is unnecessary but charming. It grates, as it were, being reminded of him." He returned to the telescope, nonplussed, avoiding another confession. "Dash is young, impressionable, impulsive. And ethereal in appearance, which is a danger. He's here on holiday to remove him from Town temptations. Much like me not so long ago, without the boundless attractiveness to contend with." Adjusting the lenses, he repositioned his eye without glancing at her. "Derbyshire with the sober earl is quite a pragmatic place to unwind."

"Young. How much younger?" She dragged her finger down a tattered leather spine. "Two years? Three?"

"A hundred," he murmured. "A thousand."

Necessity glanced to the bookshelf, the one near the back window. Left side. Capability Brown's ledgers were there, as the earl had promised. As *Stanford* had promised. She didn't want to soothe him. Ask him what his somber response meant. Find out more about him. When she desired more but did not *want* to desire more.

"Go ahead," he said, an amused rumble threading his words. He knew what she wanted. Why she'd sneaked into his library four hours before dawn. "I even dusted them off for you. Mr. Smith's brilliance awaiting your review."

She started across the room, twisting her hands in excitement. *Brown*, she thought to correct him, then gave up the fight. "I'll take them with me if you don't mind. I'll be careful as these are significant—"

"Miss Byrne, come here." He beckoned with two fingers. *Now.*

She could have said no. Told him she didn't care about gazing at silly old stars that weren't going to shift one whit in her lifetime. Told him the sky held little interest; it was the land that changed. However, his voice held a note of joy that she didn't have the heart to reject.

If she wanted to unravel the puzzle of Oliver, Earl of Stanford, the skies seemed a smart place to start.

He stepped aside when she reached him, nudging the telescope's cylinder down so she could see through the eyepiece. Grasping a leg of the tripod, he dragged the equipment closer. It was then she noted his feet were bare, his boots and stockings in a tumble by the hearth. They were long and slim, as elegant as any she'd seen outside cast in marble.

Her throat dried up until it clicked when she swallowed. *Feet, Josie. They're just feet.*

"Over there. Shift your head until a clear image presents itself. Go on, do it." He tapped the eyepiece and moved in behind her, the heat from his body circling. The feeling of being besieged was not lost on her. "You're bloody fortunate to witness such a display. I admit, I never have anyone to share my findings with."

She tore her gaze away from his endearing smile. The dimple that had once again chosen to haunt her. The intelligence shimmering from him like fog off heated cobbles. Remarkable, she thought suddenly. A man unlike any she'd ever met. Vibrant in a world of stony gray.

Flustered, she did as he asked, satisfying him but expecting little for herself. A tendency since cholera had taken everyone she loved and left her with only memories. She fit her eye to the piece, shifting for proper placement. Blinked, then again. *Oh.* She blew out a long sigh when she saw it. The sky awash with flashes of light. Flares, trails of golden dust across the heavens. Winking, streaking magic. "*Oh, my...*"

"Marvelous, isn't it?" He stepped in, not touching, but closer. His warm breath striking the back of her neck, sending a shudder down her body. "It's a fairly rare celestial event. Atmospheric phenomenon if you prefer. The first shower recorded was in 1583. This could go on until dawn. The sky lit with sorcery. The display is typically named after the nearest constellation, using a possessive form of Latin. Which is actually the only thing I learned at Harrow that's been of benefit with stargazing. I wasn't the swiftest student."

He tipped his head and gazed over hers, his low hum of pleasure wrecking her where she stood. An intimate moment between two lost souls.

I can't stay here with this irresistible creature until dawn.

Her heart was racing, her hands trembling. Choices her body was making without her consent, wrestling control from her mind. Confused and consumed, she focused on the sky, the all-consuming splendor he'd shared. Watching another rocket burst, then another. Crimson flashes with burning blue tails. She laughed and pressed closer, the telescope pulling her into the scene. His world. "Magnificent."

"It is," he breathed.

She glanced at him, a sidelong look teeming with aching awareness. From the fiery spark in his eyes, it was clear he wasn't referring to the stars.

"My father would have loved this. He liked to chart the constellations in winter when he said the skies were clearest. Like his father before him. A hobby, nothing like this." Vexed by her admission, she stepped back. Released a pent breath. "I have to go. I only wished to retrieve Capability Brown's notes. Not interrupt you. Not..."

Talk with you. Laugh. Feel your passion like a pulse in my veins. A rapid beat in my heart. What would that enthusiasm be like, she wondered, if directed toward her instead of the stars?

"I have to go," she repeated but made no effort to move an inch.

He frowned, glancing at his hands. "My father would have hated it. My mother, however, would have loved it." Releasing a ragged laugh, his broad chest rose and fell. "I can smell her scent at random moments. Lavender and a hint of citrus. She visits me in fragments throughout the day. Isn't that odd?"

"I don't want whatever is brewing between us like tea." She stalked to the bookshelf housing her hero's wisdom. Dropping to her knee, she yanked the ledgers free. There were two. *C.B.* stamped on the corner of each in indelible black ink. Anticipation warred with dread. What a possible price she was paying to look at these. Fantasies of kissing Oliver Aspinwall were one thing. *This* bit of theatre—talk of family and shooting stars—was another dilemma altogether.

She was the worst person in England for a reclusive earl who doubtless needed someone who secured every little thing she felt in a box. Only shuffled out what was needed at the moment. A minimum of fuss. Of feeling.

Necessity had never quite figured out how to lock away her emotions.

"I don't want this," she repeated, turning to see that he stood behind her. From her position crouched on the floor, he hovered over her. He moved stealthily when he wanted to, a soldier's training. Crafty devil.

"It's called intimacy, Sprite, and I don't want it, either. Not with you."

She palmed the scuffed planks beneath her feet, steadying herself. Even for her, hard-edged as she was, his insults were starting to sting. "I like plants because they change. I transform them."

"I like stars because they're constant. I transform *nothing*."

He was troubled, as desperate as she to escape this moment. But his eyes were molten. A smoky ash that spoke of tangled sheets and breathless passion. Sweat and heat and frayed moans gliding across bare skin. This much she knew. She and her bookseller hadn't been a superb match, compatible in the way she'd hoped. She'd not explored as she'd wanted or given herself freely.

But she *had* learned to recognize a man's arousal, as well as feel her own clamoring in response.

Necessity shoved to her feet with Capability Brown's notes clutched to her chest. The earl wasn't going to intimidate her, thrust her in a corner where the wallflowers resided, merely because he could. She'd be damned first. While encountering blatant ridicule and rampant contempt from London's notables, she'd made her way. *Paid* her way. Built a thriving business allowing her to secure a humble home far from the ragged fringes of Shoreditch. And not a living soul had helped her do it.

After her family died, she could have become a cutpurse. A light-skirt, twelve years old a ripe time to start. Lived above a flash house and thieved her way into a position of some dreadful sort with some dreadful man. She'd had offers. Multiple offers.

Instead, she'd chosen a legitimate path. The trickier path.

One the strongest took.

Necessity Byrne had never shied away from grasping what she wanted.

Taking the perilous path, going on blind impulse, listening to the thrumming need swimming through her blood and not the fearful thoughts filling her head, she placed the ledgers on a chair and stumbled forward, awkwardly pressing her mouth to his. Clasped the nape of his neck, sinking her fingers into the glossy hair hanging over his collar.

Trying to control him before he controlled her.

In response, he stilled, frozen, though his heartbeat burst into a ferocious rhythm beneath the hand she'd placed on his chest. A staggered breath shot across her cheek. A muffled sound that could have signaled pleasure *or* anger rolled from his throat.

She touched her tongue to his bottom lip, biting gently, her body liquifying in response. Catching fire like the kindling in the hearth across the room. When she'd never bitten the bookseller.

Stanford moaned then, unable to curb his hunger, but he didn't engage her in play.

"Kiss me back, my stubborn lord earl."

His shoulder tensed beneath her fingers. "I won't be taken in," he whispered against her cheek, her jaw, his lips setting beneath her ear. Rejecting her. But he chased her when she retreated, caught her face in his palms and brought her into the sizzling shelter of his body, unwilling to let her go.

"As if I could tempt you," was all she got out before he tilted his head and showed her why women climbed in windows to get to him.

The kiss was beseeching without being rushed. Brilliantly detailed, like his sketches of the stars. A focused assault she felt to her toes. She vibrated beneath the hand he raced down her body to attach to her waist, pulling her to him. Her senses flooded with his scent, his touch, as he imprinted his longing upon her. Tangled in yearning, awareness of him flooding her until she struggled to separate her demand from his.

Teasing with his tongue, he nipped her bottom lip as she moaned softly, his fingertips digging into her hip. Moving her against him in an age-old rhythm she recognized. Paying her back using her own tricks. Persuading in his measured way until she shifted restlessly against him. Gripped his shoulder, his neck, seeking to go where she'd never allowed herself to go before.

"There's a greedy girl," he said, letting the words slide right into the kiss. "Take me, Sprite. Take me."

Then he set about to torture. Taking *her*. A soldier going into battle. She'd been senseless to think she could win this. His hand rose to skim the rounded edge of her breast, leaving a trail of fire before returning to her hip. Her nipple puckered and she gasped, bumping against him, wanting what he wouldn't yet give. His fingers twisted in her trousers, a single layer of cotton separating them from catastrophe.

He pulled back just enough for his silky gasp to hit her cheek. "Is this what you wanted, Sprite?" But he didn't wait for the answer, roughly cupping the crown of her head, tipping it back.

All she saw was a flash of icy silver before he took them under.

He kissed without restraint, seeking to prove a point, win a match. The Earl of Stanford wasn't subtle about his intent. More than she'd received in her life, even with a man lying atop her. That elemental piece missing before sliding into place and locking them together. The mystery of yearning for that *one* person.

Her senses swam, overtaken. The sound of swift breaths leaving his lips flowing through her. The stubble on his jaw abrading her cheek. His fingers at her waist, squeezing, trapping her. Hips bumping as they sought a closeness they'd not find with clothing between them. Likely not find standing up.

She couldn't decide where to touch him. *Everywhere*. What to do. *Everything*. Her mind was spinning at a dizzying speed, the ground beneath her shifting with each beat of her heart. Deprivation forcing her down an instinctive, animalistic path while he was busy laying a bounty of delight at her feet.

For long seconds, minutes, hours, the kiss was mad, mindless. Two people clinging to each other as a storm raged around them. How unexpected. How frightening.

How wonderful.

His domination—and her submission—made her furious. Made her *yearn*. Changed her mind, completely, right there in a Derbyshire library in the middle of the night, about what she'd do to have him.

"I want you," she murmured, appalled and thrilled that she'd shared this sentiment.

His hold on her tightened as he shoved her back, pressing her between his hard body and the chilled stone wall. Without skirts, he effortlessly stepped between her legs, cradling his rigid shaft against her core. She wiggled her hips, her heartbeat exploding as she sought to ease the pulse thumping between her thighs. The shiver caught her at the base of her spine and spread like a fever. He was seducing her as she'd not been seduced, showing her a clandestine world until this moment denied her.

She rode the wild hunger and, weakened by his touch, let it rule. Sinking her fingers into his hair and tugging. Grasping his shirt in her fist and drawing him as close as she could get him.

Lower, her hand sliding down his chest, his flat, quivering belly. She wanted to feel his hard heat, wrap her hand around him and make him lose his mind.

Ruined, she realized this wasn't a simple kiss they were playing at now.

He caught her wrist before she could reach his cock. His blustery gaze found hers, his eyes having gone the dark color of burnt ash. An emotion that looked like panic crossed his face. She only had to wait a moment for it to revolve to fury. "You had to start this, didn't you? Dare me with more recklessness than I've ever encountered in a woman. Make me consider things I haven't considered in ages. Kiss me in a way I haven't been kissed in years, if ever." He slapped his hand on the wall above her shoulder, caging her in. The fingers holding her trembled. "I recall this feeling, Sprite. As it was with opium, I am *undone*."

She breathed out a ragged sigh, sickly flattered. *Heavens,* he was comparing her to the drug that had almost destroyed him.

"You wanted to see what it was like. The games we can play. How much pleasure there could be between us." His shoulders sank with a tight exhalation. "When I *knew*... bloody hell, I knew. Maybe from the first moment I met you, hunkered down by my sickbed. There was a vibration that night, a teasing touch along my spine, that had nothing to do with the wound on my face. It was *you*, and I knew it. Sometimes, darling Sprite, you have to go with the gut."

"I can't... I'm sorry..."

With an oath, he reclaimed her lips, his tongue drawing hers into furious battle. Lifting her arm, he braced her wrist against the wall, imprisoning her, heightening her arousal. Something she would not have thought possible. Teaching her a mysterious aspect about herself she filed away for future reference. She wasn't about to push him away, not now. Not *yet*. She wanted the release that was creeping up on her. The molten feeling between her thighs. The heat pressing in on her. Her arousal, for the first time with a man, had *teeth*.

She had no way to think of it nicely, like one of his society women would have. The simple truth was, his cock was as hard as the wall he'd backed her into—and his movements with his hips were hitting a particularly sensitive spot. An area ignored by her former lover and known to her only through repeated experimentations in her bedchamber.

Oh yes, there, she thought in relief and anguish. Though she didn't dare whisper it. The earl's engagement was tenuous. One wrong word, and he'd leave her alone and aching.

Wrapping her arms around him, she pressed her fingertips into his shoulders, trailing down the powerful slope of his back. His muscles rippled and flexed beneath her hands. He groaned softly into her mouth, stretching into her touch.

If his kiss is this good, how incredible will the rest be?

"You want to take me down a notch, and I just might let you." Shaken, she paused, putting space between them, enough for a breath to pass. A ragged sigh, a feather. Only to return instantly. Sliding her lips over the pulse pounding out a scattered rhythm beneath his ear, she nipped his jaw, the side of his mouth, his scarred cheek. Sucked his earlobe between her teeth until he groaned.

"Fuck," he whispered, a forbidden word she'd heard her entire life but never imagined an earl would say. A jolt of heat danced through her in response, landing in all the wrong places. In all the *right* places. Telling her what she needed to know. That he wanted her as much as she wanted him.

His lips pursed as he sighed, head dropping back to allow her greater access. He was giving her what she wanted. *Him.* She'd never been more provoked. Or more humbled. She'd never had such a man to toy with. One as enticing as the Earl of Stanford.

Wrapping his hand around the thick length of her hair, he brought her gaze to his. "You're right. I want to take you down a notch. Three notches, one hundred. Crawl atop you, pleasure you until your shouts bring down these moldy rafters. Trace every curve of your body, lick and suck and bite my way along like I'm following a map. Conspire to make you lose that dogged self-assurance, using every last ounce of knowledge I've gained along the way. And that is, although I likely shouldn't admit it, rather an impressive sum."

He trailed his knuckle down her neck, along her collarbone, and into the edge of her shirt. Scalding her skin as if his fingertip was aflame. Lifted his foot and snaked his toe into the cuff of her trousers.

She'd almost forgotten his bare feet during this wild spree. "How's that for the truth you love so much? To have you beg makes me decidedly eager. You standing before me in men's clothing once again makes me eager. When I've not been eager..." He shrugged a broad shoulder, implying that he never had.

"I've done this before," she blurted, terrified of where this was leading, hoping the declaration would make him run, when she didn't want him to run.

What if she told him she could come from this alone? If he tormented her long enough with his sensual threats. If he continued to brush his shaft against her, taunting, over and over and over again. She'd never imagined she could *arrive* while standing, with clothing on.

Didn't he understand? No matter the heat flowing like lava between them, she was a step down. Three thousand steps down. Into the gutter. While he stood at the edge of heaven.

She wanted to be conquered. But she didn't want to be *broken.*

He gave her a gentle shake, as if sensing he was losing her. Let her hair slide through his fingers like water. "I don't care what you've done." His lashes quivered against the sleepless slashes beneath his eyes as his hand returned to her hip, clasping in possession. Drawing her into a body she wanted to use as shelter. Into a man she wanted to overwhelm, to possess. "Or if I do, which I might because I've never liked sharing, I won't think about it. Don't throw regret at me now. Not when you have me in the palm of your hand. Lost in the feel, the taste, of you. Yours to take, if you so choose. In any way you choose."

His candor, when she was rumored to be the most forthright woman in England, stunned her. With a flustered exhalation, she wiggled out of his grasp, under his arm, and into the middle of the chamber, her heart knocking against her ribs in time to *his* breaths. A union of souls she didn't require.

This time, he let her go. Merely stalked her with a feral silver gaze.

"You're not the right man, my lord."

He snorted, scorn flooding eyes that shuttered while she watched. *My lord,* he mouthed sarcastically. After a charged moment, he replied, "You're not the right woman, Necessity Byrne. But I want you, anyway."

She scrubbed her fist over her brow, breathless and troubled. What a persistent idiot he was. What a feeble idiot she was. "I can't think with you standing there, towering over me. Your eyes scorching me like the embers crackling in that ancient hearth at our backs. Your body"—she swallowed, her gesture crude, straight out of the stews should he need a reminder about her beginnings—"hard."

"You *did* this, you started this. Don't judge when I'm simply responding to the hottest kiss two people have shared since Shakespeare began penning verses." He yanked his hand through his hair, sending the inky strands dancing, then grazed his wrist cautiously over scars he didn't need to worry over. They made him more attractive, not less. Nevertheless, she was *not* going there with him in this uncertain mood.

"It's never the person you think you'd choose, Sprite. My brother told me that recently, and I'm coming to believe it. Another checkmark for Xander Macauley."

"It's a price you can't pay." She patted her chest, wanting him to understand. She was close to dissolving into a puddle at his feet. Her breasts felt heavy, her stomach fluttery. Her nipples hard points scratching against her corset. She didn't feel herself. Necessity Byrne, toughest chit in the kingdom, best landscape architect in this country, brought down by a kiss. "*My* price. Because I have one, you know. If you think provisions are only reserved for ladies, think again."

Necessity should tell him. She would require things.

Dirty, delicious things.

She'd touched herself and imagined them without having any idea a man was out there who could satisfy her.

She wanted to play. Explore. Discover. The mysteries she hadn't been able to solve with her erstwhile lover. But this was a task tailored to someone of her standing. A man she could trust. A rookery bloke. Like her bookseller, except someone she wanted desperately this time. Not a tortured earl the entire of London hungered for. The only toff in England who *under*estimated his value. A sincere person deep down, she suspected. One she might end up needing more than she should.

"We don't know if I can pay until you name a price. I can't negotiate with thin air." His voice went savage. "Other men have paid, I assume. Or is this a provision reserved only for lords?"

Men, as in *many*. Her lips parted, a horrified gasp rushing forth. He believed her... *oh*. Offended and humiliated, she started for the door. She'd come back for her research. Stanford thought to judge her when he'd asked not to be judged himself. And erroneously, too, when he'd bedded half of London.

He caught her at his desk, next to the treacherous-to-her-heart telescope. Spun her around, his grip gentle but sure. "I said something stupid. Moved too quickly. Insulted you when that was not my intent. You have my sincere apology." He frowned, an enchanting pleat popping between his brows. Effortless charm she wished didn't entice. "You have me on the ropes here, Nessie. I'm not good without planning. Spontaneity is not my strong suit. I'm disconcerted by this unexpected evening even as I'm wholly and utterly captivated."

Nessie. Where had he come up with that?

Her flash of pleasure at the nickname made it hard to dispute the leaden realization—that she'd never wished to crawl into bed with a man more in her *life*. She grunted uncharitably. "You plan your encounters?"

"Usually, well, *yes*. I mean, I have a certain method. A particular style. I'm known for it, I suppose. Or I was before a drunken baron ruined my face. That way, with practice, I didn't have to think too much. Mostly, I wasn't sober. Only partially coherent. I can't honestly remember that much." He bit down hard, his jaw flexing, that sweetly bewildered expression back on his face. "This is coming out poorly. I hear the words and want to snatch them back, even if they're true. I feel like a deer in your crosshairs."

She exhaled quietly, his helplessness digging deep. How could *she* feel the teacher here? "There's only been one man. It ended over a year ago. We remain friends. I wasn't forced. It was my choice, although we didn't have enough encounters for me to develop a 'sense of style.' To find myself. To even be sure what I *like*." She licked her lips, wishing she hadn't when his eyes blazed, his body swaying as he rocked back on his heels. "I've confused you. My price..." She glanced to the sunrise bleeding around the folds of the worn curtains. Streaks of crimson and a faded, bruised blue. Derbyshire in all its glory. "My price is discovery. Someone willing to explore."

His lips parted as he blinked. "Explore? In bed."

"Or out of it. I've heard the whispers in public houses. On street corners when I was a girl. I've seen a dirty drawing or two that lead me to believe there's more."

"More," he repeated woodenly, his gaze having gone roving above her head.

"More." She shot a breath through her teeth, annoyed he was making her spell it out. "Positions, places. I don't know how to say what I want to say, especially to a man who isn't going to be the one doing it with me. I don't want marriage. I don't need it. I have my own funds and the grandest bit in this world for a woman, freedom. I just want *this*. I'm curious." Her cheeks lit, burning. Stupidly, she stepped to his telescope and slammed her gaze to the eyepiece. She could not finish this with his gaze scalding her like it was. "I never had the chance before, you see..."

He slumped to his desk. She heard the thud. "Give me a moment if you please. I want to make sure I'm not dreaming," he whispered, his voice cracking.

She smothered a laugh, desperate to hold it in.

"Here you are, in tight trousers and a wicked smile, looking like something out of a fantasy I've concocted. Revealing your, let's be honest and call them what they are, your *fantasies*. To me. The melancholy Earl of Stanford. I know you'll want to punch me for saying this, but I think I owe my brother a considerable gift for sending you to me."

She tilted the telescope, bringing the earl's incredible shooting stars into view. They streaked a sky, washing shades of cherry and gold with the coming sunrise. "Forget I mentioned it. You're my employer. In the House of Lords, for God's sake. I'm as common as the soil I love wriggling about in. I have my admirers. I'll get along fine. Because Shoreditch and Mayfair should never meet."

The silence in the room lengthened, fraught with tension. Then, "Xander Macauley is your employer. I don't live in Mayfair, and you no longer live in Shoreditch if I have it right. Not so far apart, are we? And I don't want to hear about your bloody admirers."

"You're not the man for the job," she said, his determination starting to get to her.

"This job is designed for me, Sprite. I will be *so* agreeable. I'm happy to be put through any course you want me to run to prove myself. Happy to take orders or give them if that's what you find you like. I have a month to show you everything you missed the first time around. Isn't that what you said you needed to get my grounds in order? Daylight reserved for the gardens, and the nights reserved for us."

A cascade of brilliant lights dotted the sky like diamonds sewn into velvet, and she marveled at the man who'd shown them to her. That he'd revealed so much of himself, and so freely, kept the word she knew she should utter—*no*—locked tight in her throat. There was more to him, more to her, than society had seen.

Her task was to avoid becoming too intrigued by this fact.

"You're not leaving here, thinking this way, needing someone. Running back to London and your second choice. Not when you're—"

Knocking the telescope aside, she slanted a glance at him. *Mine.* He'd almost said mine. When she wasn't—and he wasn't hers.

Nonetheless, the word settled there, blistering the air. Regrettably, there was a social mountain between them. One she wasn't up to scaling.

He recovered quickly, sensing her dismissal, devising a plan she feared would trap her if she let it. He was a soldier, probably good at that sort of thing.

Crossing the room, he grabbed Capability Brown's ledgers from the chair and came back with them in his outstretched hand. A peace offering. "Take them."

She would reject the rest, but not this. Grabbing the leather-bound volumes, she held them protectively to her chest as her body called out to the bare-footed, beautiful earl.

"This isn't a dare," she said, speculating about the mischievous gleam in his eyes. Was that what he looked like before he headed into combat? "This isn't a test. A course for you to run. Epsom or something of that nature. Upmarket games your brethren like to play. I would, that is, I desire you. My kiss showed that, didn't it? You've no need to be insulted. I'm duly fascinated by a renowned expert on the topic. It would be simple if it *was* simple, which it isn't. I can't help it's you that I..." Her words faded to a weak whisper. She felt foolish and unsure, emotions rarely getting in her way. "My body may be saying yes, but my brain is saying no. That's what I'm trying to say. You have your arrangement in the village, after all. You don't need me. I'm sorry I brought you into my predicament."

He stared in lieu of a reply, his calculated calm sending her pulse soaring. She couldn't read him, not one lick. His gaze flat, except for that intriguing spark embedded deep in his ash-gray eyes, his expression composed. He must have been a formidable opponent on the frontline. She was glad she was facing him across a ramshackle library and not the wilds of India.

"I'm glad we agree," she said because one of them had to say something. "This was a mistake. The night got away from us. Something like that." She patted her chest with the ledgers, wishing her breasts didn't feel so tender all of the sudden. "My fault. My idea. Impulsive bit of nonsense. Middle of the night bout of whimsy. I couldn't sleep. Apologies all around. That's a rookery girl for you. Decorum out the blasted window."

He looped his arms behind his back, clasping the beveled edge of the desk and resting his bum atop his hands, a lord in repose. "Fine, we agree. Apology duly noted." It sounded good, but his lips twitched in what looked like amusement.

Duly noted, but was it *accepted?*

Necessity crept toward the door, never taking her gaze off the earl.

Because a rookery girl didn't turn her back on a bloke who looked like he was waging war.

⁓

Stanford let her leave.

Scurry from the library like a mouse.

The least timid woman he'd ever met. With those silly notes from a long-dead gardener clutched to her chest like a shield.

Decorum out the blasted window, indeed. Dropping his head to his hands, he laughed into his linked fingers. Outrageous, obstinate, gorgeous, temperamental Necessity Byrne. Who would have guessed she would arrive to shake up his life? Because it appeared that's what she meant to do.

Nessie. A name that had rolled out unbidden in his bewilderment— a nickname that fit perfectly.

Hell's teeth, Ollie, what are you doing?

He scrubbed his hands through his hair and inhaled the piquant scent of her clinging tenaciously to his skin. The scent like the woman. There were reasons for his insanity, certainly, but they weren't *the* reason. That was hidden beneath a raging bundle of emotions he hadn't investigated in possibly forever.

Right now, right this bloody minute, he wasn't searching for explanations.

Massaging his aching temples, he laughed again. Although the impressive erection tenting his trouser close didn't find the situation funny in the least. At the very least, she could have mercifully pretended not to notice. He grazed his knuckles over the hard ridge, knowing exactly what he'd be doing in his lonely bedchamber in about ten minutes. The woman had managed to push his arousal to a fever pitch, and he needed relief.

Aroused wasn't a proper word for what he was feeling.

Positions, places. I don't know how to say what I want to say, especially to a man who isn't going to be the one doing it with me.

Oh, this was a dare. How could she say that to him after she'd kissed the breath from his lungs and not imagine it was? When she knew damn well how she'd affected him.

A dazed breath leaked from lips that stung from her consideration. She'd no idea what her impassioned speech had done to him. Forget about the best kiss of his life. Her frank mix of innocence, bravado, and blunt recitation had hit him hard in the chest. Striking a heart that he hadn't used much since he'd been a naïve lad roaming this dwelling in search of an absent father's love. A brother's devotion.

He wasn't accepting a bloody thing from her, either. Apology or remorse.

Aside from her possible involvement with Jasper Noble, a hoodlum she hadn't once mentioned, she was unencumbered. He was unencumbered. She didn't want marriage. He didn't want marriage. She wanted to explore. He wanted desperately, pathetically, to explore.

The simple math of it was that he wanted her. Blind, brazen want. And like every earl before him, a role he'd not truly played before, he was going to take.

Maybe she was his gift from the gods for his returning to the scene of his father's crimes. An offering from his brother, of all people. Signaling a pardon for the betrayal that had led to Xander being banished from the estate years ago.

Christ, what a tangle.

After a brief but incredible show of passion in his dimly lit sanctuary of a library, a tangle Stanford intended, after, to wrap himself in. Wrap London's foremost landscape artist in, if she'd let him.

He was determined to persuade her to let him.

Now that he knew how she tasted, her pale pink lips parted, her trim body snug against his, a better fit than he'd have thought possible, her adept mind churning, those nuggets of twisted wisdom hitting his ears, her teeth sinking into his earlobe (*that* one had weakened his knees when he was a man accustomed to sensual surprises), he wasn't giving her up. Not without a fight. Not after the personal desires she'd revealed, things a woman rarely told a man. That she'd not found what she needed before—pleasure he suspected he could provide. Better yet, pleasure *she* suspected he could provide.

Being around her without the prospect of more would be unbearable. Even if she was practically engaged, which he doubted. Her reaction to his mention of Jasper Noble had barely caused a flicker, proving the scoundrel's insignificance.

I've done this before.

Stanford would admit it to himself but no one else. Her admission burned. Maybe it was Noble, although he didn't think it was. Stanford's fingers curled into a fist. His scar itched like it did when he was vexed. Jealousy was unbecoming for an earl, for a man, so he'd lose that.

Forget anyone else had placed his hands on her. He didn't want details. Not now, not *ever*. He wanted to erase her memories until there was only him.

Which was a dare any way you played it.

It also sounded like the conceited directive of a man with the loftiest title in England outside a duke. Or a king. Necessity Byrne of the Shoreditch Byrnes would hate that arrogance; a trait he'd been taught to exhibit. To master. Beaten by his father when he'd shown compassion for the servants, his mount, his brother. It was a valuable lesson, frankly, because those who didn't have self-confidence got devoured. He'd got pummeled at Harrow that first year. Until he hadn't. A quick temper that had prepared him for India.

Necessity wasn't a part of that world—and Stanford no longer wanted to be.

For the next month, she was his. Tied to this estate and a celebrated landscaper who'd perished in the 1700s. Stanford knew this because he'd researched Capability Brown in a dusty tomb on horticulture his father hadn't sold along with the rest. He wasn't missing the importance of the connection.

A dead gardener would keep her here when the Earl of Stanford couldn't.

She'd tricked him a bit with her brazen kiss, then been rocked herself at the power behind it. That made two of them. There were issues, surely. She was unfashionably independent. Mouthy. Rude when it suited her and brutally charming when it didn't. Her clothes were a disaster and her coiffure not far behind. Although he'd sell this rambling estate to have those dark-honey strands spread across his pillow.

Not the type of woman he'd been tutored to expect or want.

Women rarely took the lead with him, either, but they rarely said no when he did. It was an earl's curse. Or his reward. Stanford wasn't sure which.

Holding her in his arms, trapped between his body and hard stone, his wish to wrap her legs around his waist and plunder, had seemed natural. Her love bites to his neck and earlobe his highest high since opium.

There were benefits. A prudent man considered every angle. She was indifferently beautiful. Intelligent. Strong, when he appreciated strong women. Intriguing. A bright hue in an otherwise dull portrait. His mouth went dry thinking about her wispy sighs striking his damaged cheek. An affliction she seemed to care nothing about. Those scandalous trousers outlining a round bottom he'd been close to cupping in his bare hands, stroking her against him and making her come right there against his ancient wall. Her warm folds, separated by mere cotton, surrounding him. He'd not been far from the thought of release himself, which would have been embarrassing and damned wonderful.

What a fantastic night this had turned out to be. One of those unexpected pleasures life tossed at you.

She didn't seem to notice his scars, but if she found out about the others, the ones buried deep inside him, it would be another story. Nightmares, addictions, regret. A crumbling estate, a past he wanted to forget, a future he feared, a disfigured visage.

What was there to recommend him to any woman?

Unbelievably, he'd told her a little. Not enough to scare her away but enough to let her know he wasn't a man to bet on in the long race.

For a short race, he'd be fine. And a short race was what she wanted.

He merely had to get her to agree to the contest.

Chapter Five

WHERE AN INTREPID GARDENER SEETHES AND AN ARROGANT EARL PERSISTS

The earl started his campaign by showing up for breakfast the next morning.

Before Necessity arrived at the salon with the lovely French windows and drippy ceiling. The scent of mildew and orange marmalade fighting for supremacy. The row of dour portraits spanning an entire wall, a miserable-looking bunch she was glad to have missed.

As if sharing a meal with his gardener was his normal routine, when she knew it wasn't.

Ignoring his penetrating stare, she visited a sideboard that had taken on better presentation since her arrival, loading her plate with sausages, sweetbreads, eggs, kippers, and toast. She wasn't going to play the feeble female without an appetite when she had a full day ahead of her. She had to supervise the planting of three rows of shrubs, the delivery of the citrus trees to the conservatory, as well as attempt to tame a lawn that had not been tamed since she was in nappies. Let him have the "dainty" meals with his mistress or the multitude of society chits clamoring to sink their teeth into his title. Sink their teeth into *him*.

Necessity bet the future countess would barely eat enough to fill a saucer.

"You're looking lovely today, Miss Byrne," he murmured without glancing up from the book sprawled open by his side. When she'd felt his gaze roasting her skin moments before. *Oh*, the man did play tricks. Such a charlatan.

She popped her plate to the table, self-conscious when she was never self-conscious. Or at least she tried hard not to be. This was her best gown, best *work* gown, and she had wrestled her hair into a tidy chignon for reasons she wasn't going to examine. Only, the heavy strands were hard to control, and her talent was limited. She supposed she looked a fright, and his comment had side meaning. "What does it matter what your gardener looks like? When she's set to get filthier than a hound grubbing about."

Hooking her heel in the spindle, she skidded her chair back. She hadn't slept well, recalling that blasted kiss and all that had gone with it. While he looked fresh as a rambling rose. A flawless portrait, for once playing the earl. For what reason, she wondered?

Thankfully, someone had poured coffee, as she favored it over tea, and placed a steaming cup in the spot she'd taken to occupying. She wasn't going to ask who for fear it was him.

He glanced up before she had a chance to sit. An exhaustive sweep that sent her senses rioting. She didn't welcome the kick in her chest or her belly, the remembrance of his lips capturing hers. Sadly, she couldn't miss the cozy glow that lit his eyes. They were decidedly cool, the color of a polished blade. When she didn't want to be sliced. He hadn't shaved; a hindrance because she thought stubble made his face particularly appealing.

Feeling like a grumpy adolescent, she slumped to her chair with a sigh, folded her napkin on her lap, and dug into her breakfast.

After minutes of silence, rather companionable if she were forced to admit this, with the echoes of an awakening house sounding around them, he asked, "What's on today's horticultural agenda?"

Taking a deliberate sip of coffee, very *good* coffee, probably shipped from the tropics by that smuggling brother of his, she cradled her cup and sat back. "How careless of me. I should prepare daily notes for my employer. Consider it done. I'll have them delivered each night for your review."

A muscle in his sculpted jaw flexed. She was coming to recognize his pique. *Ah-ha*, she thought gleefully, *got you*. The more reminders of their rank, the better.

"Xander Macauley's your employer. Send your bloody notes to the emerald chamber in the east wing. I was merely trying to make polite conversation over breakfast."

It was then her "employer" strolled into the room. A chattering, spit-mouthed lad of a year or so tossed over his shoulder. Macauley didn't miss a step when he heard his name mentioned, depositing the boy in his uncle's arms without comment and heading to the sideboard.

The Earl of Stanford reacted in a manner he hadn't known would affect her. The chemical magic they shared flowing faster when he took the wiggling child lovingly to his lap, his gaze catching hers over the boy's flaxen curls. The lad glanced to her, too, and waved a chubby, jam-covered fist. Then he murmured, *Ollie*, in a crooked baby chant as he gazed at his uncle.

And all was lost.

Necessity blew out a trembling breath and rested her cup on her saucer. The Macauley Grays, the *ton* called their eyes. They had them, all three men in the room. Xander Macauley, the baby, *Ollie*.

He's good with children—and you want children.

The thought was forbidden. Unwanted celestial advice that had her doing a fine impression of bolting when she scrambled from her chair.

Got you, the earl returned with those wicked grays as the boy's arms circled his neck and clung. He hadn't looked away and surely saw something shift in her face. She wasn't a skilled gambler, had never been good at hiding her feelings.

Macauley returned, dropping into a chair between the happy couple, his lips tilting at the energy in the air. No way he didn't feel it. Necessity's skin was dancing beneath crisp cotton, her fingertips tingling with the urge to *touch*.

The Limehouse rounder waved his fork at her, careless when there was nothing careless about him. "Don't let me interrupt. Sit, continue your discussion. Pippa is sleeping in, which it looks, from the dark slashes under your eyes, you should have done. Kit is always up at dawn, the charming devil. And last night, in the middle of the night, a time slot my darling wife managed. We're going to visit the stable after breakfast. My baby boy loves horses." He said it with so much affection that Necessity's eyes stung. Her father had sounded the same when he talked about his children.

"Um, well..." Necessity rocked from boot to boot, preparing to lie about the citrus trees arriving soon when he locked her up.

"I'd love to hear about your progress, Shoreditch," Macauley mumbled around a mouthful, ignoring her hesitation. Rolling right over it, in fact. "It's quite a job, innit? Hasn't seen much care, this place, since Ollie and I were lads running through the fields."

Stanford slanted his brother a dark look at the use of the nickname —as if she'd missed it when the boy spit it out—but Macauley only chuckled, flicked his hand as if to say *calm down*. Then he continued chewing, the smile curving his lips splendid. And annoying as hell.

Sliding into her chair, perching on the edge for an easy escape, Necessity went through her list of planned activities for the week. The conservatory windows—she smothered a secret shot of glee at Macauley's wince at the cost—the shrubs, side garden, lawns, citrus trees. Delivery and planting schedules. Deciding to make him pay for holding her here, she went into sunlight considerations, soil conditions, best timing of hydration, seasonal placement. Capability Brown's original plans that she'd gotten a moment to review, and how she'd changed her diagrams slightly to match his.

By the time she finished, the smuggler was distracted, his gaze settled on his empty plate. While the earl had given up on gardening talk altogether, circling the room with his nephew, showing him trinkets on shelves, the blue jays and robins calling outside the window. Kissing his brow at random, heart-melting intervals. Nodding as if he understood everything the boy muttered in reply.

They made a handsome pair. The earl going with a coat this morning. A cream cravat looped casually about his neck, buff trousers hugging his long legs. His tight bottom which, she decided with a laugh she covered with her fist, was one of his best features. Boots she'd wager were Hoby. But like hers, scuffed, not brand new. Country with a hint of elegance, a judgment he doubtless wouldn't appreciate.

Ollie. Last night in the library, she'd met Ollie. Stargazing, moderately affable Ollie. The reclusive, reserved Earl of Stanford nowhere to be found.

The realization rocked her.

She tore her gaze away to find Macauley's hitting her square between the eyes. He appeared torn, delighted, and concerned.

She rolled her lips in rather than say what she wished to. Like women from the dawn of time. *You dragged me here—your grand plan— and look what's happened.* Heat storming her body, her brain spinning with possibilities. Risk, *reward. Oh*, such reward. She could not dismiss the tantalizing vision of the earl's naked feet from her mind no matter how hard she tried.

Despite her unease, she didn't back down, glance away. Not for one second.

A flare of approval filtered through Macauley's eyes. Guessing how best to hit her, he went with business. "Are you going to need more assistance for the heavy lifting around here?"

"Heavy lifting" *was* a challenge with a female team. Though she hated to admit it. "I could with some aspects of the project."

"You and Pippa have discussed her business, am I right? She's got men who can be here in two days' time. Ready to assist in any way you need them. Moving trees, dirt, those bushes I've seen lying about that need planting. Digging holes two miles deep should you require it. Then they can stay on, become grooms or footmen or whatever the earl decides. If the opportunity exists, which from the look of abandonment about this spot, it does." He leaned back in his chair and stretched his legs out, all forty miles of him. "This place is light on staff, mate," he called to his brother across the room.

Stanford shrugged, his back to them. On purpose, she'd bet.

"Macauley Enterprises," she murmured, as aware of Pippa's infamous company as anyone. She rescued young men and women from the workhouse and provided positions in homes of grand stature. They were so well trained by the Duchess Society, and it was such a noble endeavor, it had become fashionable to employ them.

"That's it." His expression overflowing with pride and love. "Even I'm surprised how bleeding well it's gone over. Pippa must have tea every week with some crotchety old biddy looking to bring a 'poor rookery soul' into her household. Society grandees, such an easy mark. A charitable venture society can easily, and with low risk, get behind."

Restless, he shoved from the chair, noticing his brother's book lying on the table. Flipping through it, he scanned the pages. She wouldn't have believed it had Pippa not told her, but Macauley was quite the reader. Books all over their townhouse, his warehouse, the estate in Hampshire. He even spoke a smattering of French. A swift brain housed in that hulking body. Talk about a con.

As if he sensed her verdict, he glanced over. "Astronomy." Tapped the book with a long finger, his smile tilting. "He's always had his head in the clouds, a little. With the stars. With people, I don't know. Not so cold-hearted for what he could have been, raised by that jackal. He's a good uncle to my son, an association I want for both of them. The power of family, you know? No one was more shocked than me when he went the soldier route. Worried me, truth be told, but if he hears me say it, he'll get cranky. He tried to get on track, then the trouble in my gaming hell alley." He closed the book, his gaze thoughtful, astute. Trapping her like a bug in amber. "It's changed him, all of it."

"Is that a warning, Mr. Macauley?"

"I prefer to call it guidance, Shoreditch. Seeing as the two of you are having trouble keeping your eyes off each other. I might go knocking on the Duchess Society's door, come to think of it, offer my matchmaking services. Evidently, I have a gift." He ducked his head, appealingly bashful. A tactic she didn't buy for one second. "I remember how it started with me and Pippa. The heat that near about burnt up every space we were in. I all but lost myself in the blaze."

The Earl of Stanford, who she'd dreadfully started to refer to as Ollie in a hidden region of her mind, ambled over, his nephew dangling over his shoulder, the boy's laughter the loveliest sound imaginable. The two of them were a dream to watch, an absolute dream. "This seems a fascinating conversation I'm missing. It can't be about gardening."

Macauley shrugged, the falsehood spilling from his lips like claret from a bottle. "I was inviting her to our lawn bowling tourney this afternoon. Now that it's no longer illegal to play, ridiculous edict of

Henry VIII's. Something that, innit? Streeter and Hildy, Markham, Leighton, and their squads are coming."

The smuggler is one smooth customer, she thought. She quite liked that his brother, according to guidance recently given, was not.

Ignoring the sizzle heating the air around him, Macauley slipped a Bainbridge timepiece from his fob pocket and gave it a casual glance. "If we're lucky, Dash should be up by then." Then the sneaky devil added to the lie to rope her in. "Miss Byrne said she and Streeter could discuss their new project in Islington. An excellent opportunity to converse, isn't that how you phrased it, Shoreditch?"

Stanford turned to her, mild alarm on his face. "If you need instruction, I'm happy to—"

"I know how to play, my lord." Of course, he didn't think she could. How would a girl from the stews discover bowls? Occasionally, a rookery upbringing provided more than stuffy aristocrats guessed it did. Though she'd learned to toss in a grimy alley, not a pristine lawn. She stood, dusting her hand down her bodice for no reason, except the heat of a certain earl's gaze was closing in on her. "And I play to win."

Macauley dipped his head, too late to hide his laughter.

"I wouldn't expect anything less from a Shoreditch Byrne," Stanford said tonelessly and handed Kit back to his father.

Necessity shot Macauley a cross glance, the Earl of Stanford a silken one, then she marched from the room, three identical gray gazes fixed upon her.

Stanford watched his gardener flounce from the room.

He simply couldn't win with her.

He'd left his suave charm behind at some point. Maybe it'd been the booze and the opium fueling it... but the dry earl wasn't good with women. "I had her at 'Stanford,' now we're back to 'my lord.' Thanks for that." He snatched up his book, noting Macauley had been flipping pages. He'd lost his place, dammit. "Now I'll be stuck tossing balls around with her and the Leighton Cluster."

"Isn't that what you *want*, mate? Someone tossing your balls?"

Stanford swallowed a curse because his nephew was within hearing range, but the glare he sent his brother was decidedly unfriendly.

Macauley tucked his son on his hip, natural as could be for a knave who'd vowed to never have children. Reaching for a biscuit, he handed it to Kit. "Ah, baby brother, quit your sulking. Let her trounce you in bowls, then she'll be happy, mate. Seems the competitive sort. Pippa's always thrilled when I lose. The payoff can be nice, mighty nice, if you get my meaning. You leave the woman having to make it up somehow."

Stanford jammed his book under his armpit. He didn't want to hear about his brother and Pippa making up anything. "She *is* the competitive sort. And I might not have to let her lose. Bowls isn't exactly a talent."

Macauley rested his bum on the table, bouncing his son on his hip, his face radiant with happiness *and* amusement. "I don't think you need a solid showing. The lass is already smitten."

This news perked Stanford up like a burst of sunshine striking his face. "Truly? I'm having the worst time impressing her, although I've only known I wanted to impress her for twelve hours or so. She doesn't give a shilling about the earl bit, which is what I usually hang my hat on. Admittedly, without much effort, it works like a charm."

"The hat-hanging stories I don't need to hear." Macauley ruffled Kit's hair, blew crumbs off his son's fingers. "Good news is, she seems attracted, her gaze following you around the room today. Bad news is, she doesn't want to be. I'll be the first to tell you, Ollie, when someone doesn't want to be, it's an uphill battle. Pippa stuck in there with me until I had no choice *but* to fall in love, thank the gods. Persistent darling of a scamp. But it wasn't easy. For either of us. I fell first but still made her wait years." He grazed his lips across Kit's rosy cheek. "In the end, she said she knew I couldn't hold out forever."

Stanford hesitated, glancing up from trying to reclaim his spot in his book. He'd been preparing to read a section on newly discovered asteroids, thank-you very much. "I don't want love. Necessity Byrne doesn't want love. She wants every garden in London under her control, when the city is poison to me. This infatuation, our game, if that's what it is, isn't *going* anywhere. Get your head out of your arse, Brother."

Macauley arched a brow. "You have your lovely widow for games. I sent this chit for more lasting endeavors."

"Who told you about *her?*"

"Ah, mate." His brother often looked at him like this, disheartened by his naiveté. "Your footman. Your groom. Your housekeeper. Hell, everyone in the village knows you have a special lady friend. Kit here" —he nodded fondly to this son—"probably knows."

Stanford mumbled a curse, turned a chair backward, and sprawled into it, folding his arms along the back, book bumping his knee. "Of all the confections in London, why Necessity Byrne? She's not countess material, Xander, if I was looking, which I'm not."

"I had a feeling. You asked about her after she visited you and gave you that tonic. There was something in your voice that day. I don't know." He shrugged halfheartedly, abashed. "I'm lovesick. Infected despite my efforts to escape the disease. Seeing everyone else lovesick, I guess. Or hoping to see them." He rubbed his chest with a frown. "Blimey, have I been laid low."

"Never a truer statement." Stanford sighed, busking his hand over the stubble layering his chin. He hadn't had time to shave *and* catch her in the breakfast room. She probably preferred a clean face, which he would never have again. "It wasn't a tonic. More a poultice, I think. Feverfew. I've read up on it since then. Quite a healing aid. Miss Byrne knows her herbs."

Macauley reached for another biscuit, placing it in Kit's pudgy fingers. "The chit's spending my blunt faster than I can keep up. Bloody hell, are plants expensive. The citrus trees direct off the Duchess of Leighton's boat. She has better contacts in the Mediterranean than Macauley & Streeter do. I didn't even make any money on the back side."

Stanford cast his gaze to his grimy boots. He'd left his valet in London, one less expense, figuring he could manage in the country without one. "You didn't have to do this, Xander. I have funds, mostly, to get this place on its feet. I'm investing with you and Streeter. Partnering in the new distillery." Although those gains would take years to multiply, someday allowing him the financial freedom he didn't yet have—and they both knew it.

"Ollie," Kit giggled and wagged his arms, wanting to go to his uncle.

Placing his book on the floor, Stanford rose to his feet, taking the boy, and tucking him against his chest. Stanford's heart gave a dull thump when Kit yawned and laid his head on his shoulder. The scent of chalk, biscuits, and little boy rose to taunt him. "Don't say anything, some solemn speech about what I'm missing out on. Full of brotherly wisdom now that your life is racing along on a smooth track."

"I made mistakes with you I'm trying to solve. I admit that right out, mate, no deceit between us. High-handed but honest, innit? I'm hoping to repair the past, move away from it. India and the nightmare that followed it was an escape from *this*. From Derbyshire. I can't get that out of my mind, that I could have stopped you from having to run." Macauley held up a hand when Stanford made to argue, his jaw going tight. Everyone in London knew what *that* meant. "You, Pippa, and Kit are my family. Streeter, even those damn dukes. Dash, who I've somehow taken under my damaged wing." He dipped his chin, indicating his son settled lovingly in Stanford's arms. "*Family*. I'll do anything to protect the lot of you. Curse me if you want to. Maybe it's not right, maybe it's not fair, but my stance will never change. Get used to it."

Stanford threaded his fingers through Kit's silky golden hair, the exact color of Pippa's. Family. Something he hadn't got used to yet.

It came to him suddenly, a grim thought. Necessity didn't have anyone. The misery threading her words when she'd spoken of her family years ago had never left him.

Macauley rocked back on his heels, his gaze shooting across the room. "That summer here, when we were boys, was the best of my life, Ollie. Before Pippa, that is. I'd never seen such splendor. Such green vibrancy everywhere I looked. A world of living after the gray dying of London. Air that didn't have a stench of desperation tainting every breath. Although I have my issues with the place, dismal memories along with the good, as you do, it'd be a fair, more than fair place to raise a family. Like Hampshire for my brood."

Stanford swallowed, his heart doing a slow roll. Even if he wanted it, this demonstrative brotherly stuff was hard going. "It was my best as well." He refused to say more. Unless Xander wanted his "baby brother" bawling on his shoulder. "Your gardener sent me tea," he added, opting to share as sharing seemed the family thing to do. He tapped his temple as gently as he could. Kit had dropped to sleep and was currently drooling on his neck. "For the headaches."

Macauley hummed as if this meant something. "What kind of tea?"

Stanford smoothed his hand over the warm curve of Kit's back. "I don't know. It smells good though. Spicy and sweet. A bit like the woman, now that I think about it."

"To my understanding," Macauley said, boyish delight returning to his face, "sparring with a chit can be a pleasurable experience. Starting as adversaries leading to more. But more, brother of mine, I warn you, can strike—a fist to the chest. My *more* with Pippa brought life into crisp focus, same as those arse-chilling swims I take in the Serpentine. Removed the murkiness, illuminating the important parts. Lighting them up, moon brightness, a comparison you'll appreciate what with your stargazing. It changed what I wanted for myself, for her. My plans. Every last goal I'd devised altered in an instant. For all that we've made it to this wonderful place, me and my girl, we started in a risky one. An angry one, at least for me. I can only thank God she hung on."

"Enemies to lovers, is that it?" He resisted the urge to roll his eyes over Macauley's brand of poetry. "Isn't that a hook in lurid novels?"

Macauley took his slumbering son in his arms, pressing a kiss to his brow, leaving Stanford with a hollow ache, missing the boy already. "You have any better ideas, mate?"

"Not a damn one," Stanford muttered.

Chapter Six

WHERE A PERPLEXED WOMAN
REMEMBERS A KISS

S
he was having trouble forgetting the greatest kiss since
Shakespeare.

Necessity pressed her fist to her sternum and took the
deepest breath her rarely worn corset would allow. The scent of garde-
nias and a cloying fragrance she tagged as honeysuckle were the only
serenity to the day. She'd been made to put on her tea party gown and
the accessories she loathed to go with it, then prance around playing
games because that's what *guests*, even ones being paid for their efforts,
did when asked.

The Duchess Society had arrived at Aspinwall House an hour ago,
and this was the result. A discomfited gardener surrounded by tables
loaded with foodstuff and muted sunlight, standing on an overgrown
lawn in her Sunday finest, wiling away the afternoon as if she had
nothing better to do. Which was, undoubtedly, the situation for most
females in the world. She couldn't expect people to actually remember
she had a *job*.

Although the Leighton Cluster—so-called because of their friendship with the Duke of Leighton and the fact that they traveled in a
pack—was infamous enough for their own shenanigans not to be
horribly critical of hers.

The women worked, as she did, although the difference was, they didn't have to. Hildy Streeter and Georgiana, the Duchess of Markham, co-owned the Duchess Society. Helena, the Duchess of Leighton, owned a shipping company, scandalously inherited from her father. Pippa Macauley had her charitable endeavors and half of London's old crones, as well as her husband, in the palm of her hand.

The men, Xander Macauley, Tobias Streeter, the dukes Markham and Leighton, before being ruined by love, had been rogues of the worst sort. Only Dashiell Campbell, hiding out in the country after publishing a manuscript on deceptive gambling that had lit a fire beneath the *ton's* arses, was unattached. Leaving a barrage of over-turned carriages, midnight horse races, and pouting women in his wake.

Oh, and the Earl of Stanford. *Ollie.*

If only she could forget about him.

"You cheated," the earl said, tossing a ball the color of an emerald from hand to hand, his scowl growing with each passing second.

"As if," Necessity returned, patiently waiting for him to cede the match. "You watched my throw. Standing right beside me. Nothing dishonest about it." She'd played this game with the smoothest rocks they could find in Shoreditch's rank alleys growing up. It had taught her to be precise and not waste even one pitch. Nothing like this group, the balls rounded with a bias so they would roll more easily. She chewed on her cheek with a snort she didn't dare release. The road the *ton* traveled was smoothed in every way possible.

To add to his frustration, a bit of play-acting, she slipped a small notebook from a pocket she'd had her modiste add to her gowns and jotted a reminder to have her team construct a hot box to house the horse manure arriving tomorrow from the village. It needed to ferment for two weeks, then be distributed as compost around his roses. She laughed softly. Perhaps the earl would like to help.

Stanford observed her without comment, frown in place. A gust of wind ripped across the meadow, tugging at his tousled hair as he glanced from her ball, nudging the jack, to his, sitting a foot away. The sun had crept out long enough to highlight the silvery strands threading through inky black, adding appeal the scene didn't need to be appealing. She didn't know how long he was going to stand there, brooding in that elegant way of his, dusting his boot over the ground and whispering beneath his breath. She'd knocked his mark out of the lane fair and square with a shot even *she* was impressed by.

Xander Macauley's whistle of surprise and the cheers from the ladies had been gratifying. An official ruling, to her mind.

While the earl debated the horror of losing to a woman, his gang surrounded him, looking on with half smiles or outright ones. Four men and a baby. The tot in the Duke of Leighton's arms—or Markham, maybe it was, she couldn't say which as most nobs looked alike to her. There were another four or five children of various ages, racing about the lawn with shouts of joy. Dirt on their faces, sugar biscuits clutched in their fists, tattered hems, and dangling buttons. It was heartfelt and familial. A scene she'd not been a part of since her parents passed.

"She has you, Ollie, me boy," Dash chimed in, tossing a butter-yellow ball high in the air and snatching it back with a gamester's keen skill. "Time to offer your congratulations. I ken it's a bruising call for a man of your stature, but it did come down the line to the two of you. That should remove the sting of being soundly beaten by a wee lass. She knocked the rest of us off the peg three tosses ago. You don't see us complaining, so why would you? Your gardens are starting to look grand, guv. Take the cut like the fine gent you were born to be."

Stanford popped his ball against his hip, his tight gaze slanting her way. "Congratulations, Miss Byrne. Excellent performance."

"Thank-you, my lord." Sliding her notebook into her pocket, she kissed the ball in her hand and gave it a careless chuck, knocking his other remaining in play, a blue, ineffectual token, outside the lines. "Although I suppose you'd prefer if I let you win. Seeing as you're an earl, the kind host of this gathering." She dipped her head, never less contrite in her life. "Apologies if I blundered. I wasn't brought up to lose."

Xander Macauley's ragged laughter snaked free. Out of the corner of her eye, Necessity saw his wife, Pippa, jam her elbow in his side. The rest of the men backed away, glancing at the clouds, mumbling, one of them humming through his mirth. The Duchess Society contingent, Hildy and Georgie, looked on with what could only be termed exasperation. She'd been advised that most men didn't appreciate an uncompromising female nature.

Stanford's eyes darkened to the color of flint. Causing her to wonder what hue they'd turn if he tried talking his way beneath her skirts. His next step in the library last night if she'd not halted the proceedings. Seduction, she feared, she'd be utterly weak against.

"Rookery girls don't let anyone win, though, do they, Miss Byrne?"

She shrugged, finally enjoying the day. Sunlight warming her back, children's ecstatic shouts ringing in her ears, a dazzling earl's attention sending bad-idea flutters through her. "I've never seen a need for it."

He rubbed his temple absently with the ball, his gaze shooting to an eagle circling overhead. The charming dimple sitting at the edge of his scarred cheek flickered. She hardly noticed the damage anymore, only the beauty.

Have you tried the tea, she wanted to ask? Yet she didn't dare with this group. The men were one insult away from rolling around on the ground, throwing punches. A congenial brawl is what Pippa called it. Over tea this morning, Necessity had heard about their antics and how naturally and often this occurred. They'd already been sniping at each other over a variety of inane topics, pushing and shoving. Necessity didn't know quite what to make of it.

Just then, one of the children approached the group, a lovely girl of about seven that Necessity guessed belonged to Tobias and Hildy Streeter. The flaxen hair and blue eyes were a stunning match to her mother's. "I've a loose thread on my sleeve. I don't want to go in to cut it, but Mama says I should never pull these. This *is* my favorite gown."

Necessity acted quickly, dropping to her knee and slipping a knife from the sheath in her boot. She also had these pockets specially made. And yes, she had to show a little ankle to retrieve it, but there was no help for that. She beckoned to the girl with a curved finger. A soft smile. "I have it. No need to go in." She cut the thread, gave it an offhand pitch into the wind, and returned her blade to its home.

Only then realizing everyone's gaze was on her.

Oh. She stood, shaking out her skirt as if nothing untoward had occurred. *Goodness*, polite society was deadly business. How was one to walk across the field and not step in something disastrous?

Dash rocked back on his heels, enthralled by the display. "Well, well, well."

Stanford knocked his shoulder against Dash's, sending the Scot stumbling. "Put your tongue back in your mouth, boy-o. Or I'll do it for you."

Dash turned to Stanford with the bubbliest expression she'd seen on the man. "If I don't, guv?"

That was all it took. One tiny insult. An answering punch. A wild swing. A shove. Grunts and shouts. Until Stanford and Dash were, seconds later, tumbling about. Streeter tried to pull them apart, half-heartedly, but took his place in battle when he received a fist to the face for his effort. Macauley shoved one of the dukes into the pile, then they were tussling, too.

Hildy Streeter sighed while the Duchess of Leighton rallied to gather the children, who shrieked in joy and raced circles around the men, evidently used to the display.

Pippa captured Necessity's elbow and moved her aside. "I thought fatherhood would make my husband grow out of this. Xander talked about never marrying for eons until his friend's ears were bleeding, then when he fell in love, he expected tea and sympathy from them. I think the blows he receives are payback. Maybe earned."

Necessity grimaced as Dash landed a bruising knock—while laughing like a loon—to the earl's unharmed cheek. "What is *wrong* with them?"

Pippa urged her back another step as the men spilled across the lawn, a tangle of arms, legs, and curses. "Leighton, the duke on the bottom of the pile there, loves brawling. It's in his veins along with the blue blood. A working-class temper, which I love about him. They usually get the aggression out at Gentleman Jackson's, but I suppose this is a proper country solution. You know, Xander once tossed Leighton into the Thames. That escapade circled the gossip sheets for weeks."

"Speaking of your husband, darling, he and Ollie look more alike the older they get, don't they?" This from Georgie, the Duchess of Markham, who observed the ruckus without a hint of distress. She gave her husband, the man holding the child and standing apart from the melee, an adoring wave. "Speaking of my husband, see him looking around frantically? He's dying to get into this melee if he can find somewhere to deposit our son. I don't think I'm going to help him. I've tended his battered face enough. And you don't want to get near this, Pippa, in your condition."

Pippa turned wide eyes on the duchess, her hand going protectively to her midriff. Her smile was positively beatific. "You have a talent, Your Grace. I haven't told Xander yet. When I do, he won't let me out of his sight. Last time, he didn't even want me to ride in a carriage without him."

"Such protectiveness." Georgie pressed her hand to her heart. She had eyes the color of a piece of lapis lazuli her husband had carried in his pocket since the moment they'd fallen in love. "It reminds me of my dear duke."

"Such masculine influence, Your Grace," Necessity murmured, seeking to ignore the pang of envy rattling about in her chest. *Someday, I will have children, too. When I do, I'll ride in any carriage I like.*

"Coming from the most competitive miss in London," Pippa returned with a laugh. "I've never seen such a fierce game of bowls. I thought Ollie's head was going to explode when you got that last strike."

"He vexes me," Necessity admitted, her gaze glued to the man who currently had his arm wrapped around a duke's neck. His sleeve was ripped, the muscles in his shoulders straining. The earl fought like a ruffian, using antics employed by the unruly boys she'd grown up with. She shouldn't find that enticing. However, he looked... happy. Gaining his glad, as her grandmother used to say. For no reason she could pinpoint, she suspected he was recuperating from wounds buried deep and had had to work hard to gain anything.

It was a surprise of sorts, an unforeseen disturbance, but Oliver Aspinwall's smile when it was the real thing? Illuminating.

Pippa glanced to her, clicking her tongue against her teeth. "He does something to you, I can see. Your cheeks are as rosy as those azaleas you planted along the front drive."

"Rhododendron," she murmured, not bothering to fib and say she was unaffected by the man. "Nonetheless, I don't want it. I have my life, my aspirations. I'm only here to tend his gardens. I'm not interested in tending the man."

"He needs tending, Miss Byrne. His childhood was difficult. His relationship with Macauley mending. India. The incident at the gaming hell." Pippa chewed on her nail with a sigh, then let her hand drop, back to the gentle swell of her belly. "Because of his father and their difficulties, even caring about this place, and Ollie cares *greatly*, it is a laceration that will never heal. It's confusing to love and hate something at the same time. I know this. He's burdened with not a trivial earldom, you see, but the oldest in the books. In *Debrett's, the* book. It's worse than what my brother has to deal with if you ask me. At least the Leighton duchy isn't so well thought of. Truly, no one cares what I do anymore. Or Roan, for that matter. They gave up on my brother after he married a shipping heiress from the docks."

"It was a silly kiss. I caught him off guard, went on impulse, which always gets me in trouble." She groaned when she realized what she'd admitted, dropping her head to her hands. "I would never risk my business as I risk my contentment. I don't understand why that is. Yet, here I am, having ignited a fire I don't *want*."

Pippa snickered, even going so far as to clap her hands. "Oh my, well, this *is* delicious news. Being tactless, which I'm famous for, I'm relieved. Macauley is worried Ollie will shrivel up and die in Derbyshire. Aged and lonely, gazing at the stars, banging about this place."

Necessity snorted, unladylike to her core as well. "He has a widow in the village. He's not... shriveling, believe me. Or without things to bang."

Pippa bent into her laughter, her smile going absolutely dreamy when her husband sprinted over and cupped the back of her neck, drawing her into a rough kiss before returning to combat. *Later*, his worshipful look said. "This is the most fascinating game of bowls ever. Talk of kisses and my getting them, too! I'm having a delightful time when I expected to be bored silly."

"I have someone. Perhaps. If I want him." Her cheeks burned, but blast it, she wasn't the only person with an admirer. The earl could take his widow and... well, do whatever he wanted with her. Blinded by love,

Hildy, Georgie, and Pippa were secure with their doting husbands. Necessity's competitiveness, incongruous to the discussion, nonetheless raised its head.

"Jasper Noble," Georgie replied, having listened to the kissing part of the conversation without once butting in. Patience Necessity would never have. "The Duchess Society is looking into him as you asked us to do. Only typical debauchery is turning up so far. Nothing we haven't seen a thousand times over. Or married into ourselves." She giggled, her cheeks flushing a lovely shade of pink. "Gambling, negligible swindling, a mistress, that sort of thing. Although we haven't turned up anything, anything at all, about his childhood. The only peculiar element. It's as if he arrived in London, a man of eighteen bent on seizing the city, and that was that."

Clapping, Pippa popped to her toes in excitement. "Mistresses and debauchery! This day gets better and better."

Necessity lifted her hand, squinting into the sunlight. The rip in the earl's shirt had exposed a bit of his chest, and she didn't want to miss the sight. "I don't care about the typical men-being-men silliness. I *know* about those. Jasper's goods have been spilled across the gossip sheets much as the idiots we're watching smash each other to a pulp. It's the deeper dive I want you to take."

"Since he's sniffing around, why not just ask him?" Pippa added, proving her impropriety was a fact. "Make it a bargaining chip, as it were. I believe in forthright inquisitions myself."

Necessity drew her lips in to hide her smile. "Since he's sniffing around, I will."

Closing her eyes to the warmth striking her face, Necessity decided the day was going well.

She'd beaten the earl fair and square. She was surrounded by women who hadn't once made her feel *less*. None had cast a sour glance at her gown or made fun of her speech, which the Duchess Society had helped her improve to the point that Shoreditch wasn't readily identifiable. She and Tobias Streeter had, in fact, discussed the upcoming project beautifying his terraces in Islington. The earl's tea was tasty, his cucumber sandwiches delicious. Actually, she was having fun, when amusements hadn't been on any agenda that she'd designed for herself in years. In forever. A dewy breeze was rolling across the meadow with enough sunlight for her newly planted hydrangea and garden roses to bask in. Rain was a promise for the evening, which the soil needed. Not a hint of coal smoke or gutter stench lingered in the air. She had Capability Brown's notes to review at bedtime.

The only thing missing in this world was her cat, Delilah.

Yes, she agreed with a silent sigh of relief. The day was going well. Four more weeks, and she could go home. Never step foot in the country again, unless a lucrative project took her there. Walk the streets of her beloved gritty city as she salvaged one sorrowful garden after another.

With this bleak thought pinging in her chest, she went and made a fool of herself.

Twisted up in feelings about Jasper Noble, who she didn't want, and the Earl of Stanford, who she maybe did. When the earl was offering a month, no more, and Noble a lifetime. She understood the difference and cared little, which should have scared her more than it did. Her brain and her heart were not in agreement—for possibly the first time.

Though the brawl had calmed, the men rubbing their sore jaws and doing a lot of pointless backslapping, general masculine preening, glancing at the women to see who had noticed the exhibition, her gaze was fixed on Stanford. Of course, it was. So, she was the first to see him bring his hand to his temple, grimace in pain, sway, and drop. Racing across the lawn, she was the first to reach him, terrified, the kind of instinct that didn't let you decide about the rationale of a choice before you made it. Flight, urgent flight.

"You fools have knocked him silly," she cried and crouched beside him.

He was sprawled on his back, cheeks the color of chalk, scar standing out in angry relief. Her family's effort to elude cholera stormed her mind, those bleak days of illness and waste. She brushed his inky hair from his brow, a lingering caress. The strands were as silken as the petals of a lilac but the molten color of charred ash. The moist earth seeped through her muslin gown to dampen her knees. Was he breathing? She exhaled sharply when she saw his chest rise and fall.

Macauley immediately rushed up behind her, his features waxy. "What happened? He was standing there telling Dash what a pathetic left hook he has, then *boom*. Is he breathing? As a child, he used to have a touch of asthma."

"Fisticuffs make perfect sense, then, Mr. Macauley!"

"Don't fuss. Spot of dizziness. Not when you look so pretty today, Sprite," Stanford whispered, lashes fluttering. When he opened his eyes, she noticed the outer edge was rimmed with lavender, making the silver shine bright as a coin. When she didn't wish to be close enough to notice. "Your gown is the color of firelight. I quite love it."

She swallowed hard, her surroundings returning. "*Pretty?*"

He blinked twice, awareness flooding in. Seemingly startled that a small group of friends and family had gathered round him. Rising shakily to his elbow, healthy color doused his cheeks. His chest stuttered on a fast breath, a strong, healthy gasp. He wasn't going to expire on his lawn on a stunning spring day. "It's the headaches. Sometimes they spot my vision. I felt faint for a second there. It wasn't today's blow to the head but possibly the one in India." He grinned, the idiot, dabbing at a spot of blood in the corner of his mouth. "Dash hits like a girl. Couldn't have been that. As for asthma, I only cough when I need it. Pretense mostly."

"Godammit, Ollie!" Macauley said, as discomfited as Necessity to be caught hanging over his brother, concern shadowing his face. "Did you at least try her bloody tea?"

Necessity sank her fingers into grass she'd put on the list to have cut tomorrow if rain didn't arrive, the ground solid and slightly warm, a little moist. Glancing over her shoulder, she realized the Leighton Cluster, every last one of them, had noticed her odd behavior. Her distress over a man she claimed not to want.

That blasted kiss decided to swarm her senses, along with an enticing scent she was becoming all too familiar with. It was almost as if he'd done this on purpose to confuse her.

She glanced back at the earl, unsure how to escape. Which was a mistake. His insightful gaze recorded everything, like a deduction obtained through his telescope. Taking note, detail upon detail until, for one lingering moment, they were the only two people in

Derbyshire. He was a patient man, willing to go the distance for what he wanted. She didn't usually underestimate her opponent, but she had this time.

"You told him about the tea," she whispered, no idea why this appalled her more than the rest.

"What tea?" Pippa barreled into the closed circle, a chit unused to being kept apart from the action.

Stanford shoved to his knees, then his feet, dusting straw from his trousers before extending his hand to her. Athletic grace from a man who'd been laid flat moments ago. "My gardener likes me. Already giving me gifts and such."

"You arrogant cur," she seethed and scrambled up, not *about* to take his hand. "You bloody buffoon."

"Oh, Ollie," Pippa whispered, "have you lost your touch?"

He sighed and jammed his hands in his pockets, contrite as a lad. "You're angry, I take it." His shoulders lifted and fell, his gaze sweeping low. That perplexed vulnerability that hit her hard in the chest. "Can I blame it on being knocked, what did you call it? Silly?"

"Quit trying," she whispered so softly she wasn't sure he heard the request. "This isn't a dare. A situation requiring your legendary *talent*. Leave me be."

He hesitated, rocking back on his heels. Something she'd noticed he did when he was thinking. Plotting, the devious scoundrel. Taking her in until desire shimmered across her skin, longing roiling in her belly. When he was done assessing the situation, he shook his head and looked her in the eye, unlike most men. She would give him that much. "I'm not going to do that, Sprite. Arrogant cur that I am, I don't think you want me to."

Chapter Seven

WHERE AN EARL TESTS HIS TALENT

Evidently, if Necessity was honest with herself, she didn't want the earl to quit trying.

She jammed the spade in the mound of moist peat she was transferring into terra-cotta pots and cursed softly. Breathing through her frustration, she noted the briny threat of rain riding the air. Sitting back on her heels, she let her gaze roam the conservatory, pleased with her progress despite her annoyance. The new windows sparkled, the rows of orange and lemon trees flanking the wall a reminder of what this space *could* be. It smelled like she imagined Italy would in the spring. Fragrant citrus and the dense scent of earth.

She rubbed her aching lower back and sighed. Was her little infatuation over before it had even begun? She frowned. Which is certainly what she wanted.

Because true to her request if not his word, the Earl of Stanford had barely spoken to her for two days. Inane remarks about the weather over his massive medieval breakfast table. Flippant inquiries about the rock wall she'd hired a stonemason to repair. The copse of hydrangea blooming sweetly beneath his window. Setting the tool aside, she dug her battered timepiece from her skirt pocket. Fifty hours and forty-seven minutes, to be exact, since he'd looked at her like he wanted her. His last look as she walked away from the bowls tourney, blistering enough to melt metal.

When to be wanted was not what *she* wanted.

She should be delighted.

With a shiver of foreboding, she glanced out a gleaming window in time to see the man seizing her thoughts striding across the lawn. Dressed for comfort while still maintaining a prince's elegance, a balance he was good at. Coattails hitting his lean hip, shirt open at the neck, ends of a stark, white cravat trailing jauntily from his trouser pocket.

She squinted. He held a book in his hand and seemed to be on a mission to deliver it.

It was then she recalled buying the text on planting citrus.

And the bookseller she'd bought it from.

Cheeks burning, she snatched the spade from the ground and plunged it in the heap of dirt.

"Such aggression, Miss Byrne," he said moments later, striding up behind her. "I'm scared to ask what you're thinking."

She ignored him. At the edge of her sight, his polished boot tapping out impatience not evident in his sleek features. She stuck with the plan until she recalled his extreme fortitude. A soldier's steadfastness. Stubborn, stubborn man.

When she was the least patient person she knew.

Exhaling, she glanced up, preparing herself. At close range, with his fragrance and the sound of his breathing available for her review, her raw reaction was difficult to dispute. His bruises from the brawl on the lawn were fading, a pale-yellow ringing his right eye the only claim to the foolishness. "Can I help you, my lord?"

He tilted his head, his lips parting. On a half laugh, he murmured, "I think the better question is, will you?"

She scoured her hand across her jaw and rose slowly to her feet. The vision of him going to his knees, the catch of fear spiraling through her chest as she raced to him, had been a nagging presence. Every time she saw him hearty and hale a little burst of pleasure popped inside her. She'd seen people healthy one day, near dying the next, and this experience had not easily left her. "What do you *want*, Lord Stanford?"

He shot a cautious glance over his shoulder. "Is Mrs. Rothbottom going to leap out and whack me with her parasol? She's been giving me the evil eye all week. The woman knows my interest is... hmm, *engaged*."

She turned, putting a tall work bench between them. Grabbing a rag, she wiped her spade clean. "She's shopping in the village."

He placed the book on the bench, slid it across the scuffed wood with two fingers. Her gaze lifted. His hair held a slight wave from the damp air today. Strands she wanted to sink her fingers into and tug him off balance. Body and soul.

His eyes went dark while he stared, gunmetal gray. The want in them bleeding across the short distance.

Thankful recognition that made her very, very irate.

"There was also a note," he added lightly, resting a folded sheet atop the book. "I'm sorry to say I opened it before realizing the package wasn't one of mine. Mrs. McKinstry must have delivered it to my study without looking closely at the address."

She unfolded the missive, stomach muscles dancing. Slipping the spectacles hanging from the rounded neck of her gown to her face, the text came into crisp, clear view.

I hope the project in Derbyshire is going well. I've another volume on botany you may find enlightening. I'll hold it here until your return. Which I hope is soon. All my best, R.H.

Stanford jerked his chin toward the sheet. "So, he's the one?"

Necessity refolded the note, wondering if she should be pleased by his pique or vexed about it. Was it reasonable to feel both? "As if it's any of your business. I don't ask about the widow."

He dug his bootheel into a flagstone, a frown dragging his lips low. "I ended that. On friendly terms. The morning after you trounced me at bowls."

"Why?"

He braced his fist on the table, rocking it on its unsteady legs, his eyes flaring in the dim light. "You *know* why." Amused by his sulk, she watched as he ran his tongue over his teeth, his gaze leaving her. "Giving her up only to find your former lover sending you the occasional sonnet and romantic volumes on botany. A man anxiously awaiting your return."

"I hardly think this"—she tucked the sheet inside the book, out of sight, against her will charmed to her teeth by his displeasure—"could be considered a sonnet. Or romantic. Botany is currently the only area of science I'm allowed to explore freely. Female amateurs dominating the field because men don't want to trouble themselves with the study of flowers. Therefore, I'll take the book, which I paid for I might add, gladly. Because we ended on 'friendly terms' as well."

"What's next?" he asked, picking at a splinter on the bench. Long, slim fingers she wanted uncovering every secret she possessed. Charting the stars on her *skin*. "Jasper Noble sends a bouquet of flowers? Then you give him the choice of removing your spectacles before he lays you across his bed?"

"Oliver Aspinwall, you're used to getting what you want, aren't you?" She huffed a fast breath, infuriated and enthralled by his possessiveness. "What must that *be* like? Women are denied daily, each moment a possible rejection. Yet men stride through life without containment."

He palmed the table, leaning in until their noses almost touched. She'd become familiar to the signs of his arousal, through research she'd fought against doing but had done, anyway. The tightening of his jaw, the feral gleam in his eye. That clip of air shooting past lips admittedly lush for a man. The rapid flicker of his pulse beneath his ear. "Maybe I'm used to getting what I want, but I've honestly never wanted anything this much."

She snorted, disbelieving. But she didn't move away.

"You don't trust me." His hand rose to cradle her cheek, his thumb grazing her lower lip, setting her aflame. "When you can. When I only want, for the time you're here, to share myself with you. Give you what you couldn't find with"—he nodded furiously to the book—"*him*. No one has ever belonged to me, Nessie. Not my father, my mother, even Xander. It's foreign and unnerving to crave you this profoundly, to wish to *own* you when I know I never will. Yet, I can't help myself. In this, unlike our game on the lawn, I will submit if that's what it takes to have you."

She shifted into his touch, her breath sputtering despite her need to appear unmoved. "I don't trust myself. I'm afraid I won't be able to return to London with this hunger lurking inside me. I won't leave a part of my heart in Derbyshire, my lord." Stepping back, she shrugged out of reach. "I *won't*. I have no place in my life for this level of yearning. It wasn't like this before."

"Yes, yes, I recall. Your fucking gardens. Your dream to be more famous than the illustrious Capability Brown," he growled, lips parting, more furious words set to rush forth. But they got tangled, mixed in emotion and what looked like confusion. Indecision, *desire*. Capturing her cheeks, he brought her gaze to his. "Save your heart for someone else, then. I'll take your body. It will be enough."

"It's not that simple."

"Nothing simple about it, Sprite. I agree. I lie awake imagining you simply saying *yes*. The one word freeing us both. One. Effortless. Word." Grasping her hand, he dragged her around the work bench, tugging her along as he strode down the aisle, his new citrus trees flanking them. The scent of lemon and orange stung her nose, filled her lungs. Her breath was coming short, high, and hard. There was a pantry at the back. A door with a lock. She stored bags of mulch and seed there.

Rain began striking the roof and the windows, dull pings matching the rapid beat of her heart. *Stop him*, she thought as he stepped inside the murky chamber, kicking the door shut with his boot. *Now*, she told herself as he flipped the lock, his gaze glowing when it hit her. *Before you lose yourself.*

Conquest was clearly on his mind, lanced through the savage posture of his body. In the hand he fisted at his side until his knuckles paled. In the lips he clenched, his tongue coming out, finally, to moisten them. Readying for her.

This is what he's good at. It's a game to him. The earl is known for seduction.

"I love your hair." He gave her pathetic chignon a gentle yank, circling the honied strands around his fist as they rolled over her breast. With a smile, he slid her spectacles from her face, depositing them on a nearby shelf. "It's the color of the sunrise when it has been ignited by a midnight storm. Fiery, furious color." His knuckles brushed her nipple, then held back, agonizing torment.

She couldn't work up the strength to refuse him. Push him away. Tell him she didn't want him when it was evident she did. Her nipples were hard points beneath her clothing, the triangle between her thighs on fire. Liquid heat. So, she let the mindless passion that was likely to ruin them both unfurl.

He tilted his head, brushing the tips of her hair across a particularly sensitive spot on her jaw. She kept herself from moaning, but just.

"What's ticking?" Letting her silken strands slide between his fingers, he reached into her skirt pocket and withdrew her timepiece as her lips parted in shock at his brazen move. "Well, well. My girl and her surprises." Turning, he laid the watch by her spectacles on the shelf. "Two minutes. Then we decide."

"Decide?" Her voice was breathless, a woman provoked to the point of submission. Her hip tingled where he'd inadvertently touched her while removing her watch. Ripples of awareness flowing to hidden parts of her body that, like a weed stuck in the pavement, rarely saw the light of day.

Lifting her hand to his lips, he nipped her wrist, stroked his tongue over her beating pulse, melting her legs until she feared crashing to the straw-covered floor. "If we stop at a kiss or decide to carry it further. Me?" He gave a careless toss of his shoulder. "I'll go as far as you let me."

She opened her mouth to argue, perhaps, and he took advantage, setting out to persuade as the storm raged around them. She didn't hear the howling wind, the creak of an aged dwelling, only his harsh breaths as his lips seized hers. Her heartbeat pounding in her head, a dusky swirl swimming across her vision. She reached blindly, fingers tangling in his hair. For purchase, the hold, to keep her from collapsing at his feet. Bumping against him, she sought to crawl inside. Bring his breath into her lungs, his heat into her soul.

Closer, if she could only get closer.

His tattered groan shot through her, shattering any dismissal she'd planned to make. Desire over fear, decision made. His arm swept low with her soundless submission, curling around her back, and drawing her into the blazing shelter of his body.

He sampled, judicious but determined, tasting her, tender, his tongue drawing hers into erotic play. Then he began his campaign to wreck her. Engaging passionately, using every skill he possessed—lips, hands, that broad, amazing body—then backing off until she was frantic.

He didn't try to hide his daring persuasion. Merely kept directing the kiss until her mind was butter, her body long retreated to his side of the battlefield. Where had her caution gone? Her certainty that this path would lead to disaster? Both of them torched by the heat they generated. Lost, as he'd predicted.

God, could he kiss. The women climbing in windows to get to him knew what they were about. And in this moment, he was *hers*. Despite his plotting, he was as destroyed as she. His shaft hard as kindling, wedged against her hip, beckoning. Maybe this time, he'd let her touch him.

Somehow, she'd done it again. Made a beast of a gentleman.

She was fool to yearn for a man far from reach. A man only temporarily *within* reach. Yet yearn she did.

Necessity lifted to the balls of her feet, seeking. Her sigh of frustration circled.

"*Shush*, I have you," he murmured, his arm going beneath her bottom to draw her up and against him. Fitting them together like two cracked pieces of pottery. Quite literally lifting her feet off the floor.

The kiss took a brutal turn. Hot, hard madness. His muscles twitching beneath her fingers, her nails digging into the skin at the nape of his neck. Liking the rough touch, he groaned into her mouth, worked his body against hers, an elemental stroke and grind. There was raw power in him that she wanted to unleash, even as she feared unleashing it. She didn't fool herself. The man who'd killed on a battlefield three thousand miles away was the same man embracing her. Strong, intelligent, conflicted Oliver.

The most complicated person she could have chosen, and the only person she wanted.

One of life's mysteries.

He curled his hand around her hip, directing her movements, branding her head to toe. "Stop thinking. Designing this like one of your damned gardens."

Desire flooded her body, coalescing between her thighs. A heady thump, a vibration, a demand she was swiftly letting consume her. Her skin prickled, reason dissolving until she was nothing but a rising tide of sensation. *Wash over me*, she thought in desperation.

Going on impulse, she yanked her skirt up and, unencumbered, wrapped her leg around his waist. Silently urging him to seal the fit. He took the reins without missing a beat, clutching her hip, angling her higher, and shifting his body until his cock wedged against her moist, molten folds. Protective layers of cotton and muslin shielding them when, truthfully, there was nothing safe about this.

Aroused, mindless, she didn't care. Groaning, she arched her back and moved against him as their bodies found a rough but essential rhythm.

"You are my dream, Nessie Byrne," he whispered, slanting his head and pulling her back into the kiss. Before she could run away from him or herself. Turning, he pressed her back to the door, raising her thigh high on his hip, grinding against her. Locking them in place, her supple heat sheltering his arousal. "I want to count the stars in your eyes while I slide inside you. Exactly as I track the ones in the sky. I want that incredible hair spilling across my sheets, my fingers twisted in the strands when I come."

Such obscene sentiments whispered in that posh, privileged accent nearly drove her over the edge.

They stayed like that forever, it seemed. Tongues tangling, mouths meshed. Hands roaming, exploring, playful and demanding. Bodies meeting, backing off, then meeting again. Like coupling, she realized, yet with the tantalizing lengthening of her pleasure, better. Her nipples stiff points beneath scratchy muslin, begging for his touch. The triangle between her legs softening. Muted sighs and moans mixing with the steady drum of rain against new windowpanes, the wind whistling over the conservatory's walls.

"Our two minutes are up," he whispered, a harsh rasp sliding over her abused lips. "Admitting that since we have trust issues. Or you do."

She closed her eyes, her head tumbling back against the door. Grabbing his shoulders, she rubbed against him, an indelicate facsimile of what they'd do in bed. A grinding replica of mating. The jolt of pleasure traveled up her legs, along her spine, settling at her lower back. His hand had crept to cup her bottom with firm ownership. Whatever she was doing, *he* was doing, it was working for her. Close, she was close. "I've never... with anyone. I want to. With you."

He exhaled, startled, a hot breath dusting her cheek. "*Christ*, Nessie. Didn't he, your bookseller? Didn't you? Weren't you... I mean..."

She opened her eyes, let him see what she couldn't admit.

"But you have? Before?"

She hummed, lost in the moment. Lost in wanting him, wanting *pleasure*, more than she should. Greed, a foreign emotion that was potent and addictive, rolled over her. "Alone. Yes."

Stanford thumped his forehead to the door, then nestled his cheek on her shoulder. Kissing his way to the delicate swell beneath her ear. "Holy hell. I think my cock is about to bust my buttons."

"That's brilliant. No need to let it go to waste when you could use it on me." She wiggled against him, a rising tide racing through her veins. She no longer cared if she made a fool of herself, not if he took care of her. And she, feasibly, was invited to take care of him. "You're an expert, my lord earl. Use your talent. Show me how it's done." She smiled, a fearsome, female display. She felt his aroused reaction to her taunt, heard his indrawn breath. "I dare you."

His hand skimmed her body to her hip, perfecting the fit. Moving her along his shaft. Up and back. Up and back. Until they were both panting. "I'm not an expert, but I'm confident I can get you where you need to be. Especially as you're halfway there already."

"More than half," she whispered roughly, gratified to feel his fingers flex and dig into her flesh with her admission. She rode him, awkwardly, for another minute as they tumbled back into the kiss. Pinpoints of light exploded behind her eyelids. Her agonized groan rippling through the darkness.

With a frayed oath that blistered the air, he hoisted her high, carrying her across the room, placing her bottom on a workbench that rocked with her weight. She let go of him to grab the scarred edges, afraid the piece wouldn't hold her. He pushed her skirt to her waist, tucking the material beneath her hands.

"Hold this, that's your job for the next few minutes. Don't touch me, don't think of it. This is about you. Because if you touch me, I can't promise I'll stick to the rules. When what I want is to fuck you against the wall right there. Or on top of this"—he smacked the bench —"destroying it with our passion when it looks to be a piece still in use. *That's* what I'm known for, Sprite. On the battlefield, in the dens, in life. If I choose, if I decide, I go in with everything I have." His eyes had lost their boyish appeal, his gaze darkened with shades of grave provocation. With certainty. With power she'd undervalued.

The match was his, and this time, he meant to win.

Nevertheless, the gentle man beneath the mask stayed in the arena, giving Necessity the chance to say no. Leaning in to sweetly sample her mouth, cupping her cheek with banked hunger. When she went to touch him, he pressed her palm against the scarred wood, over her bunched gown, his fingers trembling around hers. "This will change everything, Nessie."

"Change me, then."

She wanted change. Wanted *him*. Wanted pleasure she didn't bring herself in the twilight of her lonely bedchamber. She wished to understand what being with someone she *desired* with this savage rush of emotion felt like. She wished to lose herself in pleasure. Dive beneath the waves of it and sink.

He tilted her head back, his thumb sweeping her cheek. "The expression on your face, determined and so damned sensual. You are the most beautiful, confounding, arousing woman ever tossed in my path, Necessity Byrne. I hardly know what to do with you. With myself for wanting you this much. But I'm going to try to figure it out." Stepping between her legs, he nudged them aside. His shaft, as rigid as the wood beneath her fingers, settling into the soft cradle topping her thighs.

The bench was, as he'd planned, the perfect height for such play.

Driven by impulse, she arched her body, knocking into him. His scalding gaze met hers, and she could see him debating. A bead of sweat rolled down his temple, and he scrubbed it away with his shoulder. His jaw muscles tensed, his lips smoothing into resolute lines. "Close your eyes. *Surrender*. Pursue your pleasure, darling Sprite. After all, that's what I'm here for."

She did as he asked, her lids dropping.

Without sight, the sounds of his scattered breaths circled. The plunk of raindrops and the dwelling shuddering from the force of the storm. Her tattered sigh when his hand skimmed her knee, thigh, then finding the opening in her drawers. Her body dissolved, pliant complacency, until her grip on the bench was the only thing keeping her from slithering off it.

He kissed her again, softly, as his fingers danced over her. Stroking, teasing. She murmured encouragement, words of praise when he hit a sweet spot—*yes, there*—bumping forward, chasing his touch. Groaning, selfish behavior she'd never before had reason to exhibit. He groaned himself before he thrust that first time, sliding his finger deep inside her.

"Oh, heavens," she gasped, chin dropping to her chest, pulling them out of the kiss.

"The best version of heaven." Then he bowed into his touch, into her passion, into his project, working her with long strokes, his thumb coming in to circle the tight button of skin at the apex of her thighs. His lips traveled where he could reach. The sensitive spot underneath her ear, the curve of shoulder, the swell of her breasts above her gown's rounded neck. Her cheek, light nips to her jaw. Until she lost track of him surrounding her.

"Your passion is coating my skin, Sprite, until I feel shaken where I stand."

She whimpered, a response which was no response. She simply didn't have it in her to talk. Her pleasure was arriving from multiple avenues—an earl's teeth, tongue, lips, hands, words—all coalescing at the juncture of her thighs. His finger sliding, seeking, *twisting*. A distinctive curl at the end of each stroke that made her body quiver. And his thumb, always there, pressing, circling, knowing what she needed. She vaulted into his caress, begging without speech. The stimulation stunning, sunlight sparks upon her face, her skin. The air thick as smoke around them.

His free hand lowered to her breast, cupping, his thumb finding her peaked nipple beneath layers. Not enough, but enough, when she yearned for him to suck, *bite*. When she desired the discovery of every inch of him and was being skillfully denied.

Imagining the sculpted, broad body hidden beneath his clothing, she hovered for no more than another languid second before tumbling.

He took her hoarse cry into his mouth, smothered her moans with a fierce inhalation. He seemed caught in his own pleasure, dazed and hungry. Overcome himself. He nipped the pad of her thumb when she brought her hand to cradle his jaw, causing her vision to spot. The quivers racked her, threatening to spill her from her perch. Swaying, she dragged her lips down his cheek, gasping out her pleasure against the taut muscles of his throat, sighing ardently into his shirt collar. Her muscles tightened around his finger, squeezed as she hit rock bottom, her release overwhelming. At any other time in her life, she would have been embarrassed by her response.

"Say my name, Sprite," he rasped. "I don't think you have once during this, and I want to hear it."

"My lord," she whispered, breathless and stunned, her smile growing against the fine cotton of his shirt, enough warmth to brand his skin if only he could see it.

He snorted a laugh, tipping her chin, kissing her until she felt faint. "Try again."

She swallowed past a dry throat, heartbeat erratic, pulse bumping in her ears. "Stanford."

He hummed, nipping her earlobe as she'd done to him days ago. The bite traveled to her toes, an additional heavenly tingle rippling through her. "After this"—he wiggled the finger still inside her, drawing forth another shimmer of bliss—"can we get closer than that?"

"Oliver." *Ollie*.

"That will do for now. More than, I suppose." His lips grazed her temple, his voice shaken now that she was present enough to notice. In truth, the arm surrounding her trembled.

Dangerous business, but they stayed locked in a quivering embrace longer than they should have. Luminous comfort. His heart raced beneath her ear, slowing only with his effort to find self-control. All told, a remarkably intimate encounter she'd never imagined she'd share with him.

With a forced sigh, he stepped back. Reassured them both with a hand at her elbow that she was steady. Although her knees shook beneath the skirt he gallantly lowered to her ankles.

When he was done, he gave her left boot a tap, an oddly soothing gesture. While he looked perturbed, impatient. The return of the sullen earl. His cheeks in high color, his lips plump and mistreated from her handling. The air in the cramped space sizzled, damp and heavy. Scented with her pleasure and his effort. Soil, citrus, man, storm.

"Why are you angry with me?"

He pinched the bridge of his nose and exhaled before slanting a stern glance at her. "I'm vexed with myself, darling Sprite."

"Why?" Although she had an idea about the cause of his frustration. Overlooking his pout, a tantrum she didn't want to deal with, she was close to saying, *I'll take care of you if you tell me what you like. What to do.* "It was wonderful. You were"—her face blazed, hotter than she'd ever felt it—"incredible. This was incredible."

"Hmm... we were too good, I'm afraid. Now I shall be forced to wait out the storm."

She glanced down in time to see him pluck at his trouser close. A round, wet stain had bled through the material, clearly visible. "Oh, ohhhh..."

"Alas, I'm a boy spilling in my trousers, should you be wondering about your effect on me. If we carry this further, my next smooth move will be to tup you on the staircase in a blind fury in front of my small band of servants, uncaring who catches us. Your missing chaperone, perhaps. Sounds like an unfortunate but compelling ending."

Necessity swallowed, watching him shift from boot to boot, his frown fierce, his skin flushed. His beautiful black-gray hair scrambled about his head. She knew a smile would ruin everything. A laugh even worse. Men had fragile casings, especially about *this*. Her delight at making him lose his blasted aristocratic management could be reviewed later, a gift for *her* enjoyment but not at the expense of his.

Although, she hoped he didn't have a problem. There was a man in Shoreditch, Two Dice Benjamin, who couldn't restrain himself for longer than five seconds. Not enough to have relations with his wife. Or anyone else for that matter. He'd tried to fix his problem with every light-skirt on Brick Lane to no avail.

"Has this, um, happened before?"

Stanford tugged damp cotton away from his groin. "Undoubtedly, when I was fourteen!" He gave a nonchalant flick of his hand, the slim, beautiful fingers that had set her aflame now occupied with his embarrassment. "An older lass in the village. Chased me all summer. Caught me in July or so, I seem to recall. It took a few tries before I found my footing, as it were."

Well, you've been off and running ever since, she thought a bit testily. Necessity frowned then, sitting straight for the first time since the Earl of Stanford had stepped between her legs. *Fourteen.* He'd been out and about since he was fourteen. So many women he couldn't possibly remember them. "Is that lass your widow?"

Had it been going on that long between them?

If so, it was a relationship, not just a tup. Necessity Byrne was no destroyer of relationships.

He stilled, glancing up. The perplexed facade of a man who'd annoyed a woman and had no idea why. She watched the pieces fall into place—while some of her joy at bringing him low leaked away like tea through a cracked cup.

"You're jealous." He brought his fist to his lips, an amazing, talented mouth, and laughed behind it. His eyes when they struck her were glossy silver, dazzling in the murky light. "I'll be damned. I've won a contest I had no notion I'd entered. Two contests, actually."

She jumped down, shaking out her skirts. Had to grab the blessed bench to steady herself because of her wobbly knees. "Is it the same woman, my lord?"

He considered his options. The possibilities displayed on his handsome face. Lying. Teasing. Dragging out her discomfort. He might be a hardened soldier, a lofty earl, a member of silly parliament, but he wasn't the best at hiding what he was thinking. Macauley's comment about Oliver having his head in the clouds circled back, about him being kind, undermining her already susceptible defenses. "It's not. I haven't talked to the village chit since I was a boy. She married and moved away." He tilted his head, his smile crooked and adorable, revealing more than he'd like. "I can't recall her name. Terrible, isn't it? But her face, now that lingers a bit. Her pert... ah, never mind about that." Then with a broad smile, he winked, knowing exactly what he was doing to her.

Necessity sent him a withering side-glance while tugging at her bodice. She was larger than she liked up top, and her breasts felt heavy, straining against her stays. Her thighs were moist, her skin sensitive to the touch. His gaze followed every movement, tracking as he did the stars each night. The strange and overpowering vibration continued to shimmer between them, igniting the air.

Regrettably, their unexpected sojourn had not erased the want.

"It's not my fault," she whispered, unsure why she even said it. Or what she meant by the ridiculous statement. Crossing the room on shaky legs, she retrieved her spectacles from the shelf and hooked the arms behind her ears, fitting the frame to the bridge of her nose.

He grunted, yanking out his shirttail and checking to see if it covered the stain on his trousers. "Most definitely your fault. You kissed *me*, remember? Now, I won't be able to get within two feet of you without my body going on alert. The scent of honeysuckle and dirt tied to erotic urges for the rest of my life. I can't wait to see what kind of dream this little episode brings. When I was a boy, I also used to spend in my sleep. If I'm going back to those days, I'll have to keep a towel handy by my bed."

She raked her hair atop her head, struggling to make something work with the few pins the earl hadn't snatched out. "It wasn't that much. A kiss plus, if I had to label it. Blazes, if you've been in the ring since you were fourteen, this can't be unforgettable!"

He went to her, batting her hands away. Spinning her around, he began a hasty effort to assemble her coiffure.

"Your hair is delectable." He sank his nose in the tresses and gulped a breath. "I'm quite taken with it. Gads, it's as thick as a horse's tail.

With those silver frames making your eyes look as big as amber marbles, I'm lost." Then he made her crankier by doing a fairly good job, especially with half her hairpins lying on the floor. "You shouldn't presume to know how I feel before I tell you. Before I know myself. About the kiss plus." He paused, and she was glad, as he likely was, that she didn't have to stare at him during this recitation. "I only know it feels like more. You'll have to take that for now. Like the stars, the truth comes about with time and study. Patience."

"More?" She glanced over her shoulder, catching his smoldering look. "Similar to the things I was telling you about? Positions and places we could"—her hand shot out, cutting that off, a blunder in word choice. "*One* could choose to have relations." She fumbled, lips parting, then went ahead and said it, "For a moment there, when I was on the bench, I thought you were going to drop to your knees and place your—"

Slipping his hand over her mouth, he growled deep in his throat, looking pained to his teeth. "If you start talking about your fantasies again, Nessie, I'm going to need to sit down."

"What I get for telling you." Backing away, she yanked the door open and marched from the storeroom. "Forget I mentioned them, you toad. I won't make that mistake again. There are men in London, *many*, who won't laugh when I tell them. First thing I'm doing when I get back to the city, Stanford. Find him."

"Over my dead body, Byrne," he murmured.

He caught her in the aisle, his fingers circling her wrist. "What a fearsome temper you have. Such a bite, your threats. Frankly, I'm surprised we stopped arguing long enough to pleasure each other. Although mine was a bit of a management issue." Grinning, he lifted her hand to his lips, pressing a supple kiss to her palm.

He was so damned handsome standing there tucked between two lemon trees, bashfulness and devilry in sublime balance. His jet hair a wild twist about his head. Clothing rumpled, shirttail concealing evidence of their passion. With a sigh, she admitted to the insane desire to drag him to her bedchamber and pleasure him *properly* this time.

She gestured to his trouser close. "Considering your reputation, that was surprising."

"I couldn't help myself. Yours, *ah*, Sprite, was the most glorious orgasm I've ever seen roll over someone. In. My. Life. It was like watching a person open a gift, the first they've ever received." Trepidation, slight and covered quickly, crossed his face. "I didn't try to hold back, which I guess I usually do. Bloody hell, I hope I don't make a habit of this."

"I was shocked," she confessed, casting about for a place to rest her gaze, then helplessly returning it to him, "at the intensity."

He blinked, a sluggish leak of air sliding from his lips. "Not quite the same as your own influence, is it? Better than nothing, but not like the real thing."

She chewed on the inside of her cheek, the memory of his urgent touch kicking her heartbeat into another mad rhythm. Lips at her ear, impassioned and forbidden. His words indecent and wonderful. His moan of pleasure slipping into her throat, traveling through her like honey, setting fire to her along the way.

Fully clothed, he'd somehow managed to reach every part of her. Or so it had seemed at the time.

How would it be without those barriers? With freedom thrown into the mix? Acceptance. Mental and physical. Mind *and* body. No secrets, no fabrications. She'd paid enough dues in this life to earn that.

"What if I agree? To something between us, until I leave. And *only* until I leave. We agree on each step as we go along."

His hand tensed around hers, and she realized their fingers were linked, the connection from the storeroom yet to be broken. "Is this an effort to best the widow in the village? The lass who made me shame myself all those years ago? To best *me*?"

Honestly? "Maybe."

"Damned if you don't like to win, Nessie."

"Is a competitive nature a bad thing? It's a necessary trait in the stews." It didn't hurt to remind him where she came from. Especially when they were diving into such a private undertaking. Nothing they shared in bed, no matter how incredible, would make up for the severe difference in their standings.

He hummed; a sound she now knew meant he was crafting his strategy. His gaze sharpened, fixing on her as if she were an oasis in his desert. "There's a coach house behind the stable. My mother used it as an art studio. It's in surprisingly excellent shape. No leaking roof. And only a ghost or two to contend with, the norm for a three-hundred-year-old dwelling. After dinner until dawn, it's a refuge. Ours, should we agree."

She paused long enough to gather her courage. "This refuge has a bedchamber, I take it?"

The Earl of Stanford rocked back, letting go of her hand, she guessed, before he started things up again. He had that hungry lion look on his face. "I'm going to enjoy you, Necessity Byrne."

She laughed, gaining her equilibrium. "I better enjoy *you*, Lord Stanford, after all your glowing reviews."

Temper lit his cheeks, but he didn't dispute the challenge. "That was another person. A lost soul if you can believe it. Sadly, he wasn't sure about anything." He placed his hand to his chest, as earnest as she'd ever seen him. "You're going to help me find this man. And I, in turn, will help you find fulfillment."

Trailing his finger across her cheek, he turned and strode down the aisle, halting in the doorway, rain and wind rushing in around him. He looked untamed and impassioned, a picture of a man on a mission.

A man *just* unsure enough to capture a piece of her heart.

Her fantasy. As he'd once said she was his. She feared the strength of this sentiment for both of them.

"Tonight. Come to me. I'll be waiting." His gaze dipped, his smile abashed. "I fear I'm willing to wait as long as it takes, Sprite."

Then he left her, anticipation and a rare sense of power bubbling in her blood.

Chapter Eight

WHERE AN EARL SEEKS A COMPROMISE

A roaring fire blazed in the hearth. Crisp silk covered a feather mattress he'd plumped himself. Lit tallows on every surface until the chamber was bathed in balmy illumination. Champagne for her, tea for him. Fresh wheat bread from the village baker, and the best Stilton in Derbyshire, should they need sustenance. He'd even placed some blooming flower he'd snipped from the garden in his mother's favorite vase.

A ghost of a smile curved Stanford's lips as he glanced around what was undeniably a romantic presentation. Wooing when wooing wasn't required.

Not when the chit in question had already said *yes*.

He tapped his knuckle on the rain-streaked windowpane, searching the murky darkness. He thought she had, anyway. To the west, the last vestiges of a dazzling sunset gilded the sky burnt orange and blue. The rolling hills and valleys he cherished spread beneath it. Another ten minutes, and he was going to the house to find her. If she'd decided against this gambit, which was her prerogative, he wanted to know. Blow out the damned candles and be done with this haunted place.

He was restless, like his lone thoroughbred, Mathis, before stud sessions. Stanford laughed, his breath fogging the glass. Necessity *was* a bit like an undomesticated filly—when he'd never had a gift with horses. Galloping across the meadows until his blood cooled, maybe, but never with taming. He'd never cared enough to try. When this woman made him desperately want to.

The comparison to his favored mount would have enraged her, which pleased *him*.

A blast of frenzied anticipation hit him when he saw her striding through the milky mist, a cloak of uncertain color whipping her ankles. She'd shoved a hat, an ugly, crumpled piece in her morose style, atop her head, an effort to control her mass of riotous curls.

Her hair, the color of every shade of honey, was his favorite thing about her. Aside from her wit. Her intelligence. Her temper. The sleek curve of her hip. Her smile. Her breasts. He released a tense breath and leveled his hand through his hair. Her breasts were spectacular.

He stared, his desire increasing a notch with each step she took. Fortunately, he held back when he felt like flinging the door open and yanking her into his arms. Into a dwelling he hadn't imagined inhabiting ever again. Seizing her mouth, swallowing whatever stinging comments she'd think to make, toss her on the bed and... *oh*, so many things filled his mind. An exhaustive series of lewd images. His body braced for the passionate onslaught.

She brought out sentiments long departed, a flicker of what felt like happiness. A nagging, foreign sensation in the region of his heart.

He gripped the windowpane until his knuckles paled, forcing emotion deep. Too much enthusiasm would spook the filly. And happiness with a woman hell-bent on returning to a city he no longer had any use for—that was, in fact, lethal for him—would never work.

Notwithstanding the earl-gardener-rank issue, which he truly didn't give a fig about. He was Derbyshire, and she was London, and that was that.

They had four weeks until his gardens were in boisterous bloom if her prediction held. He might be able to craftily throw her off course here and there, checking items off her erotic wish list, thereby increasing his time to five weeks. This was possible. A sound plan when he was a man who worked better with one.

Thus when she arrived, peering around the battered oak door, an invited but hesitant guest, Stanford was leaning against the sideboard, giving his best impersonation of a tranquil lover. His only disappointment? That she'd left her spectacles behind. He'd had a luscious dream the night before and been forced to bring himself to fairly fevered completion—Miss Byrne with nothing but those on. Riding him, her hair a glory around them.

Perhaps he could add this fantasy to *his* list. If she had one, couldn't he, too?

Alarm bells didn't go off until she closed the door without a word, her expression two shades past intense. She traversed the room without taking in her surroundings. He opened his mouth to say something pithy and earl-like, and she seized the opportunity. Cradling his jaw in her hands and fusing her lips to his. Similar to their first kiss but better.

Because she knew what he liked.

He had no time to plot—*hell*, no time to do anything but *react*. Her desire shattered his resistance when there had been little of that to begin with. The cup in his hand tumbled to the faded Aubusson and rolled against his boot as he palmed the nape of her neck, pulling her in.

He could tell her but would not presume to go that deep. She was the *only* reason he'd returned to a place where the scent of paint and sorrow lingered. Thoughts of his mother locked in a box he'd never intended to open again.

Kicking away the cup, he ripped that dreadful hat off her head and tossed it over his shoulder. A flood of tawny hair dropped past her breasts, tying his belly in a knot. Without an ounce of finesse, he buried his lips in the delicate curve of her neck and backed her toward the bed, her rain-and-earth scent stealing in to scramble his thoughts.

They could have a conversation *after*.

When her bottom hit the mattress, he gave her a gentle shove that sent her spilling across the counterpane. Laughing, she flipped her hair from her eyes and rose to her elbows. Her gaze swept south, focusing on his trouser close and the unmistakable impression of his arousal behind it. "Missing me, were you?"

He gazed down at her, wondering at his luck. Her hair was a disaster. She'd gotten caught in the rain earlier, like he had, and she'd done nothing to repair the damage. Her gown was another throwaway frock, the original color may have been light rose but now something close to gray. The bodice was too tight, and for his self-preservation, he decided not to think about that. She had a streak of what he guessed was dirt on her jaw. Leading him to her face. Sublime, a work of Shoreditch art. Her body, too, a wonder that didn't require a talented modiste to shore it up. Show it off. She looked magnificent in the ugliest clothing he'd ever seen.

"My eyes are up here," she said and gestured to them. Yet, there was affection in her words. Flirtatious intent with an aching note of longing that sent an arrow through his chest.

She wasn't leaving. She wasn't changing her mind about him, not yet.

Stanford took his first full breath since leaving the conservatory.

He toed off his boots, grabbing the bedpost to keep his balance. One touch or two, possibly, his golden moves, and he could have her quivering, moaning on that bed. Submitting blindly. Rote dealings, his usual methods. Successful, established effort. However, this time, he didn't want coupling to be mindless, without a part of himself in the mix. He wasn't going to trouble himself too much over why that was. Questioning could adversely affect his erection. "I have choices. For you. Leaving the practiced Aspinwall charm behind, I suggest we go with spontaneity."

She licked her lips, making his breath hitch. "Choices?"

Slow down, Ollie. Loosening his cravat, driving his need deep, he tossed it to the bed. With a wicked smile that pierced like a needle, Necessity snatched up the length and carelessly wrapped it around her wrist. The black silk shimmered against her snow-gilded skin.

"Is that on the list?" he asked in a choked voice. His heart had taken a dive to his feet with her move. "If so, it can be arranged."

Her brow winged high, a haughtier response than any he'd given. "Maybe."

She was the most fearless woman he'd come across, when he guessed she wasn't as brave as she appeared. Her vulnerability locking him in as nothing else could.

Weren't they both pretending?

Clumsily, he started to unbutton his shirt. "Would you like to do this for me? That's choice number one, by the by."

She sat up. Toed off her slippers. Instead of helping him disrobe, she untied the laces of her bodice, her gaze fixed to his. Moments later, with a lift and twist, she worked the gown over her head. Then she was sitting there in nothing but a chemise the color of a pale moon. No stays, no corset, no drawers. Her nipples rosy pink points denting cotton. Lush breasts for such a petite figure. More than she needed and everything *he* wanted. The dense, dark thatch between her legs clearly visible, calling to him.

He shivered, his mind going fuzzy around the edges. He was going to drive her wild. *Soon.* "No undergarments. Why, Byrne, you've come prepared to seduce me."

"Choice made, then."

Exactly. Reaching over his shoulder, he caught his collar, and yanked his shirt over his head. She watched it flutter to the floor before returning her eyes to his bare chest. They were the color of a flame and upon seeing him, they flared brightly. Her fingers fumbled, coming to rest on her bosom, which rose and fell with her sigh.

He knew he had a fine physique. One he'd worked like a striver to get. He'd gained two stone since the incident behind Xander's gaming hell. He didn't look like an earl underneath his clothing according to his tailor. Thankfully, he no longer looked like an opium addict, either.

When he got to the fastenings of his close, his trousers hanging on his hipbones, she halted him with a hot as Hade's stare. *Come closer.*

So he did.

Her hand was on his cock before one button had been undone. Learning his shape as best she could through buckskin and a thin pair of drawers. Curiosity and eagerness in her touch. Nothing seductive. Simple yearning. For *him.* Which gave his soul a shake he wondered if he'd recover from.

"*Nessie.*" He dropped his head back on his shoulders, his eyes drifting closed. She opened his trousers, spread the material wide. *Let her, for a moment.* It felt so *good.* He was shaky, reason blurring. "If you do this much longer, we won't get to the good stuff."

She blew an intentional breath across his belly. His shaft twitched beneath her hold. Only his drawers in the way now. "Who says this isn't the good stuff?" she murmured and hauled his trousers to his ankles, circling her hand in a sharp command. *Step out.* He followed, of course he did, kicking them to the side. Letting her control, something he'd never let a chit do. Or maybe the right woman had been the missing piece before.

He'd never found one who wished to lead, that much he knew.

When he *liked* it. He was lit up like a rocket about to go off.

She gazed at him, her eyes fever-bright, the color of a bonfire or a stormy, rosy sunset, caressing him but making no effort to remove his drawers. "I think there's good stuff, and then there's low-level good stuff. Which is this?"

He swallowed, losing focus. *What?* His skin had ignited about ten seconds ago with that scalding breath she sent across his midriff. And his cock had given up the game minutes before that. "*Well...*"

She hooked her finger inside the waistband of his drawers and gave it a wiggle. One untied loop, and he would be naked before her. "I think your choice, and mine, will be to mix the stuffs up. Activities in this bed are one choice, right? That's high level, to my mind. Top shelf." She drew the material down an inch and kissed his hip. Let her tongue linger, slide lower, into the dent at his pelvis. He couldn't have repressed his ragged groan if he had a knife pressed to his neck. "Maybe next time, you catch me in the stable, and we have a brief session in a stall. Or even simpler, low level but not, I use my mouth on you in, say, that linen closet on the second floor. Or the pantry off the kitchen. If the door locks. Or maybe even if it doesn't." She dug her teeth into the skin of his thigh. "For fun, you could give me a limit. Five minutes? Like a game. And we see who wins."

She tugged his drawers lower until his cock was threatening its containment. Batted her lashes as she gazed at him. Taking her sweet time to nibble, lick, suck without going near where he wanted her. With his breath shooting fast from his lips, telling her everything. "I have lots of ideas, Ollie. *Lots.*" Seducing him as he'd never been seduced.

"Where did you *come* from?" Though he didn't for a second allow her to answer. He was too busy climbing over her with her laughter ringing in his ears. Catching her beneath her bottom, he hauled her up the bed with him.

Seizing her lips with a hunger he couldn't hide, he yanked her chemise over her head, heard a seam split. "I'll buy you a new one," he said, then dove in, pressing her deep into the mattress.

Her game. His game.

Because it was fun when it had never been *fun*. The spontaneity he'd promised her, he allowed himself. Rolling across the bed, wrestling, kissing, groping, muffled sounds of pleasure rending the air. Her active hands testing her skill while learning his boundaries. Fingers in his hair, nails scratching his scalp. Gripping his hip and guiding his rhythm against her.

Insistent yearning. Tasting the flavor of each other for the first time.

At some point, she demanded he remove his drawers, and together, awkwardly, they got them off, where they landed in a puddle on the floor. Then he took her arms over her head and, locking them on the mattress, laid his long body over hers.

They stilled, skin-to-skin for the first time. Both of them searching, he could see, for what to say. Her eyes were as dark as whisky circling the bottom of a glass, wide and full of wonder. She shook her head—*no, not now, I can't*—tugged his mouth to hers, dragging him under.

He explored, similar to his quest in the skies each night. That much curiosity and passion behind it, which wasn't the norm for him. With his lips, his teeth, his *tongue*. Charting every curve, freckle, crease. Her breast filling his hand, his thumb circling her nipple, nails flicking the hard nub until she groaned into his mouth, arched into his touch. He moved to the other as he trailed his attention along her collarbone, tracking her pleasure, each ripple and shift of her body. Going further, backing off. Smiling against her creamy skin when she groaned, frustration evident.

At the last, he blew a hot breath across her skin. He could tease, too.

"Is this payback, Stanford?" Her voice was slick as morning dew, swelling with lust.

He captured the peaked bud, sucked, licked, soothed. "Maybe, Byrne," he whispered with her nipple caught in his teeth.

She grabbed at him but lost her grip as he moved down her body. "This is what you imagined while I had you on the bench." His words were smothered against the rounded curve of her belly. He didn't hesitate, seduction long gone. *He'd* been the one seduced this day. Murmuring his desires into her taut thigh, her piquant scent rising to tangle him in a knot, he feasted, setting his mouth to her core.

She tasted like ambrosia. Far more potent than opium, the high of her.

Her back arched, her fingers clamping in his hair, pulling, pushing. "If you... don't stop... we won't get to the good stuff." Her voice was thready, trembling. Her breath gusting from her lungs, her legs shaking where they held him, clenching his shoulders.

"Who says this isn't the good stuff?" he returned against her moist flesh, his cock so hard he could have hammered a tap in a wine cask with it. Knowing his time was limited, he set out to destroy her, make speech and thought impossible. Make her come quickly with his mouth before sliding inside and pleasuring her properly.

He angled his finger into her silken heat. Added another when she signaled that he could. A dance in tandem with his tongue, a dance he loved. A dance he was good at. A mixed tempo to keep her on edge but never falling over it. Not yet. Details, always the details. One must never forget them. *Overlook* them. And he didn't.

Glancing past her truly astounding breasts, he found her eyes closed, back arched, her hand—the one that wasn't fisted in his hair—tangled in his sheets. The long, lovely slope of her neck that he'd bitten on his way down was flushed ruddy red like the English roses she loved. Her hair a golden glory around her, a shade lighter, he'd discovered, than the delicious thatch between her legs.

This image made him dizzy with desire.

Returning to his task, he drew her into his soul, senses aflame. His skin tingling, a sizzle of sensation brewing at the base of his spine, along his back and legs. Tongue grazing her sex, he took the swollen nub between his lips, sucking gently, then not so gently. He used what he'd learned with the most generous of intent, wishing for more pleasure for her than he had any other living soul.

She sobbed in response, quivering, whispered pleas, dire commands. *Now faster, there, Ollie.*

"Not yet, not *until*." He thrust his fingers, licking, tasting her, aware she was close. Pleasure arriving with her trembling thighs, the mewling sounds spilling from her throat. "Then, we'll get to the rest."

With a hoarse cry, she dropped her leg over his shoulder, holding him to her as she shattered. Hands tugging at his hair, guiding him. Rising against his mouth, his stroking hand, sending everything deeper. She rode the orgasm through his efforts to extend it, until she gasped and pushed him away, boneless, broken. Chest heaving, her hands tumbled to her side, complete surrender from a woman who never surrendered.

Her release continued to ripple through her like waves across a channel. He took a playful nip on her quivering thigh and laughed softly when she growled an unintelligible response. The sounds still echoing about the room, her instant of raw, uninhibited bliss was one he'd not forget in this lifetime. He felt as if he'd climbed a mountain, conquering her if only for a moment.

Before he thought too hard about his own thunderstruck reaction or the nagging, relentless yearning crowding the base of his spine, he crawled up her body. Cradled her jaw, tilting her head. "I want to see the color your eyes turn after you come." Such a dark amber they were nearly black was the answer.

She exhaled brokenly, swallowed hard. "I knew you'd have a smug smirk on your face." Her voice was wobbly, liquor-fueled he'd have guessed if he didn't know better. "You've vanquished the headstrong rookery chit, my lord earl. Made me beg when I've never begged in my life. Turned me into a raging addict for your touch. Congratulations. I concede defeat. I am humbled by your prowess."

He laughed, fondness and rare delight filling him. Even after this superb performance, and it had been *superb*, with her scent clinging to his cheeks, her dew to his lips, his own body halfway to the pleasure gates, she was trying to bedevil him. Trying to *win*. Or sulking because she hadn't. "My darling Nessie, I accept your compliments."

An aggrieved spark lit her eyes. "You don't have to look so proud of yourself. I liked it. It was good."

Good? He almost laughed at the description. It had been fucking amazing, and they both knew it. "Hmm," he murmured and rolled to her side. "Well, then. At least a man can try."

She grasped his shoulder, trying to bring him back. "Oh no, you don't, Lord Stanford. I want the rest. I have a list, remember? We had a deal."

With a lazy grin, he propped his cheek on his fist, trailing his finger down her chest, over her ribs, finally, gingerly, circling her nipple. Watching it bud while giving himself thirty seconds before he clamped his teeth around it. Minutes before he made her come again. Her lids fluttered, her body rising helplessly into his touch. He had her, the poor darling. "If it was only *good*..."

She cupped the nape of his neck and drew his lips to her nipple. "You are such a dirty fighter. Low-down like a lad born on the docks," she groused, then sighed happily when he took her between his lips, laving her with his tongue. "But oh, *God*, Ollie, was it good. So, so good."

He let her nipple pop from his mouth. "Good is great, then?"

She pinned him with a hot glare. "Are you sure you remember how to *do* the rest?"

"Ah, darling Sprite, do I ever," he said and rolled over her, pressing her soft, sweet body into the mattress.

The kiss they created was surprisingly tender as their bodies locked into place. A shared confidence. Unique and extraordinary, a thought he kicked to the back of his mind.

Skin slick, they began to shift against each other, bumping, grinding. Sending the old bed creaking. Heartbeat, breath, and movement rising in pitch and speed. Her plump breasts in his hands, his shoulders, his forearms, in hers, nails biting into his skin. Scraping and clawing. He drew her thigh along his waist, pinned it high on his hip, and settled between her legs.

There they created the rhythm that would carry them through, rehearsing for long, aching moments before she groaned low and reached for him. Her fingers circled his length, stroking, thumb sweeping to tease the rounded head. Her touch flowed to his toes, a swell of lust catching him hard in the chest. And gentler feelings, frightening ones he wasn't ready to admit.

Stilling, they gazed at each other, a startling moment of intimacy. Chests rising and falling in a synchronized rhythm, legs entwined, hips touching. With a tender kiss, he laid his hand over hers and moved his shaft into place.

No words passed between them as he slid inside, the slowest entry of his life. Her gusty sigh ripping across his cheek. Her soft fingertips at his back, slipping down his spine, gripping his waist and urging him on. Her tongue coming out to lick his bottom lip, her throat pulling in a delicate movement. Her body, perfect and desired, lifting to reach him.

The meeting of their bodies was exquisite.

Eventually, he closed his eyes to the intensity, her flaming amber gaze striking too hard, hitting too close. Silken threads, a wealth of emotion he longed to reject, wrapping around him as he surrendered.

Losing himself until there was nothing between them.

Her earth-and-rain fragrance filled his mind, where he saved it with his cherished memories. He left the kiss as he lifted her up, hand to her lower back. Instinctively, her legs circled his waist, securing them in perfect accord. Open to him, his thrusts increased in depth and speed. Long, slow, delicious glides from tip to base. He held at the end of the thrust, buried so deeply inside her, felt her muscles tense and clench around him. With a moan, he dropped his face into the bounty of her hair, kissed her neck, her cheek, before returning to ravage her mouth.

Then he took them to places neither had gone before. Giving her everything.

"*Ollie.*" Her arms locked around him, bringing him in. Legs tightening about his waist, body lifting, settling in, they flowed into each other with natural ease. Born to be with each other. Made for each other.

Their bodies bumped, stirred, moans and cries mingling with the sound of rainfall striking the coach house windows. The hiss of a roaring fire. The aging creak of a bed being put to brutal use. Echoes beyond his senses—yet ones reverberating within his soul. A dizzying swirl of awareness, his skin flushed, his fingertips tingling as they stroked her jaw, her cheek, swept into her hair, that glorious, untamed hair. Her nipples, her waist, her tummy. Down her body and back again.

He was wild with the abundance of her.

His pace got away from him. His plans away from him. A pinch at the base of his spine caught his breath, his orgasm circling. He paused, gasping, struggling. She felt so incredible, her body spasming around his. Her hair stuck to his skin, her hands on a quest, all over him. The scent of her slicing like a blade. Her moisture slick on his cock. Affectionate, brazen, willful wonder of a girl.

He couldn't think, could only feel. His reckoning for letting her get close, for letting himself *be*. For inviting her in. Doomed if he let himself be.

"Quit thinking, Ollie." She cradled his cheek, drawing him into a kiss laced with fury and hunger. With dogged persistence. "Stay here. Right here. With me."

He dropped his brow to hers as he worked himself inside her, again and again, agonizing strokes until she rose, pelvises bumping, boneless souls pleading for fulfillment. The ancient headboard spanked the wall, and as he figured to touch her in a way he *knew* would end this thing, she began to climax like a pyrotechnic exploding beneath him. Muscles clasping around him, her frantic cries twisting him up until inky dots swarmed his vision. Until the air in his lungs shot out in a gasping surrender. The blood in his head draining to his feet.

He said something as his pleasure raced in behind hers, he was sure he did, driving into her with such force that they slithered up the bed. Shaken, he gripped the headboard, attempting to halt the tremors wracking his body and comfort her at the same time. Perception vanished, any plan for three seconds in the future. Sparks of sensation, blind ecstasy, and the woman still moving languidly on his cock were the lone remaining pieces. Breathless and dazed, he could only hang his head and gulp air, his hand grasping the brass slat with enough strength to crush it.

Mindless and sated. For the first time, utterly destroyed by passion.

Necessity leaned up to playfully nip his twitching biceps. "You can let go now, my lord earl. Before you crush the headboard. You've completed your mission."

He collapsed—melted, in truth, a puddle of masculine content-ment. Tunneling his arm beneath her, he rolled to his side, and fit her against him. Her head fell to his shoulder, her lips shooting pert sighs over his throat. That glorious hair, *ah, God,* flipping across his face. The bed gave an unholy groan and dropped two inches on one side, threat-ening to spill them to the floor.

They curled into each other, laughing, though Stanford waved away discussion. He didn't know what he'd say in this condition. This depleted, roar-filling-his-head condition. His body was hers—and his heart was straining to reach her, too.

When that was simply too much to give up.

Too soon, he reminded himself, exhaling past the ragged shudder in his chest.

He'd never felt connected after. Satisfied, certainly. And impatient to leave. To inch away, flee into the night. He'd never stayed with anyone, not until dawn, never dared with the nightmares. Never wanted to. It wasn't the *point.*

"Sleep," he whispered and dragged his delightful horticulturist as close as he could get her, not once considering letting go.

Chapter Nine

WHERE A HORTICULTURIST REALIZES
SHE'S IN EMOTIONAL TROUBLE

Necessity remembered the first time she'd slept on silk sheets. The first time she'd had tea at Gunter's. Thanks to the kind ladies at the Duchess Society, her first sentence spoken without dropping a single H. Her first official contract signed, for development of a narrow patch of loveliness behind a baron's townhouse on Curzon. She recalled the moment she'd had ten pounds to call her own, stuffed beneath her mattress in a leather sack that had been her father's. Enough funds to purchase two gowns from a modiste instead of doing with those she made, poorly, herself. One an atrocious mulch-brown the seamstress had been holding for someone who never picked it up, and the other some odd tangerine color that looked horrible with her skin.

She'd made do. Built a life.

She remembered a lot of things.

And for the entirety of her days, she'd remember *this*.

Laughing quietly because she couldn't contain it, she propped her chin on her fist, making a mental documentation of the earl's total and utter fatigue. The hearth burning low and hot at their backs, the reliable tick of a clock somewhere in the chamber.

And the gorgeous earl, dead to the world beside her, exhausted breaths slipping from his lips.

She'd finally worn him out.

Those feral silver facets pinning her to the bed all night shut off in sleep. His eyes had glittered, searing like an ember as he climbed over her, claiming her. His hunger feeding hers. A remarkable, incredibly dazzling sensation to be wanted and to *want* with such intensity. What a match they were in this arena.

A struggle, a battle almost. To slide deeper. To thrust harder. To grab pleasure and run away with it. To wring every wobbly pulse from every spent vein. Every thready beat from a drained heart. Untamed and inexplicable, their evening. She was decided about one thing, if *only* one thing. There could not be another man to fit her this well, to desire her this much. To make her blind with a rush of such yearning that it tossed her off her feet.

When she was the most grounded girl she knew.

Beggars were never choosy; they didn't have the right or the option. She'd never expected to have anything close to this. A man like him to explore.

Astonishingly, she and Oliver, fourth or fifth or twentieth Earl of Stanford, ancient title with a medieval burden falling down around him, were opponents outside the bedchamber, possibly, but quite compatible partners *in* it.

Despite her avowals, here she was, caring for more than his gardens.

She sighed and tugged the sheet she'd retrieved from the bed they'd destroyed to his waist. Combating the chill racing through the window he'd thrown open when the heat in the dwelling had become unbearable. When the scent of their lovemaking had taken a firm, ferocious hold.

She should have been uneasy, lying there on chilled planks atop a threadbare rug of once-luxurious origin. Instead, she wished to never leave. She wished to entice her delectable partner into going a third round. He'd whispered in her ear seconds before her last release, possibly triggering it, about taking her against the wall. Holding her up while he thrust inside her, making her see stars brighter than she could through his telescope.

The remembrance shimmered, a dreamy finger across her skin. A slow puff leaked from her lips.

Well, it was settled. She was weak. Obsessed. Captivated, partly against her will. Addicted like he had been to the drugs.

Maybe she could be forgiven for taking him. He was a hard man to overlook. Such contradictions. Clever, with a mind turned to the heavens. Gentle, with a heart buried beneath layers of heartbreaking experience. Temperamental when it suited him. Elegant, even in slumber. Handsome, goodness. *More* than. Coal-black hair tangled about his brow, the damp strands curling enticingly about his ears. The threads of gray bringing him close to perfection to her mind. An unforgettable face, a warrior's body.

Truly, no earl in the *world* looked like Oliver Aspinwall did under his clothing.

Taking care not to wake him, she traced the mark her teeth had made on his biceps when he'd been hanging on to the bed for dear life, her gaze sweeping the length of his long form tangled up in the sheet. *Blazes.* A greedy, possessive evaluation. She'd about fallen off the bed when he took off his shirt. No man outside the docks had a physique like that. Her bookseller was scrawny in comparison, when she hated to compare, but she was pitiful, so there you had it.

Also, the earl was, which she suspected a little irritably that he *knew*, a highly inventive lover. Precise *or…* she hummed and let her gaze roam him again. Just very detailed, like he was with his celestial notes. He'd taken time to draw out her pleasure until she was a length of cord pulled to the limit, about to snap. Touches, caresses, *oh*, his hands. And the *kisses*. Necessity fanned her face, exhaling hard, her body heating thinking about them.

They were *combustible*. After all, they'd smashed the blasted bed with the first round.

The only round to her expectation.

Then he'd teased her, playful and laughing (another surprise) after depositing her on the counterpane he'd spread before the hearth. As if they were having a picnic on a sunny hillside instead of fleeing a faulty bed.

Although, in the end, he'd touched her carefully, with the thoughts she'd told him to kill rolling about in his head. They were plainly visible, his concerns. She shrugged and drew a languid circle on his broad chest. But he'd still touched her. Been unable to deny his need any more than she could deny hers. His teeth scoring her neck. His breath hot between her legs, across her nipples, sliding like honey down her throat. His shaft hard as stone in her hand, and later, harder still thrusting inside her.

Bringing her atop him, astride, in control. Another first. Fisting his fingers in her hair and whispering about his love of it, if not her, while he plunged into her. Teaching her to ride. Their gazes locked for most of the battle.

Breaking down barriers she *knew* he didn't want to shatter, until there was no division between them. None at all. Naked in more ways than one.

Her body gave a quiver of fevered tribute. *Dear heaven*, how he provoked her.

He was an enigma. A confounding man. A tad mercurial when she preferred steady. A fast temper that smoothed into mirth in the blink of an eye. He'd placed flowers—dianthus, a simple blossom but one of her favorites—in a vase in a room he'd invited his lover to. Brought champagne and cleaned her skin with gentle care after he bedded her.

Such effort. When no one had ever sought to please or protect her. Not since her family's death. She didn't know what to do with it. Or the fact that she was seeing a man utterly dissimilar from the posh gent she'd sketched in her mind.

Like a rare plant, she wasn't sure he was going to thrive under her attention. She wasn't sure she was good for him.

Drawing a calming breath, the faint odor of paint lingered from the space's previous use as an art studio. She wondered if the scent bothered him. He hadn't said anything about his mother, but anguish was evident in his sorrowful glances, the way he seemed to be walking over glass around his estate, fearful of stepping too hard on the past.

As if he heard her thoughts, Stanford's heartbeat skittered beneath her hand. Eyelids twitching, he moaned, and not in pleasure. His lips parted, words coming too quickly for her to catch them. *East division. Artillery. Blood.* She shook him, her hand going to his cheek, the scar rough beneath her palm. "Ollie, wake up, it's only a dream."

Though she knew it was a nightmare that had him in its talons. A much different dilemma.

He thrashed once, then woke instantly. Half sitting, the sheet tumbling, he took her wrist in a punishing clasp and drew her roughly against his body before he fully woke. His eyes when they met hers were the color of ice, his sight still thousands of miles away.

"Ollie," she said, twisting her arm from his grasp. "We're in the coach house. It's Nessie. I'm here, in Derbyshire. India's gone. It's over."

With a vicious oath, he flopped back, his arm going over his eyes to hide everything. His withdrawal, the same choice she'd have made, filled her with anguish. More discomfort than she imagined possible over a man she'd only truly met seven days ago.

Her mind spinning, she catalogued what she knew, determining how best to react. Subtlety was required to soothe the beast. But before she could reply, he was out of the bed, winding the sheet around his waist, and giving it a brutal tuck at his hip. It hung low, a crumbled roll of silk layered across his flat belly. Moonlight snaked in the open curtains to bathe him in silver nearly the color of his eyes. Highlighting hollows and valleys, muscle and sinew. Scars from the war. Golden skin and the trail of inky hair meandering down his chest.

And when his gaze met hers...

Her mouth went dry, the blood draining from her cheeks. *Oh*, he was a vision.

"Quit looking at me like I'm a bloody confection," he snapped and prowled to the sideboard, the sheet trailing along behind him like the train of a gown. His sulks didn't bother her—and they never lasted long. Her father had been of similar temperament. Quick to ignite and cool. Ollie's anger was nothing compared to *true* anger, the kind she'd grown up seeing in the stews. His rants were protective, a shield to hide his vulnerability. It softened, not repelled.

And she *had* been gazing at him like a sweet she wanted to devour.

He poured tea, then tossed it back like whisky, which she guessed he'd rather it be.

"Do you want to talk about it?"

He laughed raggedly, his gaze diving into his teacup. "You never shy away from the bad stuff, do you?"

"I guess I don't see the help in running."

He glanced her way, briefly, before moving off. "When the nightmares come, always in the middle of the night like cowards creeping up on me, it's a mix."

At her silence, he gestured with the teacup, the sheet fluttering around his legs. "A mix of here and there. India and that alley behind Xander's gaming hell. Blood flowing into my eyes. That's India. Glistening on the cobbles." He spread his fingers and stared at his hand as if he could see it there even now. "That's London. The dull roar of voices and my heartbeat sounding in my ears. Men on a barren field, skin torn to shreds, dying around me. Fathers, brothers, sons. Me, slipping away with them. I must tell you that the scent of death never leaves you once you've encountered it.

"Opium, you see, let these images retreat. For a time. But Xander wouldn't give up, and maybe I didn't want to. His men covertly retrieved me from the dens, then paid the owners to refuse me entrance. It was quite a game. Until my addiction became a harder fight than I was willing to tolerate. My brother *is* persistent. I'll give him that. Even with my betrayal, letting him be banished from this place when I knew he'd done nothing to deserve it, he still hung on."

"Ollie," she whispered, emotion he'd surely reject thickening her voice.

He poured more tea, his hand shaking. "*Don't.* In that torn voice that makes me want to cry right along with you. I'm only explaining so you understand. Why I'm here, in the country, hiding if that's what it is. Why I can't *be* with anyone. Why I don't plan on marriage. It's not the scar, what society believes. It's the memories. Although they're everywhere here, so conceivably that makes me a fool to return to them. At least I was able to leave India on another continent."

She sat up, wrapping the counterpane clumsily about her. She wasn't backing away from a conversation he'd never had with another soul. Necessity was as sure of this as she was that her heart was breaking for him.

Cradling his cup, he watched her with sorrowful eyes. With heat. Want. Yearning. *Oh*, he'd hate knowing his need sat there so clear for her to see.

"Your accident"—she dusted her cheek—"only makes you more handsome. The rest, I suppose, you're going to have to work through. Coming here, that's a start. Talking to me, another. As I said, I don't see the benefit in running from what *is*. You're facing what is."

"Scars make the man," he murmured after a lengthy pause. "You meant the ones inside, am I right? I didn't realize that then. What a wise young woman you were."

"What was she like?"

His posture stiffened, that solid, silent connection flowing between them. "My mother?" He trailed his hand over his heart to his belly, a slight smile twisting his lips when her gaze dipped, tracking the movement. "She was gentle. Too gentle for the man she married. Loving, that I recall. She was the only daughter of a viscount, her immense dowry bringing her to my father's eye. He was older by twenty years, maybe twenty-one, and taken with her wealth, then her beauty. She loved painting. I remember sitting in here with her for hours. Napping, playing with this little red cart I had. I don't know what happened to it. The earl gave her this place and, after she had me, hoped she and I would stay here, out of his sight."

Necessity tugged the counterpane to her neck, forcing herself to stay where she was, not go to him. His walls were rising brick by brick before her eyes. "And then?"

"There was a fever that swept the village, and she was gone. I was five." He sipped thoughtfully, his lids lowering to hide his reaction to what he was sharing with her. "Then it was simply the two of us, my father and me. Buying a commission was my way of getting away from him. Away from Derbyshire. Away from what happened with Xander. Sometimes, my darling Sprite, running does exactly what you wish it to."

"I had love, a wonderful family, though it was taken away. But I had love. Poverty, true, but in some strange way, contentment. I'd wish that for anyone. The certainty of knowing where you belong. I think it's what kept me going... during the hard parts after. When I was new to being alone. I'm sorry, dreadfully sorry, you didn't experience that, or at least, not for long."

Glancing back, he ran his tongue over his teeth like he was capturing the taste of her. This inexplicable thought flickered through her mind. Suddenly nervous, Necessity swept her hair into a loose knot at the back of her head and searched about for her hairpins. The counterpane gaped, exposing her to a gaze that had seen it all.

"Leave it down. *Please*." He sighed upon hearing his forceful tone, his smile tilting. "If you don't mind. For your notes. Further seduction of the earl."

Laughter tripped from her lips. "Me?"

He leaned against the sideboard, cool elegance though his eyes were scalding. "I've never been more thoroughly seduced in my life, Sprite." When she continued to stare, he shook his head in wonder, his irritation easing away. "Mix the stuff. Do you recall that bit of whimsy while your finger was tangling in my drawers? Good advice, by the by. We killed the damned bed trying to mix the stuff. You'll have to repeat your lecture of the low and high levels, or whatever it was, because my mind was engaged with"—he hummed—"other things. I wonder where tupping by firelight, you riding me to fevered completion, would fall on your list?"

"Have you brought her here?" Necessity closed her eyes after she said it, gave her thigh a hard pinch. *Impulsive fool. Now he'll know.* Know what, exactly, she couldn't say. Nevertheless, embarrassment burned her cheeks.

Stanford grinned, his good humor, as it always did, returning. "The widow?"

With a scowl, she rose to her feet, shaking out the counterpane like it was a ball gown. If he kept teasing her, she was going to smash his teacup over his head. "Never mind. Forget I asked. It's ridiculous of me to ask. You can do whatever you'd like, of course, here, there, or anywhere."

Setting his cup on the sideboard, he crossed to her. Halted before her, hands at his side. No effort to touch her, throw her off track with one of his stunning kisses. His smile, luminous and amused, remained, *damn him*. "I've never slept with anyone all night. I didn't dare with the nightmares. And never anyone, *ever*, here. I'm only now coming to claim this place myself."

She clutched the counterpane to her neck, twisting the silken material into submission. There wasn't room for anyone else here, is what he meant. "It doesn't matter."

"There's no need for jealousy, Nessie darling."

She bared her teeth at him. "I'm not *jealous*."

He cupped her cheek, bringing her eyes to his. They'd gone the color of leaves turned bone-gray in the winter. She wanted them to blaze again, hotter than metal. "Maybe it does matter. I don't know. I can't say. Not yet." Leaning in, he tugged her bottom lip between his teeth and sucked gently, forcing a tremor through her. She wanted that talented mouth on her. Doing all the wondrous things she was finding herself addicted to.

She closed her eyes and leaned into his touch, giving in, giving up. Her capitulation wasn't a comfortable conclusion, but it was a valid one. Her need was stronger than her fear.

He trailed his finger down her collarbone, over the rise of her breast peeping over the top of the counterpane, melting her stance and her resistance. Her nipples puckered in anticipation of his touch. "We're well and truly alone, except for your easily eluded companion, for a week or more. Free to meet when we'd like. As often as we'd like until you leave for London. Explore your list, the low and high levels."

She swallowed hard, weakening by the second. "Your family?"

"My meddlesome brother has vacated to Streeter's for business and such they have to conduct. Dash took the morning coach to Oban. Says he's checking on a distillery they're considering purchasing, although he raced to Scotland before the arrival of Theo and her fiancé, the dull but steady Edward, if you ask me." He pursed those gorgeous lips, looking for all the world like a man set on negotiating. "I'm even open to discussing your plans for the western garden. The orangery and the back meadow. The conservatory's sparkling new windows perchance? Soil conditions in Derbyshire? Location for the trees you talked about planting along the drive? Elms, am I right?"

She shook herself from her stupor to find his smile aimed at her. His fascinating, crafty smile. "You cheat. As if this wasn't enough." She tossed her hand out to indicate the chamber they'd destroyed in their passion, yanking at the counterpane when it slipped low. "You go and dangle the things you know I want to talk endlessly about, before my face like a carrot."

"If it's to be endless, I'd like a reward for listening." He tugged the silken material from her fingers and peeked inside the V. "Your breasts, I know it's indecent to admit, are glorious. I'm desperately obsessed with them." He pressed a kiss to the plump rise of one, sending a shiver through her. If he moved his lips one inch to the left and down a little, he would hit her aching nipple.

She grunted, faltering, flicking his hand aside.

"How about it?" he asked, his tone light yet his expression anything but. "We discover each other until you leave?"

Did he truly think she'd say no?

"There *are* things I want to do that I've never done before." Wrapping her lips around his cock, for one. She'd mentioned it, briefly, when he'd been inside her the second time, and he'd responded by thrusting hard, then coming apart. Confirming the power of suggestion. And his love of having his member sucked.

His lips flattened into stiff lines, his body rocking back. "I don't want to hear about your damned bookseller. What you have or haven't done, thank-you. Can we leave that bastard in London?"

"You hypocrite. When you've been bleeding ink all over the broadsheets for years with your affairs. Your torrid reputation walking in the door ahead of you it's so massive." Although the thought of Ollie doing what he'd done with *her* with anyone else made her want to punch him, Necessity shoved that emotion deep, cupping the nape of his neck and fusing her lips to his.

He was *hers*.

For a second, he didn't respond. Stubborn scoundrel. So, she whispered something truly filthy in his ear, and then, by heaven, he took her under. Tripped her back, the counterpane and his sheet spilling free, mouth seizing hers in urgent demand. Hand at her hip, her breast, kneading, caressing. Coming to rest with her wedged between the wall and his hard body.

"Teach me something," she whispered, her breath streaking free when he circled her nipple with this thumb. *So, so good.*

"I don't think I have anything to teach you, Sprite." He sounded petulant, slightly vexed. Men didn't like when women fulfilled their desires under their own power. However, if she'd waited to meet him, he would have been her first for everything. The thought tore at her heart, but such was life.

Hoping to change the emotional tide, she dragged her pinkie down his chest, over his belly, to his waist. Playful, drawing delicate circles on his hip as he rocked into her. She could go lower. Show him what was what. He was rigid and ready. The man had amazing recuperative abilities. "Be my tutor. I never had one of those, like you did."

He grunted softly, but his smile was spreading, his eyes ablaze. His hands on a quest to turn her inside out. "I suppose I could although I loathed most of mine. Or they loathed me."

"My lord earl"—she turned and backed *him* into the wall, his look of astonishment whizzing like one of his stars through her—"this time, I guarantee you'll enjoy the lessons."

Chapter Ten

WHERE AN EARL DECIDES LOVE STINKS

He was falling in love, in the least likely place for love to catch him.

His mother's goddamned art studio in the wilds of bloody Derbyshire.

His cozy hideaway. Unbelievable considering his childhood, but a place he felt safe in. Was coming to cherish even. A dwelling he was currently inhabiting in keen anticipation of his gardener's arrival.

Possible arrival. Nothing was certain about this tender friendship.

Lifting his gaze from his telescope, Stanford stretched with a groan, giving the rapidly-becoming-charming coach house a sardonic appraisal. It was clear to him what was happening, though he prayed it wasn't to anyone else. There were clues spread about the room. Blunders Dash had devoted an entire chapter to in his fantastically popular gambling book. Mistakes a man ought not to make if he wanted to protect himself.

Tells. This chamber was loaded with tells. Secret bits of him on display.

For one, he'd moved his folios and astronomy books from his study in the main house to a space still reeking of his mother's *paints*. His favorite Bainbridge watch rested on a table beside a bed he'd crawled beneath after his first encounter with Nessie and shored up himself. He couldn't have her spilling to the floor while astride him, could he? They got lost in each other—and lost quickly.

Also, he couldn't tell a servant why the bed was half collapsed, either. Unlike most of the *ton*, and he was thankful for it, he was handy with a hammer.

Across the room sat a vase currently overflowing with lilacs, without comment from his darling Sprite, though he *knew* she enjoyed them. He'd found her sticking her nose in them yesterday and drawing a covert breath. Maybe more revealing, she'd moved her notes and diagrams here, too. Her lists of flowers, plants, and such and—his mouth tightened, his hand rolling into a fist—her new botany book along with the rest.

Squinting, he crossed to the escritoire he'd rescued from the attic, a dusty area full of furniture from eras long past. And ghosts if he cared to acknowledge them. When he told her, without one hint of sentiment, mind you, that the desk was hers to use for the entirety of her stay at Aspinwall House, her delight had, well, delighted him. It wasn't a *gift*. It merely made sense that they each had one.

Shoved between the pages of the book her first lover had given her was a scrap of paper. A crude bookmark of some sort. Opening the volume, he gazed at the sketch. A rough outline of the winding gravel drive leading to his estate with her initials, *NB*, scratched in one corner. She'd noted locations for shrubs and trees, items on a list for his future gardener. His *permanent* gardener. She'd stressed this point yesterday morning while wearing his shirt and nothing else—that image enough to stop his heart—as if he didn't recall she was leaving in one week.

While he...

He swore softly, fiddled with the scrap of paper, debated, then shoved it in his pocket.

...was hoping she'd never want to leave.

If Xander got any idea about his growing feelings, *hell's teeth*, Stanford would have peace in absolutely *never*. Pippa, who he'd come to love more than an actual sister, was already hinting about his children growing up with theirs if only her dear brother-in-law, that of course being him, would hurry up the process and have some.

She didn't seem to realize he actually had a countess in mind.

He fingered the folded crease of the bookmark, considering it as he had for days. Maybe since the first day. A little girl with a sturdy temper and eyes the color of tarnished gold? His jet hair and love of stars? What could be more picture-perfect than that?

However, the lady wasn't willing to be a countess. Or a wife.

To be tupped five ways to Sunday, yes, but to reside in Derbyshire with a broken-down earl on an estate that needed a lifetime of repair, no. Necessity Byrne of the Shoreditch Byrnes was headed back to London and her thriving horticulture enterprise. She'd been discussing the project with Tobias Streeter, that set of Islington terraces he was designing, for the past two weeks. Another request for her services had arrived yesterday. Some horrid mess of a viscount's garden near Primrose Hill that needed the "Byrne touch." She'd beamed when she'd read that statement, a sunny smile making him feel like a brute for his reluctance.

Stanford laughed and dropped his head to his hand, gave his temple a squeeze. The Byrne touch, indeed.

He was suffering mightily from the effects of it.

Walking to his desk, a plodding stride because he knew where he was headed, he opened the top drawer. In the back on the left, hidden out of sight, was a velvet box. Faded to the color of whatever flower it was she'd planted last week beneath his bedchamber. Hyacinth?

Because he was punishing himself in a manner he hadn't since his private opium war, Stanford thumbed the box open, the contents enough, to this day, to take his breath.

The ring had been his grandmother's on his mother's side. It had come to him upon her death, and even then as a boy of five or so, for some odd reason, he'd wanted it. A simple gold band capped by a trio of small diamonds. The diamonds surrounding an emerald rumored to have royal connections. It was dazzling and, in turn, delicately lovely.

Like the woman he wanted to give it to.

Better than a fucking book on botany, wasn't it?

He snapped the box shut and jammed it in the drawer, as far back as it would go. About the same way he was handling this love bit.

But then, throwing him off balance, her remarkably reliable talent, Necessity stumbled into the room, into his heart, her unfettered hair a tawny glow around her. Someone he wanted for more than sex. A first. Hell, wanted for *everything*. A woman who didn't desire his money (modest) or his title (considerable). A woman forging her own path without need of a man mucking up her plans.

Lamentably, the disingenuous role he'd performed for years but wished to no longer play was sticking. He had nothing to offer that Nessie wanted aside from pleasure.

She closed the door and sprawled against it, her smile crooked. Illumination from the sconce winked off the lenses of those delectable spectacles. As usual, her gown was nothing to speak of. Sad and faded, bright yellow at one time. Formfitting in the bodice and the hip for his viewing pleasure; something to be happy about with her threadbare frocks. His body came to life, images of their lovemaking in this room and in various spaces across the estate roaring through his mind, a train on loose tracks. Checkmarks on that list of hers, bunches of them in the past two weeks.

He realized she was foxed when she beckoned with a clumsily curled finger. Not surprisingly, he went at once. Adoration, there was no other word for it, beating out a steady drumbeat in his chest. Love, a rush of feared feeling through his veins. Unfortunately, he was on this island alone, experiencing so much without her. As he'd been for much of his existence.

Another tell, but one he would hide. For now.

When he reached her, a nagging cautiousness in his step because intoxicated chits were to be dealt with carefully, she erased the disquiet and threw herself into his arms. He caught her against him, pulled her in, her place now, cradled to his chest. Dropping his head to her hair, he breathed in the scent of her. Honeysuckle from the soap she used. A spicy aroma he couldn't define layered beneath. And the wine she'd had at her dinner with the ladies of the Duchess Society.

She smelled delectable, and he wanted to take a bite.

"Miss me?" she whispered, her lips going inside his open collar to press a moist kiss to his collarbone. "I love when you don't shave. Umm...." She snuggled his jaw, his neck. Taking small, sharp nips that were undermining his vow to return her straightaway to the main house. "Your stubble against my thighs feels so *good*. Have I told you that? I think I have. You look like a pirate, all swarthy. Set to pillage." She giggled. "Pillage *me*."

He stepped back, took her shoulders in hand. Slim but strong, capable, every bit of her. "You're half-sprung, darling Nessie. More than half, I fear."

Her eyes were the ruddy hue of a lost sunset when they met his. Laughing, she swayed into him while managing to unfasten a button on his shirt. "I had a second glass when Hildy Streeter felt the need to review polite topics of conversation at a dinner party. I have one coming up next week at Baroness Enderby's. Her garden is wretched, and no amount of polite will change that. Only my services will. Even if I'm unsuitable, she'll hire me. Then, I had a third glass when Georgie, the duchess, Her Grace of Markham, declared that men don't like boozy women. Although they were boozy, too. The duke had to lead his duchess to bed. Tobias Streeter was kind enough to escort me home. He's very much a gentleman for a rookery crook turned architect."

"I suppose," Stanford said, trying to control her roving hands. Trying to disregard that she'd called Aspinwall House home. She was as loopy as a sick crow, for God's sake.

She popped another button, her finger circling his nipple while she watched for his reaction, her gaze sizzling and getting hotter by the second. He contained the ragged sound filling his throat, but just barely. His nipples, perhaps an unusual thing for a man, were extremely sensitive.

"I didn't even go inside the house, Ollie. Merely waited for Streeter's carriage to roll down the drive I'm beautifying for the first time in centuries, then I sprinted here. Creeping alongside buildings, in shadow, like a thief. Apologies for the dirty slippers and ragged hem. I encountered a bramble bush in the darkness. Some type of berry from the stains on my skirt. The Duchess Society delegation would not be pleased." She giggled again, her breath streaking across his chest, tearing down his wall of resistance one stone at a time. "Or with you. Earl Rogue of Derbyshire."

He clasped her wrists in one of his hands, his body blatantly responding to her exploration. He was helplessly hard, shaky breaths darting from his lips. A shiver forming its own storm at the base of his spine. The warning signal to his losing control and reason.

Her eyes widened at his powerful hold, her gasp of excitement piercing the air. Bumping against him, she managed to secure his earlobe in her teeth. His vision blurred. "Oh, Ollie, *yes*, like the stable. My hands over my head, remember? Until I begged you to let go. Take me like that and—"

"*Nessie*," he pleaded, really, *truly* hoping to, for the moment, overlook that she liked to be bound. A series of experimentations they were conducting, cravats and his hands had so far been the only restraints. He didn't know much about this type of play despite what society assumed. He was merely going as they went along. Lost in her enthusiasm and his desire. Before Nessie, he'd honestly been an in-and-out kind of gent. Not before the lady found her pleasure, never this to his remembrance, but nothing layers deep, a spot he worried he'd not find his way out of. Like being tossed into a chasm without a rope.

Giggling, she yanked a hand free. Tugged his shirt from his trousers while nibbling at a vulnerable spot beneath his ear. Dirty politics now —when she knew that maneuver drove him wild. "I love the silver in your hair," she said in a honeyed tone before driving her fingers into the strands and slanting his head for easy access. "Soooo delicious, lying against that hard jaw."

For one stumbling, unsteady breath, he fell into the kiss, into her. Hand palming her lower back, bringing them hip to hip, where he was hard and she soft. Lips parting, famished, tongues touching, then tangling. Vexed as always because he couldn't *quite* figure out how to gain the upper hand, a piece of this game he'd welcome having. With her, the world scrambled. Passion and heat and light. The moment better than a thousand stars whizzing across the sky, once his only dream.

He wanted to take each moment and hold it close. Remember her always.

She swayed again, lips sliding down his jaw, reminding him she was too foxed for this. "Darling, Sprite, *stop*." He trapped her hand against his hip before it moved lower, took her shoulder, and backed her toward the bed.

She brought him down with her in a tangle of arms and legs. There was the distinct possibility that he let her. "I'll keep on my spectacles. Nothing else. As you like."

Rolling to his side, putting enough space between them to slow her down, he propped his cheek on his forearm, gazing at her, the wash of moonlight through the open curtains a crystal spill across her delectable body. *If only*, he thought. If only she wanted more.

She sulked, lips pouting, drawing crazily sensual designs across his chest. His yearning for her was spiraling, running races along his skin, and heading straight for his cock. He wanted her to touch him, lower and lower still, feast on him, but he wasn't going to allow it. He'd take care of this once she was asleep. Lying beside her while he touched himself wasn't the worst plan he'd ever come up with.

"You're being honorable, aren't you?" She released a full-cheeked huff. "It's something no one but me and that smuggling brother of yours know about you. That you're *kind*. *Sweet*. *Generous* beneath the scars and the scowls." Her eyes glittered when they met his, hot as the embers in the hearth across the way. "Gentleman earl when I want a dirty ravenous earl ripping at my clothing. A bed-breaker. Destroyer of chemises. I think I've met him here before."

She wanted a ravenous scoundrel, did she? He debated, calculating just *how* soused she was when she confirmed her pitiful state by hiccupping.

He sighed, amused and frustrated. Skimming a tangled, golden strand from her face, he lingered, caressing her cheek, the delicate curl of her ear. Her hair fascinated him. "I'm going to get you a glass of water. Take off those filthy slippers. Undo your laces and let you sleep. Then before dawn, return you to your bedchamber. Your companion will never know you've strayed. Toast and tea for breakfast is my advice. Light is best. I'm extremely knowledgeable about the repercussions of overindulgence."

"My honorable knight," she murmured, her lids slipping low, seeking even with his gentle rejection to burrow into him.

As he settled her for bed, his mind went to the purloined bookmark in his pocket. The clandestine love orbiting his chest. The things he was starting to hide from her to protect his vulnerable heart.

Perhaps, he was not so honorable a knight after all.

Chapter Eleven

WHERE A GARDENER'S SKEPTICISM
CREEPS IN

Ecessity's head was throbbing.

But not as badly as before the prescribed toast and tea.

Two things had set her in motion. Mrs. Rothbottom sent a note that she wouldn't be arriving today due to an unexpected birth in the village. Secondly, Mrs. McKinstry, the earl's capable housekeeper, claimed she'd last seen the earl in the early morn when he'd been riding out to check on a tenant's cottage. A damaged roof from the recent storm.

Necessity didn't want to add to the Earl of Stanford's burden when she was already going to add to his burden. An out of sorts female was not what he needed to balance on his already overwhelmed shoulders.

Stanford—

She halted on the front lawn and cursed. Loud and free because she was alone. Because it felt good. She added a kick to the grass that was an acceptable length, thanks to her management, wishing the move hadn't reverberated through her aching head. Incensed with no cause, she reached and plucked a perfectly lovely azalea bloom from a shrub and tossed it into the wind.

Ollie.

She hadn't thought of him as Stanford since that first amazing night. An escapade rolling into many amazing nights. And days. Stolen mornings and afternoons. Every second they could seize, adrift in each other. The linen closet on the second floor. Check. Stable stall. Check. Beside the narrow stream running through his property in the misty pre-dawn. Check. And oh, the coach house. Their refuge from the world.

Check, check, *check*.

There they had learned, taught, explored.

Stalking across the sloping meadow, no clue why she was irked aside from being denied what she wanted—*him*—the previous night, she counted off the ways they'd turned each other inside out in the past month. Tumbled beds. Ripped clothing. Laughter.

More laughter than she'd experienced in years. In forever. Working, discussing his stars and her plants. They slept together almost every night. Tangled around each other, not on separate sides of the bed like her parents.

Ollie had done his best to fulfill her wishes, discovering her body with obvious enthusiasm and freely sharing his. He was open to suggestion and never minded if she took control, as men often did. He didn't think he knew every little thing about lovemaking, though he was good enough at it, *amazing* actually, for her to imagine he did. He didn't order her about or make her dreams feel small. He listened. When men never listened to her.

She lifted her face to a deadly blue sky, her heart giving a leaden thump. Reality was pressing down on her. A wave set to roll past and wash her away from him.

She had a meeting the following week. Thursday. A bold, black circle around the date on her calendar. A possible project with Baroness Enderby if she didn't offend the old crow more than was permitted. Gardens that needed as much care as Ollie's had. Another discussion the following week with Tobias Streeter regarding his Islington terraces. Necessity was assembling a team, had already made plans reaching into the following year. Ordered supplies, bricks, plants, trees, shrubs. Too late to change her mind, to change course. She was committed to London for the foreseeable future, yet her heart had started to crack, part of it landing at an earl's feet in Derbyshire.

Her step slowed as she approached the coach house. In the way of things of late, she knew he wasn't there.

She entered with a cautious step, brilliant images roaring through her mind. Ollie's body rising over hers. Firelight glimmering across his muscular shoulders, turning his skin a dusky, golden hue as he made her his. His knowing smile saying things he couldn't. Conversation after, unlike any she'd shared with another soul, sitting across a counterpane snatched from the bed in their fury. Intimate picnics before the fire in their love nest.

Crossing to her desk, a gift that *wasn't* a gift that had melted her heart, she found her botany book open, the sketch she'd left as a page marker missing. She flipped it closed, considering. Could the earl have taken it? And if so, *why?*

Maybe he's as besotted as you are, her mind whispered.

She'd gone further than she needed with this experiment. Watching the man while he labored, nose buried in a dull astronomy text, those talented, ink-stained fingers skimming the page, wasn't required. Lusting after him, his long body angled over his telescope, lips moving soundlessly as he recited the findings churning through his swift mind. He was content in the country, discovering his life away from the tumult—and palpable hazards—of the city. A philosopher at heart. She now understood what Xander Macauley's warning weeks ago about Ollie having a tender core meant.

The Earl of Stanford had been forced down a confounding path, in an effort to escape a legacy he'd eventually embraced with an open heart. Such was the man. Courageous but not the warrior he portrayed. Not at all.

Twisting her skirt in her fist, she glanced at the bed. That marvelous bed that he'd repaired. He was sleeping better, the nightmares retreating. A bit. She didn't know if it was her influence or his contentment over rediscovering Derbyshire. The estate was shaping up finally. He had deep roots here. While she had no roots, not a single one since her family's death.

Crossing to the most important thing in the room to him, aside from his mother's paintings, she pressed her eye to his telescope, seeing blurry nothingness. Yet feeling him there beside her. Because this space was him. Now it was also *her*.

Studying him while he slept, strands of her hair draped over his body, wasn't going to help her leave him. Listening to his feathery breaths and wondering what her Bond Street bedchamber would be like without that sound shimmering through it.

He'd tricked her with those sad smiles, the dimple that charmed her drawers off. Gloomy tales of his time in India and growing up on this estate alone, making her cuddle him close in the darkness where they'd still be tangled up come morning. The joy of being with him a brighter glow than she'd anticipated feeling in this lifetime. She was burned by it. Scarred, like his beloved cheek.

Frightened at the thought of being without him when she'd never been frightened before.

This slice of fragility infuriated her.

He could have been less open, and maybe she would have been, too. Forced to retreat or hide from him. The bookseller hadn't wanted to know the name of her cat. What her flat looked like. Her aspirations for her business. Her parents' names. How many siblings she'd had.

Oliver had. In fact, he seemed to want *everything*.

She needed to return to where she belonged. Did Ollie not see that? To a dwelling she leased with her own blunt. To her cat, Delilah, who her neighbor was taking care of while she was away. To Mr. Limpet, the baker on Birdie Street who sold her fresh malt loaf each morning. To the treacherous docks and putrid lanes of Shoreditch, even if she didn't live there anymore. To her life, not *his*. It wasn't surprising when she considered how handsome and clever he was, how agreeable and delightful he could be—when he *wanted* to be—that her feelings were scrambled like an egg.

Jasper Noble didn't ask these things of her. He wasn't trying to change her. Get inside her heart or her head. Only her drawers. He was *safe*. He knew the score about being a rookery brat. He understood how hard she'd worked to be simply presentable. He would let any societal mistakes she made pass without blinking an eye because he'd be making them himself.

Best of all, her pulse didn't kick every time she saw him.

Of course with those contrary things running through her mind, when she left the coach house in search of the earl, Necessity was livid.

He was leaning against a fence in mid-repair at the edge of the woodlands, a tattered rag tossed carelessly over his shoulder. The beauty of Derbyshire, the sweeping meadows, and grassy plains laid out behind him. Wind ripping at his hair, the silver threads glinting in the sunlight. He was filthy, streaked with sweat and grime, his untucked shirt billowing. Trousers hanging low on his hips without braces to hold them up. She could picture his children running wild in these fields. His countess taking him by the hand and leading him away.

Necessity could never be a *countess*. The idea was preposterous. Like a Shoreditch girl becoming a queen. A farce, a dream.

He hadn't seen her yet, and for one second, she didn't want him to. She'd filch this image as she'd done a nob's purses back in the day. It had taken a time or two before she realized she wasn't made for thieving. Fast hands were not a skill. Nor a blank expression that hid secrets.

Wiping his brow with the rag, he tilted his chin into the fading light, a slight smile lifting his lips. She knew him. Recognized that expression. Contentment, satisfaction. His eyes, the ashen color they turned when he shattered into a thousand pieces around her. A little darker then, perhaps.

Her heart cracked in two, breath leaving her in anguish.

He loved this spot, his legacy, and she could never ask him to leave it.

Looking over his shoulder, he spotted her. Before he could stop it, delight lit his eyes. Turned them glassy. He took a fast step forward, then ducked his head, finally, blasted *finally*, hiding what he was feeling.

Much too late for both of them.

When she got close, he braced his fists on the fence and leaned into it, burly shoulders flexing. As nonchalant as a man with a title older than God and the body of a stevedore could. He looked tasty enough to swallow whole. Her mouth watered; her thighs quivered.

She was glad the wooden barrier stood between them.

"What did I do?" he asked straightway, no hedging. It was then she noted the cheroot jammed between his lips when she'd never known him to smoke. It bounced elegantly with his scowl. This little piece of him shouldn't have made her want him more.

She feigned ignorance, annoyed that she'd let him witness her annoyance. "Nothing. I was merely taking a stroll."

He snorted. Rudely. Eyes smoldering as hot as the tip of his cheroot, he dropped to his haunches to gather a pile of rotten slats. "Stubborn chit," she thought she heard him whisper.

She climbed on the bottom rung of the fence and hung over the top. The wood felt slightly damp beneath her fingers but was sturdy. He was good with his hands, the earl. "I had a list in my botany book. The one in the coach house. It was a diagram of your front drive. I need it."

Shrugging, he didn't look up from his task. "You'll find it, somewhere. Try another search. One conducted when we're not naked."

Necessity exhaled, squeezing the slat hard enough to split it. *So that's the way this is going to go, is it?* "I sketched it for your new gardener, Osgood Hagen."

He made that dismissive sound again, gaze fixed on his task, sending her temper soaring. "What kind of name is Osgood?"

"He's capable, talented, and desires the country life. I've worked with him on multiple projects. Employed for years with the Duke of Leighton before seeking lesser positions. You can check his references. I've left him detailed notes for continued repair of the conservatory. The vegetable garden we discussed. Timing of plantings, where and when and how. Miss Palin-Wise is staying on to assist for as long as he needs her. For continuity. I find it helps keep the design on track, to have an original team member remain." She added this next piece to light a fire under him. "Still on your brother's bill, this bit, so I went through him. You and Macauley really need to connect on your horticultural agenda."

Oh yes, that got him.

Stanford shoved to his feet, then evidently got one of his rushes to the head. Rubbing his temple, he shot through clenched teeth, "Xander and I connect *too* often. You know what, Nessie? You can bill him for the rest of his damned life. Forget I said anything. Osgood sounds perfect. Let him make Aspinwall House his masterpiece. Tell him to spend thousands of pounds, in fact. He should be thrilled. Seeing as he desires the *country* life." He hopped the fence in an agile, muscle-shifting move she tried very, very hard to be *unmoved* by.

"Which you don't," he tossed over his shoulder as he strode past her.

She raced to catch up, realizing he wanted a fight. Suspecting she did as well. "I have to get back to London," she huffed, hating the desperate blade fashioning her words "I have meetings. One next Thursday with Baroness Enderby."

"Yes, yes, you told me about that one. In bed. Cantankerous spinster, depressing garden. That's all I recall before you climbed atop me."

Her cheeks burned, but she kept pace—two steps to his one—because it was true. She'd told him all about her plans for his estate while they were knotted like thread around each other. Hours of conversation in the dusky dawn, skin to skin. Conversations leading to more, always more. They could not seem to get enough of each other. "There's also my project with Tobias Streeter. The Islington terraces. I have my team assembled. You know he's become quite the item in the architectural world. Possibly a novelty with his rookery upbringing, not so different from my own except for the viscount's bastard part, but he doesn't seem to care. He wants clients even if they've come to sniff out the Prince of Limehouse." She sighed, running out of steam. "Or whatever silly nickname they gave him. I guess I feel the same, let them stare, comment, judge, as long as they're willing to pay."

"Rogue King of Limehouse." Tossing his cheroot down, Stanford ground it beneath his bootheel. Right there in a patch of newly sodded grass! "You forgot to mention getting back to the lover gifting you botany books."

Crimson colored her vision. She was going to pummel him like one of those dukes he grappled with in the dirt. "It wasn't a gift! I paid for it."

He kicked an elm branch from his path. "I bet you did."

"Oh, you *brute*." She snatched the back of his shirt and gave it a feeble yank, doing little to stop his forward progress. "Arrogant arse!

Conceited cur! After your antics, the women, the brawls, the lurid stories, racing carriages and tossing men in the Thames, you have a lot of nerve. I heard a woman ambushed you at the opera once, right in your private box!"

"My fucking *brother* did the river tossing, Sprite. I was busy then in the dens." He halted suddenly, and she stumbled into him. Spinning around, he grasped her shoulders and gave her a gentle but forceful shake. "I have nerve, Necessity Byrne. With you, I have loads of nerve. So much that I don't recognize myself half the time. Livid one moment, panting after you like a hound the next. I'm even considering coming out of hiding because it may be what I have to do. I think about you when you're not with me, a thousand queries a day. I'm bloody sick of them, actually. What is she doing? Where is she? What time is she coming to me? And by God, you've come to me. Come *beneath* me. Atop me. Beside me. I'm wrapped in your sweet, little fist when no other woman, though there've been fewer of those than you think, have held me such." He tipped her chin until her gaze centered on his. His eyes were pale silver, almost white. "I dare where you're concerned. With all my nerve and not an ounce less. I don't have it in me to give you less. Although less is what you seek. That's the trouble, I'm finding."

Her lips parted, heart hammering. His impassioned speech wasn't a declaration. A proposal of any kind. It was longing cloaked in anger. Desire. Disbelief. Emotions shimmering over his face like sunlight had moments before.

What was she to do with this?

He growled and seized her hand, turned, and started across the lawn. She knew where he was going. She followed, tripping behind him, watching as he took care where he stepped, even in his ire, fury she'd ignited, caring for her safety. *Oh, this man.* This obstinate, proud, kindhearted man.

He made her heart ache, her body tremble, her head spin. A future she wasn't prepared for unfurling like a ribbon around her. She suspected he felt the same.

But this didn't mean she had to be *happy* about it.

So, she would take. One final act of thievery, then she was finished stealing from him.

He burst through the coach-house door and kicked it shut behind them, instantly crushing her against it, filling his hands with her. Speechless, when she didn't want words. Ollie's unique brand of poetry did silly things to her. Punched holes in walls standing stout and strong since she was twelve years old.

She needed her wits about her to survive this tumult.

They made fast work of fastenings, loops, ties, excellent architects of the hasty encounter. Her skirt yanked high. His trousers opened. Simple mechanics. Blind need. Fumbling fingers, scattered breaths. Hands twisting in hair, pins flying. His touch, making sure—*there, yes, please*—she was ready. Her teeth nipping his lower lip, drawing a ragged moan free. Mindless, she wished to mark him, leave her brand on his skin.

Slapping a hand to the door for leverage, he lifted her, linking her legs around his waist, bringing their bodies chest to chest. Reaching, fitting his shaft in place. Hard meeting soft, moist, hot. Sliding home. A languorous glide, his fight for control etched in the deep grooves on his face.

Then he lost himself, submitted to the storm. Taking her lips, his kiss matched the rising rhythm of his thrusts. Arching her back, she rocked with each stroke, doing her level best to participate. Meeting, lunging, pursuing.

Giving. As he'd wanted, every ounce. Did he not perceive her surrender?

Heat spread, igniting until the laden air sizzled. Until she felt she could sprout wings and fly over the estate. Their tangled groans battled for relief, ringing through the cottage. The sounds of the wind whipping through the row of sweet gums outside, the tick of his pocket watch across the room, were lost to their passion. Strong arms bound about her, calloused fingertips digging into her skin. His heartbeat raced through layers to reach hers.

It felt as if this was the only man for her, the only who would ever touch her in this way, which she accepted, *embraced*, shoving aside fear, regret, despair.

Unfettered, she nipped his jaw, the slope of his neck, his earlobe. Harder there, as he liked. He'd not shaved this morning, the most erotic thing in the world that abrasion. He moaned and shifted with the action, lifting her higher, going deeper. Bottomless, their connection.

Senses awhirl, she snatched every morsel. Hips bumping, the knuckles of his hand paling to the color of chalk. Blinding, blazing light streaking behind her eyelids. Her pulse a steady thump in her ears. The door creaking, his harsh breaths striking her cheek. The world closing in, compressing to a constricted bubble of heat and sensation.

Groaning, he gripped her hip, angling her higher, closing in on his release. Always, as was his way, ensuring she found hers first. By now, she knew the signs. The stutter in his breathing, his body trembling. His full-length glide, again and again. A pounding, glorious assault, moist skin slick with passion. In response, she grabbed his shoulder and buried her cheek in the warm, salt-scented cotton of his shirt, struggling to stay with him.

"Let go, dammit," he whispered in the curve of her neck.

The incensed plea, the ragged thread in his voice, snapped her restraint. Clutching him, head swimming, she broke, gasping, cresting, peaking. One set of blissful ripples spinning to her toes, destroying her, then another following just behind. Leaving her shattered in pieces, like pottery hurled to stone. Murmuring unintelligible words against his jaw, the sweet taste of his skin flowed through her, a pleasure wash.

Unable to hold back, he plunged his fingers into her hair, brought the tangled strands to his face as he dropped off a cliff. Driving himself into her, seeking to conquer when she'd submitted ages ago.

For moments, time slowed to the uneven keel of their breathing, the creak of the door he had their weight braced against. He shook his head, struggled to collect himself, exhaled long and hard into the hushed silence. Shaky, both of them clinging to each other, which pleased her. Their further unraveling. She'd not expected more sexual inventiveness. Not after the past month of discovery. Yet here he was, arousing her, challenging her, to the point of madness.

Well, hell. She would never tire of his touch. That much was settled.

Tears pricked her eyes, but she swallowed them back. Dug the heel of her hand into the scarred planks of the coach house's oak door and gave him the signal that she could stand. When she wanted to rip his clothes off, crawl into the bed, and sleep for centuries. Until answers were easier. Until answers were *there*.

He wasn't any better. His forehead pressed to the doorframe, chest heaving, hand by her head flexing as if he'd lost feeling in his fingers. Skin damp and streaked with dirt. His unique scent, sweat, pine soap, and Ollie, tunneling through her.

They were wasted, ruined. Held up by bone and sinew—and little else. Hurt feelings and the realities of life enveloping them. Vastly dissimilar social standings worming destructive holes in the precarious foundation they'd created in his mother's art studio. Their pasts were littered with shards more harmful than the one that had sliced his cheek.

She knocked her head against the door, lifting her gaze to the ceiling. Angry sex was spectacular. *Bloody hell*, as Ollie would say. *Bloody, bloody hell.*

However, the *after* promised to be problematic.

No cuddling and laughter arriving in this room.

As if he heard her judgement, Ollie released his hold. An agonizing slide over every ridge of firm muscle he owned. His evident pique now a punishment for her obstinacy. For being truthful, or scared, or whatever emotion wasn't allowing her to take what he was, perhaps, *maybe*, offering. In his reticent, halfway-certain, bashful earl's manner. Vulnerability, stubbornness, devotion thrown on one plate and served to her. The potent mix that had gotten her to this fearing-her-heart-was-no-longer-hers place.

He stayed with her until she was steady, knees mercifully holding her upright, then he was striding across the room, gulping water from a pitcher they kept for such an occasion, his posture stiff with umbrage. Chilly, when the air was humming warmly with what they'd done to each other. Invisible threads tying them together, both parties resisting the pull.

The slip of paper was on the floor, near a button she'd torn off his trousers in her frenzy. The sheet was rumpled, obviously having been crammed in his pocket. With a wobbly crouch, she went to her knee to retrieve it. Hesitated a moment before taking the button, too.

Her list. The diagram for the front drive. He'd had it all along.

"Why were you keeping this?"

Slanting a side-glance at her, he cursed soundly and stalked back to her, ripping the note from her hand. "*Mine.*" Tucking it in his fist, he scrubbed his hand across his mouth, where a drop of water clung to his bottom lip, inviting her to lick it off. "Like your damned botany book, I think I've paid for it."

His inability to see any side but his own was infuriating. Obstinate toad. Hadn't the intense pleasure they'd shared smoothed his temper at all? "Ollie, be reasonable."

He jammed his hands in his pockets, dragging his trousers low on his hips. Her gaze roamed the length of him. Dear heaven, his body was enough to make her weep. "Don't 'Ollie' me. I know where that ends up. With me doing whatever *you* desire. From digging a trench for some fancy rose bush to licking cream off your thigh."

She huffed an aggrieved sigh and jacked her thumb over her shoulder. "It already went there, you oaf! That's why we're standing here, bewildered and breathless, about to spill to the floor. Because we tupped each other within an inch of our lives against a door that has seen this act before. Once, at least."

"Twice," he growled. "We're first-rate standing up." Releasing a tight breath, he tipped his head to stare at the ceiling, same as she had when she'd been trying to flee. His eyes were smoldering, deep, dark, and stormy when they circled back to her. "You can change course in life, Nessie. Alter plans depending on the situation. We're taught that as soldiers. What you expect isn't what you necessarily find after going into battle."

"Are we at battle? If we are, that might be part of the problem."

He brought his hand to his mouth and laughed roughly behind it. "As if Necessity Byrne of the Shoreditch Byrnes can do this dance without fighting for every scrap she gives. Or gets."

Vexed, she went to punch him, lightly but nonetheless with feeling, then realized the error in reasoning and dropped her arm by her side. With his gaze blazing with unspent passion and arousal simmering like a pot on a cauldron inside her belly, touching him would be a mistake. Her inability to purge him from her system confounded her. How could she have had him in so many ways for weeks and only want *more*? The answer hunkered in the shadows, taunting her. She wasn't ready to shine a light on it yet. "You're livid because I won't, immediately, without thought to my own wishes, obey your command. Bow and scrape like the rest of society because your title is one step below a king's. When his lord earl has yet to even tell me what he'd like me to do!"

"It never occurred to you to ask what I was willing to give, did it?" He gestured violently to the space they'd made their own. "After weeks of revealing ourselves in a way neither of us, I'm convinced, has done before. Did you even *consider* deviating from your plan to restore my gardens, then race back to London? You assumed exploring your body and your goddamned list was all I wanted. Because it's what's thought of me, a Lothario and erstwhile addict. I'd hoped for better than this easily peddled theory from you."

"Why would you hope for better from a rookery girl of all people?"

His fingers curled into a fist, the words rushing forth in a brutal exhalation, "Because I let you see *me*."

Necessity's heart fluttered, her gaze shifting over his shoulder to a picture of the Derbyshire countryside his mother had painted. Had she considered altering her plans? She wasn't sure. Maybe not. Her thighs were quivering from his touch, his taste lingering in her throat, his scent coating her fingertips.

She. Could. Not. Think.

With a snarl, he spun on his heel. Adjusted his trousers, tucked in his shirttail, preparing to depart. Preparing to run.

Thinking to delay him somehow, she pinched the bridge of her nose, *his* usual move, a headache brewing behind her eyes. "I need time. Can you please manage not to be so angry with me while I ask for it? I don't want to hurt you, hurt myself."

He marched to his desk and yanked a beaten leather satchel from the floor and began stuffing items—folio, astronomy book, random sheets of foolscap—inside it. "I'm not waiting around while you decide if you want me, want *this*. You're reckless with your heart and mine, I'm realizing. I don't think I'm willing to accept that."

"Reckless? What are you proposing, Ollie? Can you tell me? *Are* you proposing? If you are, it's not very romantic. Even for a girl from the slums. May I suggest revisions, flowers, and moonlight perhaps? Although it is memorable."

His step slowed, his satchel banging his hip. The side-look he shot her was bewildered, packed like his satchel, but with hesitancy, not supplies. He glanced away as an edge of fear sliced through his gaze.

She leaned into her mirth, though it caught her like a blow to the chest. The least funny thing imaginable. Laughed until there was no breath left in her lungs.

He had no idea what to do about their love affair, either.

Opening the door, he glanced over his shoulder. A looming sunset of violet and gold lit the space around him. A splendid aura befitting an earl. Befitting the man she suspected she was in love with.

He lifted his hand, his chest giving a hard hitch. *Goodbye.*

Her heart hit the floor. *Wait.* "You're leaving?"

He gave his shoulder a stiff jerk, moving away though he stood in the same room with her. "No, Nessie Byrne of the Shoreditch Byrnes, you are."

Chapter Twelve

WHERE A LONESOME GARDENER IS STUNNED BY THE NEWS

Ravenous society mamas will rejoice to learn that the Scarred Earl has returned to our fair city, taking up residence in his ancestral townhome. In search of a countess mayhap? Or his runaway gardener, some say. One never knows, but the streets of Mayfair are abuzz. The Leighton Cluster is swarming with children and delight, reformed rakes proving to everyone's surprise to be loving fathers and loyal husbands. What's one more changed man among them?

Although this cagey lord might be tricky to capture...

—Society Tidbits

Choking on her tea, Necessity slapped the morning edition of the *Gazette* to the small breakfast table jammed in the corner of her equally petite kitchen.

Ollie was here. In the city.

Blocks away, possibly traveling Curzon or Brook right this minute. Maybe stopping along Bond for a silk cravat or pair of kidskin riding gloves. He could look up and into her window if he knew where to find her. She lived above a glove maker's shop, in fact. One of some esteem. Not where she purchased hers, as these were much too dear, but they looked lovely in the window.

Her mind whirled, her stomach taking a riotous leap. The Scarred Earl—this name made her furious for him—had a house in Mayfair. A detail she'd not known but should have. Of course, he did. Titled nobs were overloaded with properties, usually to their dismay, due to lack of funds to maintain them. With estate business and solicitors and newfound family to deal with, it wasn't like the Earl of Stanford could avoid London forever.

Although six weeks had seemed like it.

Actually, there'd been news of him.

Trivial tidbits she'd held on to like a child would sweets. Greedily. Hildy Streeter and Georgie, the Duchess of Markham, had spoken of him in conversation with Pippa Macauley and her half sister, Theo. Something about his estate, asides not directed toward her. This occurring at the weekly teas they'd begun to invite her to, where she was forced to act like she didn't desire information about any earls. Was there merely to practice pouring and engaging without enraging, as Hildy called it. All the things that bored her silly but were going to help her business thrive. The humiliating things she did to see it succeed amazed her most days.

Moreover, one of his crew of misfits was expecting again. Hildy had mentioned it. The Duchess of Leighton, Necessity believed, though she couldn't quite recall. The Cluster was indeed swarming with tots. A very prolific group.

A nagging sensation had her rereading the snippet, heart sinking to see the reference to her this time.

Bloody, bleeding hell. *Runaway gardener?* She'd not run away, *he* had. Although honestly, her foot had been out the door.

Both of them terrified of the emotions staring them in the face.

Delilah snaked through her legs, winding about her ankles. Necessity reached down to give her cat a head scratch, her chin a tickle. Delilah purred and sprawled on the floor in a bright spill of sunlight, her favored morning spot.

Unable to stop herself, Necessity rose, crossing to the bureau she'd purchased from a baron while working on his gardens. A wife, three children, a mistress, and a run-down estate had been bleeding him dry.

He'd been forced to sell his furnishings, jewelry, and an unentailed manor in Scotland to keep everyone afloat.

The desk was gorgeous. A mahogany masterpiece, three hundred years old, something the baron had tossed aside without blinking when it was the nicest piece of furniture Necessity would ever own.

The invitation sat on top of a neat stack of unanswered correspondence. With a cautious caress, she traced the embossed lettering, pondering her options. She didn't have the multitude of requests a duchess would, but she had some. Enough. Invitation to an outdoor gallery opening in Hyde Park next month. Tea with the Dowager Countess of Newberry. Horse race in Newmarket next week with Jasper Noble. This one she hadn't declined, but her heart wasn't in it.

She wiggled out the bottom card, her pulse jumping. An invitation to Lady Bedivere's salon party. Billed as part musicale, part lecture, but assured entertainment. Necessity snorted, giving the edge of the paper a flick. Music that was sure to be horrid, the possible highlight being Dash Campbell's lecture. He trotted his gambling book out like a carnival owner with a pet monkey, but the tome *was* flying off the shelves and into every parlor in London. She understood having to sell oneself. It was part and parcel of owning a business.

She'd only been invited because the Duchess Society had bandied her name about enough, as a friend *and* a client, that she'd begun to be added to the random society list. The *ton* liked to have the occasional working-class soul in attendance to emphasize their liberality. She was, after some modification, an acceptable choice.

Dipping her hand in her pocket, she grazed her fingertip over Ollie's trouser button. She allowed herself to do this five times a day—this was three. And once, if she was weak, before bed. Then it went into the dish on her bedside table until morning.

If Ollie was in Town, he'd plausibly be at Lady Bedivere's fete. It wasn't his type of party, considering what she knew of him, but he *was* friends with Dash. Xander Macauley was sure to be there along with the rest of the Leighton Cluster. When one arrived, the rest piled in behind them. They indeed traveled in a gang.

Reckless with my heart.

She whispered the words to herself for the thousandth time. How could one be reckless with something they'd not been *given*? She'd only been trying to survive the sure sense of falling in love with a man she couldn't have. Survive his realization that she could never be his countess. Struggling to keep her hard-worked-for life intact. She had no one else to rely upon. Not a farthing stuffed beneath her mattress she hadn't earned on her own.

Their parting would have been bearable if he hadn't gone and been all Ollie about things. Sweet and clever and so, so handsome. Vulnerable, his anger only crisping the edges of his kindness. His eyes sorrowful ashen pools she couldn't help but trip into. The reclusive, cantankerous Earl of Stanford nowhere in sight.

The last time they'd talked, he'd had that dreadful look on his face. Clearly as baffled as she was about what he was feeling. Trying to keep her but telling her nothing to make her stay.

Remembering made her cross and lonely, more in love with him than ever. *Blast it.*

She couldn't believe it had been six weeks since she'd touched him. Since she'd felt the weight of his body pressing her into his mattress. She'd loved that feeling. Weeks since she'd watched him sleep or tucked a damp strand of hair behind his ear. Kissed him until her legs went boneless. Laughed and talked until dawn. She'd had a friend, the closest of her life, for a few short weeks in the wilds of Derbyshire.

She would go to Dash's literary bash, she decided, and placed the invitation in the "yes" pile. It was good business. Interacting with potential clients. Polishing her social skills. She had a new gown, two actually. Beautiful where, before, not so much. A modiste with panache, according to the Duchess of Markham. With talent, to Necessity's mind. She'd had them made in the event a situation arose. That was all. Not in hopes of seeing the Earl of Stanford again.

She nodded, released a held breath. Patted her trembling belly.

She was content. Fine, in truth. Pleased with her business and her life. If she woke in the middle of the night and reached for Ollie, once or twice, maybe five times at the most, this could be expected. If she looked him up in *Debrett's*—sixth earl, two fat paragraphs of notations about his family—it was mere curiosity. If she studied a map in Hatchards to chart the distance to Derbyshire from her flat, it was boredom. If she had a drawer of letters she'd addressed to Aspinwall House, she'd count that as madness.

Researching *facts* wasn't a sign of anything but inquisitiveness.

She sighed. The letters, she couldn't quite explain.

Strolling to the lone window in her flat, she bumped aside the curtain to gaze at hectic Bond Street. The crowds of people marching to and fro, hat boxes and parcels in their hands, the wind ripping at bonnets and beaver hats. The sound of horse hooves clipping cobblestones, shouts of street vendors, and excited children. While she searched the avenue for a tall man with silver threads in his hair. A scar she thought made his face the most exceptional in England. A shy, slow-release smile that lit up her soul when she let it.

Annoyed, she thumped the windowpane with her knuckle.

She wasn't going to avoid the man when it benefited her business not to. This would be a solid test—*if* he showed at Lady Bedivere's—to prove she was on the road to recovery. Getting over her adventure in Derbyshire. Getting back to normal, whatever normal was.

Maybe then Necessity would be able to accept Jasper Noble's invitation to the horse race. Dinner. Theatre. Opera. He'd asked numerous times without a hint of dejection when she'd refused. Cocksure bounder. They'd been friends for a long time... and could perhaps be more. He'd made it clear he would be open to the idea. Though she wasn't sure if he was pushing for something he *thought* was a good opportunity, rather than one he wanted with the type of desperation she'd got accustomed to in Derbyshire.

As if he was running from something, too.

She gave the windowpane another furious tap. The thought of touching another man, or one touching *her*, sent a queasy ripple through her. Made her question if she was prepared to have a series of lovers as she'd planned. Her enterprising, independent future. Woefully and despite her fantasies to the contrary, visions better served in dreams than reality, she only wanted one man.

Her memories of Oliver, Earl of Stanford would have to be enough.

This avowal, like the earl's button nestled in her pocket, remained her little secret.

"Have you seen the *Gazette* today, mate?"

Ollie glanced away from his taciturn sentry at his brother's warehouse window. The streets of Limehouse were positively mad with activity. Like bees in a hive. Stevedores, dockworkers, light-skirts, cattle, horses, carts, children, dogs. The vibrations flowed along the pitted lane, unswervingly rising to his perch two stories up. He could see why Xander, the most compelling man he'd ever met, loved this frenetic, fascinating place. When he felt a bit shaken to be back in the center of the folly. "No, should I?"

A bemused smile crossed Macauley's face. "Maybe."

Ollie crossed the room, snatched the paper from his brother's desk with a ragged sigh. *God, what had they printed now?*

"Runaway gardener," he whispered when he got to that part, wishing he'd kept the utterance to himself. "Fuck."

"My thinking exactly." He yawned behind a meaty fist, light on sleep. The baby was waking them up every three hours. Xander Macauley, unlike most fathers, adored helping with the feedings. Pippa was one lucky wife. "Not likely to appreciate the mention, Miss Byrne. Spot of petulance in her. Reminds me of a female Leighton, which is frightening." He shrugged a broad shoulder, a giddy grin Ollie wanted to erase with his fist sliding across his face. "Don't worry over much, boy-o. A man can't help who makes his mouth water. And temper can prove beneficial if you know how to use a spitting feline to your advantage."

Ollie hummed beneath his breath, ignoring the bait. Temper, yes. Care for society, no. If Nessie saw this rubbish, which she might *not*, she'd likely toss it in the hearth without an itch of concern. Recognizing a brilliant idea when he stumbled across one, he strolled to the hearth and chucked the paper in the flames.

"There's a suitable response, innit? You get more like me every damned day, lad. I'm proud as a papa over here."

"Bloody vultures," Ollie said through clenched teeth. Dropping into the closest armchair, his gaze circled back to the crisping newsprint. The flames were getting to the runaway bit. "I should be used to it by now. You are."

"I've had more practice, mate."

He rubbed his temple and sank lower in the chair. The Scarred Earl. Wasn't the first time the moniker had been bandied about. He lifted his hand to his cheek, the rough skin abrading his fingertips. His legacy along with the nightmares, a decrepit estate, a disturbing past. Why would a beautiful, intelligent, self-sufficient woman like Necessity Byrne want to even consider shouldering those responsibilities? His biggest asset, the earldom, was a burden not an advantage.

The truth was, she didn't require anything he could give her outside his talent in the bedchamber. Skills he almost wished he didn't have— because how he *got* them had, in part, pushed her away. A slender shade of doubt passing through her eyes at key moments. Across the breakfast table. While walking the meadows before dawn. Asking herself what she meant to him because he'd done an abysmal job telling her.

The thing was...

Sighing, he gazed longingly at Xander's glass of whisky. *If only...*

He missed her with a ferocious yearning. Raw longing that had him staring at the stars each night, trying to comprehend how he'd once had such a woman and let her go. An ache that made living difficult, locating a slice of happiness more so. Every day there was something he recalled that was now absent. Her sly laugh. The slight crook of her front tooth. The sluggish, erotic circles she traced across his chest when she was thinking. The way she crinkled her nose to keep her spectacles from sliding down it.

The part he missed most? The impassioned conversations about life in a space he'd vacated the day after she left. Their refuge, the coach house, now gone silent. Those impromptu picnics before a blazing hearth, scenes that often ended with him climbing atop her. Or she atop him. The scent of paint, rain, and earth was too much to conquer. His mother and Nessie, ghosts he didn't have the heart to fight. Not with the haunts that arrived regularly during the night.

He had to conserve his sanity for the proper struggles.

Shoving his hand in his pocket, he checked when he knew it was there. A scrap of paper that had become his talisman. Like a lovesick fool, he carried Nessie's gardening note everywhere. Because he felt he should, he'd taken the time to share it with Osgood Hagen, his *permanent* gardener. Although Ollie hadn't let the man take it when he'd asked to add the diagram to his burgeoning folio.

A bit of whimsy, perhaps, to keep it. But what good was having a title, when earls and dukes and so on were known for foolish eccentricities, if he couldn't play along with the gambit? Mr. Hagen was a perfectly charming gentleman with a face like a trout and a hawkish gaze that didn't miss much. A man bursting with delight over finding a position in the country with an employer who said yes to every request he made.

The project was on Xander's shilling, after all.

"I remember that sorrowful look in the mirror, mate, damned if I don't."

Ollie rubbed at his stinging eyes with a hand that shook. A dream the previous night had woken him hours before dawn. A murky sky over his London townhome, not a star in sight, and no telescope to provide relief in any case. "Shut it, Xander. No one wants to hear about the splendor of your and Pippa's love story. I've ridden that train before. So many times, I can recite it verse by verse as we zip along the tracks. Let's start with the knife you got her for her birthday, years before you fell in love."

"It was splendid, *is* splendid, but enough about me, my darling wife, and my truly remarkable gift-giving. I don't kick a man when he's down. Especially my brother." He cracked his knuckles, the pops ringing through the room. "How 'bout I round up Leighton, Dash, Streeter, blokes you can plant a facer, without having to worry about it hurting a fraternal relationship. Markham's a lover, not a fighter, you recall, but he's happy to watch."

Shaking his head, Ollie dusted his hand across his bruised lip. "That was yesterday, remember?" A friendly brawl that had nearly got the Leighton Cluster pitched from White's. He owed Baron Nelson a coat. It *was* his blood that had gotten smeared across the sleeve, no arguing there. Leighton and his remarkably sturdy left hook. And blood never came out of material no matter what you did to remove the stain. He was surprised *that* story hadn't hit the gossip sheets. It would eventually. A duke and an earl knocking over tables and shattering glass at the most prominent club in London? Sounded like a sensational tale to him.

He wondered what Nessie would think about his scrapping in public for the first time in years? Probably figure he was up to his old antics and firmly agree with her decision to never speak to him again.

Women got vexed quickly, it seemed. All around him lately. Theo had been mad as hell when they stumbled into Leighton's house, which was closest to the club. Best choice to wash up, bandage the contusions and such. Most of her ire had been directed at Dash. Ollie didn't know what was going on with those two. Their gazes tangling, then one or both storming from the room. The encounters left a charge in the air, like lightning during a storm. Ollie recognized it as he and Nessie sure shared it.

Attraction could be *felt*, he'd learned. Maybe Dash was suffering from the effects of wanting a woman he couldn't have. *Good*, Ollie thought, resentment ripping through him.

"I'd kill for a whisky right now," he murmured, then recalled whose warehouse he was sitting in. His gaze lifted to find eyes the same color and shape focused worriedly on him. "I'm not, Xan. I *haven't*. I mean, I think about it. Fantasize about the dens, mostly. Not booze. Being able to forget was a gift for a while there. Lost in London's putrid haze night after night. Although..." He dropped his head to stare at a ceiling of metal pipes and fittings that Tobias Streeter, architect of this building and every other his brother owned, had painted a cheery, vibrant red. It struck a daring note, that was certain, one that fit his brother. "I don't want to forget as much anymore."

The pinch of satisfaction was startling.

He sighed out a gratified breath. Despite his best effort to muddle it up, it appeared he was healing.

Ollie closed his eyes, the salty sting in the back of his throat his misery and his alone. Necessity Byrne with her bold smile and even bolder touch had helped him. Given him something he needed to step back into the light, out of the Aspinwall groove.

The key move would be to *stay* out.

Like he'd started it, he was going to finish his journey alone.

The teacup brushed his hand, and he flinched, rising to a sit. He hadn't heard Xander cross the room. "Thanks," he whispered and cradled the cup in both hands as warmth, and a silent show of support he'd not known he wanted, flowing through him. His brother was a paternal creature, by God if he wasn't.

With a grumble, Macauley threw himself into the armchair across from him, legs sprawling, boot coming close to knocking Ollie's. "I'm sorry if I mucked things up, mate. I thought a simple flirtation might bring you out of your slump. A woman worthy of your wit, you worthy of hers. Harmless attraction if it was even there. A verbal dance, sparring you seem to enjoy. I *like* her, is what I'm trying to say. Rookery chits get my vote every time. She does excellent work with plants and trees and such. Streeter loves what she's doing in Islington. Labors as hard as any bloke, he says. I wasn't setting either of you up for failure. I never expected, that is, I—"

"Stop, please. You're killing me. I'm... grateful you sent her to me. Thrilled my gardens resemble something from a book or will someday soon. A *botany* book." Laughing at a joke his brother would never get, he tossed back his tea, images of Nessie in his bed, her skin glistening, her eyes shining the color of burnt honey, sweeping him like a fever. Her body rising over his as she grabbed hold, taking him to a wondrous place he'd never been before.

If she touches the bookseller again, I may resort to violence, he promised with a sour smile. "I think I'm grateful. Ninety percent certain."

One *hundred* percent of the mornings he woke without her, however, were as gloomy as London's coarse, coal-choked mist. Simple, inarguable math there.

Macauley wiggled a cheroot from his pocket and jammed it between his lips, no intention of lighting it, Ollie knew. A habit his brother had mostly given up prior to his marriage. Given up for good after Kit was born. It was a delay tactic, anyway. Smooth negotiator that Xander Macauley was on the business front, he wasn't skilled at dealing with emotions. Nevertheless, he was getting better, surrounded as he was by the demonstrative Leighton Cluster and their thousands of children.

"You have me spellbound," Ollie murmured, rotating his cup in his hands.

Macauley's lips curved around the cheroot, while he pondered his words. "Could have handled this estate business from Derbyshire, am I right? Been a year or more since you dipped a toe in Mayfair."

Ollie stared into the cup, nudging a soggy tea leaf with his pinkie. He was starting to regret stopping by the warehouse. A frank effort to postpone his meeting with his solicitors when this conference was turning out to be almost as deadly. "And your point is..."

Macauley re-pocketed the cheroot, then smoothed his hand down his plaid waistcoat. He'd taken to wearing brighter colors since marrying Pippa. The vibrancy inside matching the outside. "Dash's latest literary jubilee is tomorrow. Might as well go since you're in Town. You haven't had a night until you've heard him work his rookery magic. It's a prime show, it is. The boy has society by the short hairs. All the while building a tidy bankroll with those slippery fingers of his. Lady Bedivere's the latest to want a piece of him for her collection. He doesn't mind selling himself, true enough."

Ollie fingered Nessie's note in his pocket, thinking a literary reading in some old hag's drawing room sounded worse than dental surgery. "Thanks, but no. I'm only here for a day or two to..." He let the words drift away, no need to lie when they both knew why he'd bloody come to Town.

Macauley buffed his nails on his trouser leg, whistling a jaunty tune. He was the very worst of actors. "Your gardener was invited. Can't say she'll attend for sure but can't say she won't."

Ollie's head lifted, interest leaping like a panther into the room.

"Jasper Noble is expected to be there, too. The rat bastard never turns down an opportunity to bump shoulders with his betters. Signed a contract last week with Lord Bedivere, shipping vases from the Pacific Islands, a deal Streeter and I wanted, by the way." He swore and tunneled his hand through his hair, shadowed streaks of exhaustion sitting beneath his eyes. "The baby was up until dawn the night before my meeting. A slight fever, worrying us to pieces. As things go, I fell asleep in the middle of negotiations, practically tumbled out of my chair, insulting Bedivere from the looks of it. It *was* a poor showing. Otherwise, Noble would never have got the jump on me."

Even as his heart gave an illuminating, possessive thump, Ollie flattened his lips into a withering tilt he prayed showed no emotion. It was a gesture he recalled his father tossing out many times. "If we're talking truth, Xan, aren't they *your* betters, too?"

Macauley turned a dazzling grin on his brother, the edges sharp enough to slash through brick, demonstrating the canny charisma that entranced every person he met. Charmed a duke's sister into happily attaching herself to him for life. "I have an earl's blood flowing through these veins"—he tapped his wrist—"blue and steady. I'm half acceptable in their priggish eyes, and now that the connection is verified, thanks to you, I'm going to use that association for every pound it's worth. I'd sell my connection to our father like whisky if I could. Pour it down the *ton's* throats. All it was ever good for."

The last came out harsher than he'd intended, his smile dying.

He and Xander waded into conversations about the deceased Earl of Stanford like they were surrounded by sharks.

"I'm sorry, Ollie, ignore me. I still get mad thinking about him," Macauley said after a lengthy, helpless silence. "When he might have been good for something, for you. I wasn't there for much of it. I hope he was."

"He wasn't good for me. Good for anyone." Ollie pinched the bridge of nose, warding off a headache, the past thickening like fog around him. He hadn't brought Nessie's medicinal tea to London; another needle beneath his skin every time the scent of chamomile drifted into his nose. "You have half that's untouched, in some way, when I'm full in. The name, the eyes, everything."

"Go get her," Macauley advised in a strident tone, that worrisome brotherly note creeping in. "Unless you want Noble to get there first. Don't let anything you think your father placed on you keep you from finding happiness, do you hear me? He's not worth it, Ollie."

"It's complicated, Xander. I'm complicated. More than she wants. More than she *needs*."

"I've come to think it's not all love, mate, but the way a person makes you feel when you're with them. And if you're already half in love with her—"

Ollie laughed, a harsh, aggrieved sound. Scrubbed his hand across his jaw, wondering when he'd last shaved. "More than half, I'm afraid."

Macauley blinked, his lips parting in amazement. "Then what the hell are you sitting here with me for?"

Ollie shrugged. "Fear?"

Macauley cursed and shoved to his feet, pointing out the window toward the lusher sections of London. Where Nessie was this very minute. "Fight for her, boy-o. Use those smooth words, just keep them honest. You can spend time in the city, banging around in that manse our dear papa left you. If that's what it takes to secure the girl, it's a minor exchange. I go to bloody teas for Pippa. Seems like one a week with all her charitable endeavors. Drury Lane. Museums. *Christ*, she carted me to Gunter's last week. All for love, Ollie. I do it gladly for love. Easy solution, innit?"

Ollie sank lower in the armchair, a defeated slump. "Pippa isn't Nessie. My gardener only wants me for, well, you know. Not to be indiscreet when, hell, of course I'm being indiscreet, but um, frankly, I got pretty good at it. Women. Lots of practice, which the gossip rags rolled into more than it was. Most I don't remember, but that's another story. This is how I'm repaid for my attention to detail, by the way. It's now the finest thing, maybe the only thing, about me."

Macauley burst of laughter nearly knocked the paintings off the walls. "Do you hear yourself, mate?"

"I hear myself. Loud and clear."

"You sound like an idiot."

Ollie flicked his hand, dismissive. *Yes, yes. Agreed.*

"Did you at least ask her to marry you? Some pretty, groveling speech with a little earl slickness thrown in? Flowers? Jewelry? I have ideas I can share that I didn't use. I had to try twice with Pippa, you know. Remember the story about the signs for her office?" He rubbed his hands together as if he was preparing to roll dice, excited by the match. "If you at least got this ball rolling, we could be close to closing the deal. Blimey, when the *ton* finds out, I want a front-row seat. The scarred lord and his runaway gardener will be the story of the bleeding year. You did get the ball rolling, right?" Macauley slapped his hand to his thigh. "Right, Ollie?"

Ollie glanced up, catching the flagrant exasperation in his brother's gaze. "No, I only made things worse. Issued an ultimatum that didn't go over well. Like a lead brick, truth be told. Something along the lines of, 'Stay in Derbyshire, although I can't tell you why I want you to, or lose me forever.' A plea with absolutely no tender words backing it— and certainly no flowers." He deposited the teacup on the table at his side. "Mostly a diatribe of panicked apprehension, now that I think about it."

Macauley dropped into the armchair he'd vacated with a whimper. "You gave that hard-headed chit an ultimatum? Necessity Byrne, girl from the stews? Dogged free spirit? Digger of dirt and grower of plants? The most tenacious woman I've yet to meet, and when you consider my darling Pip, that's *saying* something. *Hell's teeth,* Ollie, I don't know how you got so capable at bed play if you've been employing these bargaining skills to make your way beneath the sheets."

"It's the soldier fascination. Tragic hero, tormented earl. Worked like a charm. This before the gaming hell incident if you can believe it. Now with the scar, I worry it would work even better." He blew out a fatigued breath, staring at the raindrops making a sluggish slide down the warehouse windows. His heart felt categorically heavy, perfect for this weather. "Nessie didn't care for any of my routines. I had to go off script."

"This is a pathetic case you've brought to me. We have a lot of work to do, brother of mine, to get your sorrowful foot back in the door."

"She shut the door. That's what I'm trying to tell you. I'm not reopening it." Which wasn't completely true. He knew where she lived. Had paid an investigator a laughingly modest sum to locate the information. If he'd walked down Bond more times than he needed in the past two days and stared up at a particular window with cheerful blue trim and neat little curtains, it was... well, he wasn't sure what it was aside from a pale shade of insanity.

But he'd put his heart out there once, and she'd failed to take it. He would only reopen their door if she came to *him*. Certain circumstances might necessitate it. They'd been careful but not entirely. No method was full proof. She could be expecting his child; an occurrence they'd not discussed once. He tried that one morning, three days before she left, and lost his nerve. As he recalled, she'd seized his lips beneath hers. Touched him in a way that made the blood drain from his head. Whispered a lusty appeal that had blown every thought from his mind.

Something like that.

Watching the play of bewildering emotions cross his brother's face, Macauley tunneled his hand in his waistcoat pocket, snatching out his cheroot. This time, staring at it like he might light it. "If your absurdity makes me smoke this, Pippa will kill me. And then I'll kill *you*. You and Shoreditch are perfect for each other, I'm sorry to say. Two pigheaded fools."

Ollie closed his eyes to the certainty of that statement.

Chapter Thirteen

WHERE AN OBSTINATE EARL MEETS HIS MATCH

No matter how much his brother harassed him, Ollie decided he wasn't attending Dash's silly arse literary gathering. When he stuck his toe back in that foul pool, he'd choose something notable. A lecture on the findings of William Herschel, perhaps. Or an event supporting the new astronomy exhibit at the British Museum.

With a new face and new *feelings*, and the possibility of running into his runaway gardener, this occasion seemed too overpowering a mix.

In any case, he'd already read Dash's manuscript, *Proper Etiquette for Deception*. Been given as a gift, along with the rest of the Leighton Cluster, a signed copy. A typical show of Scottish bravado if he'd ever seen one, although the book was quite good. Entertaining and provocative, with an academic bent. Theo's influence if you asked him, which no one had. Ollie had actually used a technique from chapter three to cheat at *vingt-et-un* at Xander's gaming hell the previous evening.

Therefore, spending the evening in the dreary Mayfair townhouse in the Aspinwall family for a century and one-half was his final verdict.

Until he read the morning edition of the *Gazette*.

Is a gardener of note becoming a Necessity for a certain roguish yet Noble rookery gent? Their jaunt through Hyde Park was viewed as such by many.

That ridiculous spot of journalism had sealed the deal.

And who would want to be named Necessity Noble, anyway? Maybe he could save her from herself.

Ollie gazed across the sea of people crammed into the Bedivere's garden parlor, his height giving him clear sight over the waves. The French doors were open to allow a breeze only marginally stained with the scent of coal smoke and burnt sugar from the sweet shop around the corner. The clink of crystal and low shrill of hushed voices flowed over him. The scent of lemon verbena and bergamot. Someone was playing the pianoforte in the music room, a bouncy melody drifting down the hallway that didn't match his mood.

He was cranky. Stunned by his continued appeal to the mamas and daughters of the *ton*. Thirsty when an alcoholic beverage was never coming his way again, not even a swallow of abysmal ratafia. Sweating beneath more layers than he sported in the country. Bored by the conversation going on around him, inane chatter hitting him from all sides. Vigilantly watching each doorway, there were two, *and* the veranda entrance for the arrival of a dirt-smudged termagant with amber eyes that made his heart crack.

Antsy, Ollie rolled his shoulders and took a sip of juice reserved for children and old ladies with a heart condition. The only interesting element of this evening was Dash Campbell. If Nessie didn't appear, he'd remain the only interesting thing. Which made Ollie in turn disgusted and depressed at the way his life was shaping up.

As part of his presentation, Dash read a section taken from his book, then showed the crowd the accompanying move. He picked an easy con, a straightforward cheat, like slipping a card beneath his sleeve. Many of his dupes required complicated sleight of hand, which was the only way he'd been able to publish such a scandalous text as most people would never be able to undertake the frauds.

The crowd clapped and giggled like they'd forgotten he'd once robbed them blind. The entire spectacle was as irritating as the slick look on Dash's face. His so-pretty-it-hurt-to-look-at face. A visage that drew a bigger crowd than the double-dealing workshop.

Ollie sipped his virginal drink and sighed. What a bloody burden.

Like the weight of his title.

Regrettably, Ollie had his fair share of females circling. An earl, even a damaged one, was rather appealing. In fact, Lady Marston-Germaine had become something of a problem. He'd been trying for five minutes to get the Duke of Leighton's attention as he stood the closest. Markham would do. Tobias Streeter. His brother even. *Someone* to come and rescue him from her clutches. Dash couldn't be counted on to help because he was busy selling books.

"Lord Stanford, what are your plans for later this evening?" Lady Marston-Germaine whispered near his ear, getting right to the point. Why waste anyone's time, right? "My husband is visiting our estate in Oxfordshire until next week. I have a lonely terrace in Regent Square all to myself." She tunneled her gloved finger in the split between his own glove and his cuff, the only patch of bare skin she could find unless she touched his face.

He turned, caught in a masculine dilemma as old as time. Young boys dreamed of salacious offers until they started receiving them. Then it became a quest to figure how to turn them down.

Lady Marston-Germaine smelled faintly of citrus, which wasn't distasteful. Her eyes were a watery, seeking blue. Her face lovely though thinly drawn. In the past, he would have gone home with her, he suspected. Spent an hour or two in a strange bed, expended the requisite amount of time after the fact soothing her while planning his getaway. Staring at an unfamiliar ceiling and wondering why his chest felt hollow.

He no longer wanted exploited moments like these to be the lone ones comprising his life.

Decision made on that score if nothing else, he was reaching to push the lady away, not pull her closer, when Nessie stepped into the room. His breath sputtered, catching in his throat.

This, he understood immediately, was what she'd been hiding beneath those grubby gowns. A diamond of the first water dressed in a frock a modiste with *talent* had created. Finally. Deep rose that brought out the honied threads in her upswept hair, the shimmer of amber in her eyes. The bodice perfectly fashionable but scooped to highlight the most gorgeous breasts in England.

He was ashamed to contemplate such a base thing about the woman he loved to pieces, but there you had it.

Of course, he was sunk. Doomed by circumstance.

Nessie took one look at the scene—at the same time Xander did with an exasperated exhalation Ollie didn't have to be close to translate—and made her decision. Her cheeks flushed with indignant discernment. Then, Jasper Noble strolled into the room behind her, a hint of possessiveness in his stance. He was tall, possibly taller than Ollie, broad of shoulder but lean everywhere else. Dark hair glimmering in the candlelight, his gaze fierce, he looked like a panther set loose in a salon. Ollie hadn't looked that predatory with an English army pistol in his hand. A stargazer, he didn't have it in him.

Deciding they didn't look ill-suited, Ollie's eyes flared as blistering as hers. He felt them ignite. He tipped his head toward Lady Marston-Germaine. *I'm fine without you.*

He didn't want to make use of the chit, but she'd placed herself firmly in his orbit.

With a determined tilt of her lips, an act that should have frightened him, Necessity turned to Noble and gave him a smile that was flirtatious. And fake. Not that a rookery gambler would have any idea about a gardener's false promises. She glanced back, her smile predatory. *I'm fine, too.*

That's when the game commenced.

Not a game he'd ever wanted to play, but he couldn't back down now.

He competed for as long as he could, one lady after another trying to capture his attention. Lady Marston-Germaine had gotten the clue and drifted off like mist. He didn't recall the names of the others. He made no new friends. His only desire was to carry Nessie away from this pack of predators, slip that delicious rosy-sunset gown off her body, and show her the confounding, marvelous things swirling through his heart.

He ignored the efforts of Hildy and Tobias Streeter to nudge him across the room where Nessie stood. Xander tried, too, then gave up with a whispered oath and call for another glass of champagne. Pippa merely smiled in her teasing way, enjoying the display. A little sister relishing the preposterous quandary her brother-in-law had landed in. The dukes Markham and Leighton didn't help. After the brawl at White's, mostly his fault, they probably figured he had more grief coming. They'd fought their own love battles, and he'd heard the stories. That left Dash, who merely winked and kept peddling his merchandise.

Let her see what it will be like if I don't marry her.

When this comment fluttered through his mind, Ollie knew he was going to give in and talk to her. Grovel, beg if necessary. Damn his pride. And damn *hers*. If she didn't want him, then she didn't.

But it was time to see if she did.

Her scent struck him five feet before he reached her. Spring rain mixed with a floral swell that made his belly tighten. Hers and hers alone. It wasn't the easiest fragrance to capture in a room of ribald aromas, but he managed.

Nessie glanced up when he got there, a dead shot look. He loved that she didn't think too much of his title or the rest of the rubbish, but it would have been nice, for once, to have her bend a little. "Well, well, if it isn't the sixth Earl of Stanford. How are your gardens? I've had positive reports from Osgood. He said the lemon trees are making strides in the right direction, though it will be a year or two before they produce citrus. The window in the conservatory that was leaking has been repaired. The trees along the drive are adapting well to the replanting."

Ollie held back a grin at Jasper Noble's mocking smile. If he thought Necessity was selecting *him* with this flippant conversation, he didn't know her well.

She baited the man she *wanted*.

Also, he didn't know her well enough to catch her mistake.

Ollie filched a glass off a passing footman's tray when he wasn't planning to taste a drop. He was well past the self-destructive behavior. However, he needed something to do with his hands. "Did I ever mention that I was the sixth, Miss Byrne? I don't think I did."

Which meant she'd looked it up. Looked him up. In *Debrett's*. A book she'd once laughingly called the Journal of Nincompoops.

She blinked, stilled, realizing her error. Her gaze lifted to his, the faintest trace of crimson shading her cheeks. For a split second, the world around them ceased to exist, and they were back in the coach house, stretched out before the hearth, skin moist, bodies replete. Mentally, he reached for that contentment, the passion and breathless anticipation, while they stood staring, lost.

He asked her a thousand questions in those charged seconds but uttered nary a one.

"You've left a few stragglers on the refined side of the salon, Stanford," Jasper murmured, his expression amused. His eyes were the color of lava that had hardened centuries prior. Black, but not quite. "They look in need of the sixth's attention. Lady Marston-Germaine appears particularly bereft."

"Sod off, Noble." Ollie took a step closer to the man than was hospitable. He hadn't been sparring for two years with that crew of Macauley's for nothing.

Jasper drained his glass with a mocking glance that said, *Don't you wish you could do that?* It wasn't a particularly biting quip when everyone in London knew about Ollie's addictions. "Not that I'm a member of White's, unacceptable considering my upbringing, but wouldn't this be round two for you this week? Didn't release your ire at Gentleman Jackson's with that stylish circle of yours? Two dukes in the mix is glamorous indeed." He leaned in, a flicker of combativeness seeping into his voice. "I'm happy to entertain the notion if you didn't. I'd assume I could wipe the floor with you, like most of the gents in here, but seeing as your brother is a bloke from the stews and likely taught you, I won't go that far in my guesswork."

Nessie stepped between them, knocking Ollie with her shoulder and bumping him back a step. "Jasper, can you locate something edible on the food table? The cucumber sandwiches didn't look horrid. Avoid the sweetmeats."

"Dearest, you haven't tasted the sandwiches yet."

"Be charitable," she returned with a smile that was, this time, the real deal. "Someone on our side made them."

Shocked to his teeth, Ollie realized they were friends. Nessie and this near criminal who called her dearest. A criminal who was on *her* side.

Which placed him firmly on the other.

His blood boiled as he pushed a punishing breath through his teeth. This was the wall she'd erected between them? Their positions in society?

Ignoring Ollie's scalding look, certainly not the first he'd been dealt in his life, Jasper hummed a cheery reply and elbowed through the crowd, going after palatable foodstuff.

"*Dearest*," Ollie growled the minute the criminal was out of earshot. "How dare he, the brash mongrel."

Nessie plugged a finger in his chest. "How dare *you*, arrogant boor. The mongrel and I come from the same district, three streets apart. You insult him, you insult me. You know nothing of Jasper Noble, nor he you, frankly. You're not at all like the other thinks. I know you both well. I can attest to this."

Ollie cracked his glass on a passing footman's tray, the untouched contents spilling over the side. "We're all misunderstood, Sprite. Compassionate and loving under the scars and armor, is that it? I'm damned glad to hear you know him *well*."

"Don't take that tone with me, my lord earl. You've known half of this *salon* well."

"Why are we always arguing?" he whispered, rubbing his eyes, which were salty with exhaustion. "You're either spitting insults at me or ripping my clothes off. Like me, hate me. There's no in-between with you. Though your unpredictability is as tempting as opium, and I'm clearly hooked. I must be demented as I seem to love not knowing what I'm getting from one day to the next."

Because I seem to love *you*.

Right or wrong, complicated and in some way so bloody simple, he loved Necessity Byrne. Her mind, her body, her untamed spirit. He'd been chasing his tail for weeks when the answer was written in the many remembrances scattered across his heart. Xander had said, solid brotherly advice, that you didn't choose the person who made your mouth water. The person who *healed* you. This would be the added piece when he doled out advice himself someday.

Although love was left unsaid. Because he couldn't tell her here.

In this room of sycophants, the aroma of brandy and macassar oil a stain on his senses. A plinky pianoforte melody ringing in his ears. With his brother watching, when Macauley's avowals to Pippa were legendary. The dukes Leighton and Markham wagering about his chances to win the girl because of course they'd won the girl. Tobias Streeter composing his theorem on romance right this minute.

The verbal thrashing he was going to take from the Cluster, his extended family, made him vaguely queasy. He wasn't used to having people care about him even if he secretly adored it. Furthermore, he didn't enjoy being on stage, his private desires on display. It was enough that the *ton* knew about his troubled past, humiliations anyone connected to him had to endure.

He wasn't unaware of the trials Necessity faced if she let herself love him.

When he suspected, hoped, she *wanted* to love him. Maybe it would help if he gave her a wee push, as Dash called it. How hard a push was the question. The chit didn't suffer fools quietly.

As they stood gauging their next move, Necessity's tawny eyes darkened, musings hidden from everyone but him. She didn't disagree with what he'd stated, claiming they got along splendidly, or she hadn't ripped his clothes off on multiple occasions. She merely released a spent breath, mint and rainwater drifting past, and folded her arms underneath those magnificent breasts, awakening memories of circling her peaked nipples and sucking as she spiraled. His hands full of her. Her cries of pleasure, her body tightening around him. Awakening an ache that he longed to soothe immediately. Patience wasn't a talent.

"If you keep looking at me like a starving tomcat, my lord earl, they're going to know."

"I don't care if they know," he said, realizing he'd never spoken a truer statement. "I have nothing to prove to these people. They gave up on me years ago and I, in turn, have given up on them."

She huffed a sigh, tapped her slippered toe, making her gorgeous gown swish. "Well, maybe I do. Care, that is. I came for business, not in hopes of seeing you, should you think otherwise. You see, they're fine hiring me to restore their gardens. But sleeping with one of their earls? That's a no-no."

He laughed; he couldn't help it. His grin widened as a flush spotted her cheeks. Embarrassment or anger, he wasn't sure which. For the first time in weeks, his heart lightened. She didn't sound certain about why she was there. Actually, she sounded tentative as hell. So, he threw her a bone. "Aren't you going to ask why I came when you know I've read Dash's book twice already and hate these sorts of events?"

Her lips parted, a spark of interest entering her eyes. She swallowed her response, her sleek throat working with the effort. She wanted to ask, but stubborn chit that she was, she wasn't going to. Unconscious of the movement, she leaned in, a clear *tell me* without words.

A skill he'd evidently mastered, Jasper Noble strolled into the scene at the worst time. "I'm uttering the code word, as you recommended, if you were getting mired in society muck." He extended a plate loaded with sandwiches, biscuits, and one lonely grape. "Derbyshire."

Necessity's lids lowered, her groan ripping free. "*Jasper*, dear God. Are you trying to start a war in this parlor?"

"Only following orders, dearest." He slanted a tight glance at Ollie. "You'll thank me for it later."

Ollie reacted exactly as planned.

With possessive recklessness. Masculine idiocy.

Anger rolling through him, painting his vision crimson. He grasped her wrist, her pulse racing beneath his fingertips. "What did you tell him? What did you bloody tell him?"

Betrayal was fierce, a blinding sea rushing over him. The ground beneath his feet shifted as he realized he might not understand Necessity Byrne of the Shoreditch Byrnes after all. That the handsome devil standing there with a menacing expression knew her better.

"Hands off, Stanford, or I'll be forced to start the war Miss Byrne mentioned. I'm outnumbered, every friend you have in the room, but I'll take the chance. It's the rookery lad in me."

Ollie didn't have to be told twice. Blood thumping in his ears, he released his hold on her in more ways than one, gave the severest bow of his life, and marched from the salon without looking back.

Necessity grabbed the first glass she could get her hands on.

The champagne bubbles burned her throat, hitting her brain with a thud. Her gaze focused on Ollie as he stalked away, lean and easy in formal black, as elegantly dressed as she'd ever seen him. Candlelight striking his hair, the silver threads glistening. Broad shoulders and those muscular arms testing the seams of his ultrafine coat. The hurt she always seemed to bring, twisting his features.

She would have told him, *could* have told him if he hadn't reacted so quickly and so crossly, that she'd shared nothing of her time in Derbyshire with Jasper Noble.

Too late, in any case, as he was gone seconds later. Only his familiar fragrance remaining to haunt her, bringing forth the memories concealed behind her heart. For good gone, possibly, after this debacle. The Earl of Stanford had been abused enough in his life to readily flee more neglect.

What she wanted, wasn't it? For him to leave her alone?

"Dirty dealing, Noble," she whispered after letting a rousing cadence of applause for a horrid pianoforte medley die down. Tears stung her eyes, grew thick in her throat, but she forced them back. She was *not* crying in front of this sea of sharks. Her future clients. People she would take money from in exchange for her services, but they were not friends, not a one, ever.

The Leighton Cluster she excluded from this grouping. That crowd, she was coming to like. If Ollie rejected her, however, they might reject her, too. Bringing another twist of despair to her belly.

Not now, she promised herself, *but certainly later in your cozy flat, tears are allowed.*

"You told me to do it if he got too close. Keep you from falling for his racket." Reaching over her head, Jasper snatched a flute from the tray before the footman prowled past them. "But the thing is, you didn't really want me to do it, did you? You might have mentioned one word to get me off the hook, dearest. *Abort*. Not like I enjoy fencing with the Scarred Earl. Had enough trouble in this life, hasn't he? I have no disagreement with him.

It's his brother and Tobias Streeter who are on my list. And me on theirs."

"Don't call him that." Her voice wavered, spilling too much, more than she wanted, into the salon. "Don't you dare call him that."

Jasper sipped dispassionately, but his jaw tensed in aggravation. "You've only created difficulty for the older brother, darling. In ten minutes or less, when he realizes the miserable earl is gone, and he hears whispers about why he left, Macauley will be forced to send his men to check the Cable Street opium dens, making sure to keep a certain addicted peer out. Like he's done so many times in the past. What a waste of effort on all sides." He grazed the rim of the flute across his lips, thoughtful. "Maybe this would be a good time for me to create a spot of mischief at his warehouse, while he's on a do-gooder mission. Something Xander Macauley seems unable to keep himself from, sticking his hand in everyone else's pot."

Necessity coughed, startled, champagne fizzing up her nose. *Oh, heavens*, she'd never considered this outcome. She glanced around wildly, looking for a place to set her glass. She would find Ollie, talk to him, talk him *down*, before she'd ever let him go down that hole again. While making sure to tell Macauley to post extra guards on his warehouse, in what she could pose as an anonymous tip.

"I suppose that answers it," Jasper muttered, sounding thoroughly disgusted but otherwise unmoved. "Our love affair concluded before it began. I should have known better than pursuing a friend. Simmering pots don't always boil, do they? Now I'm left with strumpets. The occasional actress. Widows. That sort of thing. There's a French modiste with a shop near your flat who sent me a pair of silk stockings with a *very* interesting note attached. Might be time to take advantage of her offer."

Necessity slanted a sidelong glance at Jasper, wondering how many verbal blows she was going to receive today. He was the perfect combination of swaggering sophistication and ill-tempered charm. Tall, lean, hard, handsome. Intelligence flooding eyes a deep, almost blackish blue. A menacing persona softened by innate refinement he carried about like his portmanteau.

And despite his allure, a tidbit she'd keep to herself, her pot hadn't come *close* to simmering once around him.

Someday someone's pot would boil over because there were mysteries to be revealed. The story he'd told everyone about being born in the stews didn't match her memory. Jasper Noble had simply appeared one day, ten years ago or so, roaming the docks and back alleys. Building an empire, then fighting to keep it. Always with that refined air about him.

He'd no more grown up in Shoreditch than she had Mayfair, but it was his secret to keep, not hers to expose.

"What do you mean, 'that answers it'?" Mostly she asked to see if he had it right about her. About Ollie. A prudent way to gauge how much she'd shared without trying.

Jasper gave his cravat a yank. Sighed. Dusted the toe of his boot over a thread in the rug. Took another sip, then glancing into his glass, opted to drain it dry. "You love him. And he loves you. You're debating how quickly you can trot after him, and what it means when you catch him. You see, dearest, when the two people in question can't see the situation, but everyone else *can*, fate has stepped in. Meaning you must give up. It was that way with my parents. The only two souls I've ever known to be so connected. Walked into a room with them and you felt the pulse. My father often told me that when he met her, stumbled into such sentiment, he never expected to recover. And he didn't."

Necessity wedged her empty glass behind a fern, wondering how bold it would appear if she showed up at Ollie's home and knocked on his front door. She wasn't above sneaking in a servant's entrance around back. She could pick a lock when picking a lock was called for. It might even come down to her searching the dens herself.

First though, she had to ask, simply *had* to. "I thought you said you were an orphan?"

Jasper glanced up, his midnight blue eyes widening for an agitated second before he got hold of himself. His lips curved, amusement mixing with scorn, both self-directed. "Score one for Miss Byrne. I guess that's part of the story I spin to keep the real one tucked up and out of sight. Gains more emotional traction, my telling. After all, who can refuse an orphan?"

She laid her hand on his wrist, wanting him to know. *Needing* it with the slice of misery cutting through his gaze. Put there for no reason she could comprehend, but his pain looked real. "We're friends. You weren't mistaken about that. I'm here when you need me, whenever you need me. We rookery brats stick together."

He covered her hand with his and gave it a squeeze. "You are a wonder among women." His way of thanking her for not asking more. For letting the story he'd fashioned for society hold. "Now, let's go find a lovesick earl."

She stumbled, startled to her bones. "You're going to help me?"

He shoved the champagne flute in his coat pocket and executed a military turn toward the door. "I'm not letting you go haring around London by yourself, busy practicing your apology, or preparing how you'll react to his. Too, I know what you're thinking in that razor-sharp mind. 'If I don't find him at home, I'll check the dens myself.' You're a tenacious chit, courageous to your core, the kind of reckless audacity I thought meant we were perfect for each other."

She hurried alongside him, avoiding the Duchess Society's stares burning into her back. Hildy and Georgie were going to demand she take additional lessons in propriety after this unseemly display. "We're not perfect for each other, but there is someone out there. For you. Your other half." Her cheeks burned to recite such idealistic drivel, unrehearsed poetry, but she felt Ollie was hers. She only needed to show him. Tell him. *Love* him.

If he'd let her.

Jasper flicked his hand, a nonchalant flutter like he was shooing a fly. "Oh, I met her years ago. The other-half, ideal chit you're bandying about. Childhood obsession if you can believe it. Doesn't sound like me, am I right? Adoration at first sight nonsense, a green lad stumbling upon the person he wants to spend his life with. Who believes in that rubbish?"

"I do," she whispered. *Now*, I do.

"Dearest naïve child. True love is a flimsy plot, except in my lurid novel, the heroine married someone else after the hero, that's me, ripped his heart out and laid it at her feet. Never again, I say. It's why I thought the friendship angle with you was brilliant." Waving aside the livered footman who tried to do it first, Jasper opened the front door and bounded down the marble steps, propelling himself into London's ether. "Don't be offended, dearest, but I'm definitely going back to strumpets."

His grief swam through the distance separating them, and Necessity could only think as she watched her step, trying to keep from stepping in one of the many puddles littering the street, *not me*. I'm not losing Oliver. I'm not leaving him. He's not crawling back into his solitary hole never to be heard from again. If he feels he ripped out his heart in his bashful, the woman-isn't-even-sure-he-loves-her manner, she wasn't rejecting him.

If he hadn't, if she was mistaken, then she would correct the situation. By ripping her heart out and placing it at *his* feet. She was courageous enough to do it.

As Ollie had once said, after tearing her diagram from her hand and stuffing it in his pocket...

Mine.

She felt the same about him.

Chapter Fourteen

WHERE A ROOKERY GIRL FORMULATES A PLAN

J asper knocked a branch from his face and pressed his nose to a smudged windowpane on the front side of the earl's townhouse. "Blasted hydrangea." He sneezed into his sleeve, then dug inside his waistcoat for a handkerchief. "I used to have horrible allergies as a boy. Quite a pathetic sack I was. Gangly and pale-faced. Hope that problem's not rearing its ugly head again."

"Viburnum," she murmured. "People often confuse the two."

"Who cares? Oh, that's right, *you* do. Since I've known you, plants were the obsession. Now, it's a bloody earl." He sneezed again, knocking his brow against the window ledge. "Dammit, Necessity, this is madness, even for me." He rubbed his temple. "And you want me to do *what?*"

Necessity bounced up on her toes, peeping into the window of what she thought was Ollie's study. A sconce tossed a dull yellow glow across faded paneling. Books and ledgers lay in a muddled spill across a massive cherry wood desk. She strained to see into the far corners. No telescope. Macauley had mentioned that his brother didn't have one in the city. A strange comment she thought he *wanted* her to overhear. Her gaze skipped past a settee and caught. Tracked back. The coat

Ollie had been wearing this evening lay in a tumble over the arm. She had a momentary image of bringing it to her face and pressing her nose into the fine wool. Drawing his teasing, tantalizing scent into her being. She could smell him from here.

"I want you to find what I asked for. *Tonight*. Bring it to my flat and put it on the roof. Have one of those hulking brutes you employ by the hundreds help you. I don't care if you have to steal it. Whatever it takes. You owe me, so I'm asking for a return of the favor. I got you in the door with Lord Spellman, talked you up whilst creating that ridiculous wall of bamboo the countess insisted upon. Now you're shipping his purchases from Asia on the regular. Quite a pretty penny, I bet."

She turned to him, waited patiently for his perturbed gaze to meet hers. She meant business, and she wanted him to know it. The shimmer of moonlight couldn't soften his displeasure, but one man was all she could worry about at the moment. "You claim to have the nimblest hands in England, Jasper Noble. Years of larceny under your belt. Prove it."

"You can't march up to an earl's front door at this time of the night, dearest. Even you. His butler will have a spasm or something. A scandal-induced apoplexy. And the next morning, every butler in Town, they all talk, the haughty mongrels, will know."

"I'm not planning to, but thank-you for the advice."

He shoved off the brick, flipped aside his coattail, and crammed his handkerchief in his trouser pocket. "Where in the hell am I going to find a telescope before dawn?"

She held up a finger.

He muttered an oath beneath his breath. "A *good* telescope. Spectacular, even."

Necessity picked at her nail, wagged her head from side to side. She clicked her tongue against her teeth, suddenly nervous about enacting her plan. "I realize it's a huge ask. I'm sure Streeter and Macauley Shipping or whatever they call themselves, can locate one without delay. Never mind. I'll head over to Pippa's right now. A midnight knock on her door won't cause a ripple of concern. Her staff is used to chaos. Perhaps you can even give me a ride."

"As if that isn't the shrewdest tactic you've ever used against me. How low you'll go, Byrne. Like I'd let Xander Macauley best me at any damned thing. Even outright thievery."

She grinned, fluttering her lashes. "I have no idea what you mean, Jas."

He grunted, dragging his hand through his dark-as-night hair. "My carriage is parked in the mews around back when you need it. The driver has been instructed to wait. Do *not* travel alone if you please. I'll walk, thank-you, as I set out on this ridiculous caper of yours." Snubbing her gentle sensibilities, Jasper swore roundly and manhandled his way through the viburnum shrub. "I feel for the Earl of Stanford, the luckless bloke, if you manage to find him. I really, really do. How I thought I could manage you for a lifetime, I'll never know. I must have been out of my bleeding mind to consider coming clean on this matrimony deal. And with the runaway gardener of all women."

"If I'm not there, you'll find a key under the yellow flowerpot," she called as he disappeared into the mist. "The door sticks, and you have to give it a good shove to force it open. Before dawn, it must be before dawn, don't forget!"

"I don't need a bloody key," he shouted back.

Necessity dusted her hands together, satisfied for the moment. Dealing with Jasper's tantrum was oddly unraveling the nerves circling in her belly. "Well, friend, I don't, either."

It was a skill she frequently used in her line of work. Gardening sheds with rusted locks in need of negotiation. Conservatory cabinets with missing keys. A sealed desk drawer here and there merely for the fun of it. She'd learned to pick after her family died, when her future, and how she was going to make enough blunt to survive, had been an open question.

She halted by the domestics' entrance, rattled the knob, unsurprised to find it bolted. It *was* nearing midnight. She kept the leather roll in her boot. Specially made, the pocket. Tools in the right boot, knife in the left. It was touch more than skill, she thought, sliding the tension wrench into the keyhole. Closing her eyes, Necessity wiggled the metal probe until she felt the tumblers shift.

The strategy once she got inside Ollie's townhouse wasn't clear—

but when she'd seen his coat lying across the settee, getting *to* him was it for her. He hadn't run back to his past, finding comfort in the dens, or hopped into the bed of an actress or strumpet.

Her grand gesture was set to take place four streets over at her flat on Bond. *If* Jasper Noble did his part. Her part was getting the earl there, so she could make her offer. Make him understand.

Jasper would find a way to help her. Friends were wonderful like that.

She was stepping into the manse, prepared to creep down the murkily lit hallway, and find her man when she realized she wasn't alone.

Ollie braced his arms on either side of her, trapping her between his body and the doorjamb. "What have we here?"

She turned in the banded circle of skin and muscle, her cheek brushing his flexed biceps. His scent, only Ollie, forever Ollie, threading into her lungs. The heat between her thighs was instant. A sizzle that crackled over the crisp night air.

She missed more than his laughter and his wit. His jokes and his generosity. She missed his *touch*.

His smile was shaded with tones of confusion and delight. Longing washing through his eyes, turning them the color of spent smoke. "Was that Jasper Noble I saw climbing my hedge?"

She figured an indecisive hum was the best response until she came up with a better one.

He lowered one arm while keeping her confined with the other. Plucked her tools from her hand, his eyebrows lifting. "A thief as well as a betrayer. Interesting. You *and* your friends."

She made a grab for the leather bundle, but he held it high above her head. "I didn't share anything, my lord earl. About us. If you'd stayed long enough, I would have told you."

"You have a code word as a means of escape. Why, then?"

"Because." She swallowed, her throat suddenly dry. All the things she wanted to say to him, she'd wanted to say on *her* terms. With him smiling or laughing, her lips plump from his kiss. Not with his tilted in indecision and doubt. His eyes clouded with uncertainty.

"Why, Nessie?" His voice was cold, hard, the earl in him stepping to the forefront, pushing the gentle man she loved with everything in her aside. He grasped her jaw and tilted her chin high until her gaze hit his. "*Why?*"

She wrenched from his hold, sought to wiggle past him.

"Not this time." He shifted until his body pressed hers to the jamb. Unrolling the leather set of tools, he took a thin metal pick in hand. "I lie awake at night aching for you. My body mourning, my heart heavy, like someone died. I haven't felt the like since Xander left all those years ago, disappeared from my life, and left me with my father. I've missed you more than I'd imagined, more than I'd intended. More than I'd dreamed I could miss anyone. More than I *like*."

He placed the pick's pointed tip above her breast and dragged it slowly over the curved mound, circling the faint rise of her nipple. Her skin caught fire, a ragged sigh ripping free.

"I'm ready to tell you everything that's in that heavy heart," he murmured, circling, circling while black dots flashed across her vision, her knees threatening to let her slide to the step. "More than ready. But now, at this moment, I want you gasping. I want you begging. I want your breath in my lungs. Your sweat on my skin. Your fingers in my hair, your legs squeezing the life from me. Your moist core milking me dry." He leaned and took a patch of skin beneath her ear between his lips, his teeth, and bit down. Tenderly but without purpose. When he sucked hard, surely leaving a mark, she moaned, uncontrolled *want* wracking her body, his grip on her all that was keeping her standing.

He pulled back, trailing the pick down her cheek, throat. Using the tool in a way she'd never envisaged, he popped a button on her bodice with a ragged knitting stroke. A saber's upward thrust. Another button flipped away into the night.

His eyes were icy, his mouth held in imposing lines she imagined he'd employed on the battlefield. But his cheeks were flushed, his breathing erratic. The hand holding the pick trembled, sending it dancing down her jaw. He wanted her as badly as she wanted him. What could be more tantalizing?

Seeing him lose control was almost enough—*almost*—to make her come right then and there. What would he think about that?

He needed her. And she needed *this*. Power, love without words. To share their fascination. To step into passion and lose herself before she told him things that would change her life. Change his. Where they'd be together or be *ruined*.

She wanted to be wrecked, wanted to wreck him.

Before she told him she was never leaving him again.

Going on instinct, she dropped to her knees, slipping past the welcoming enclosure of his hold. Leaving him, but only for a moment.

"Nessie," he said, an urgent thread in his voice. The leather pouch hit the floor with a thump.

She batted his hand away as he sought to bring her to her feet. "Let me, Ollie. I want to."

She'd done this once with him, in bed, briefly. Before he growled, rolled her on her back, and took her places she'd only dreamed of going before meeting him. He'd tasted wonderful, slightly salty, his cock smooth and silky, pulsing and hard, a vexing contrast. She wanted more. She wanted to know him in every way, *this* way.

Effortlessly unfastening his trousers, having mastered the task weeks ago, she stroked him. A languid glide. This skill, too, she'd mastered, his spend flowing over her fingers the time they'd experimented one morning in his study. It had been the most erotic act of her life, watching him tremble and erupt. An event that, before then, had happened inside her, away from view.

Blowing a hot breath across his skin, she caressed until his body quivered, his knees locking to hold his stance, his hand going to the doorjamb with a smack. When he breathed out a ragged groan, she added her lips. Enfolding them around his head, sliding her mouth along his shaft. Her tongue dancing over the underside. Something, though she would never tell him, she'd read in a French text long ago.

And had never tried until now.

He talked to her then, threadbare pleas and hissed longings. Bold threats. What he was going to do to her, what he had *yet* to do. The many ways he would help her find pleasure. His fingers tangling in her hair and guiding her as his hips thrust to meet her motion. They found a fluid beauty in the crude splendor that was his need and her hunger.

She scraped her nail across the top of his thigh, his skin damp beneath her fingertips, and he jerked, swearing. When she bit lightly, using the edge of her teeth, that was it. Control breaking, he yanked her to her feet. Shoved her into the house, their panting gasps a resounding echo down the deserted hallway.

"Turn." Chest heaving, he spit out that directive, nothing more. Spinning her, pushing her body against the wall. Gentle, but with power he was holding in reserve. Moving in, he stepped between her spread legs.

He yanked her skirt high, around her waist. "Hold it," he whispered against her shoulder, his teeth nipping the nape of her neck to drive the point home. She gathered the crumpled silk in her hand as he worked past her drawers, ripping, tearing. Sliding his finger inside her, testing her. Two fingers. His words—*wet, tight, perfect*—riding like an angry gust through her.

She palmed the wall, bumped back, wanting him to destroy her. It was a miraculous feeling to wish for such obliteration. To beg in return —*now, now, now, Ollie*—without a care for what his assault would do to her.

He caught her around the waist, tilting her pelvis. Fingertips digging into her hip, he thrust in one determined, steady stroke. Then he molded his hand around her breast with a sigh of what sounded like relief. He loved her breasts; she knew he did. It made her smile despite the maddening fever of his touch. Despite the blurred vision, the scattered breaths backing up in her lungs. Despite the fact that she could no longer feel her toes or most of her fingers. That a line of sweat was working its way down her back, and in a moment, he would know. Her skin tingling in a way that meant she wasn't long for this act. The sounds spilling from her throat raw and animalistic, hardly human.

The night called to them regardless, the world continuing to spin around them. The screech of an owl, the settling of a house with old bones. The tick of a clock down the hallway. He thrust, having slowed to tease, laughing when she reared back. *More.* Lifting her arm above her head, he held her. Didn't let her go when she yanked, although she didn't want him to, and he knew it. She liked it, this play. Games they were only starting to discover.

His mouth hit her ear, his exhalation scalding her cheek. Panting now. Thrusting, no more games.

They fumbled and fought, surged and tumbled, sliding down the swell of a monstrous wave of passion. She turned her cheek to the wall, cool when everything was blistering, burning her up. Her muscles quivered when her climax arrived, her knees giving way. He held her, arm snaking around her waist, his words—primal, vicious, savage—ringing in her ears.

She gasped, moaned, brought her hand back to catch his hip. "Ollie... Ollie." Her mind lost, her body taken. She felt her muscles squeeze his shaft, his agonized groan following.

They stumbled back, and he held them steady, still linked. Panting, grasping for air. Trembling limbs, churning lungs. Whispered sentiments neither could respond to. Understand. Process. She wasn't sure walking was ever going to be allowed again, much less speech.

His mouth streaked down her cheek, damp skin melding. Then giving up, he slid to the floor and brought her down atop him. Collapsed, a tumble, bodies tangled.

They were an absolute mess.

It was delightful.

Seconds passed, a patent coolness chilling moist skin. The hallway was drafty. Silent, thank heavens, except for that blasted clock somewhere down the way telling her she was a part of the living world. That Ollie hadn't tupped her past the point of breath. Past the point of *being*.

She stretched, sated, lying there partially under the Earl of Stanford. His long body trapping hers once again, this time against his faded runner. It was late enough for the servants to be abed. What if one of them had heard them? What must *that* ruckus have sounded like?

She had no control over herself, she thought with manifest wonder. She was a puddle of spent desire.

"Are you laughing? When I'm shattered, never to recover. I can't possibly make it to my bedchamber, much less carry you. We'll sleep here until the housekeeper finds us, although she's nearly blind."

Necessity flopped to her side, rolling off him. Somewhat. She extracted her left leg as best she could. Her right arm was wedged under him and fast asleep. Her gown gathered at her waist, torn in at least two places, the hem hanging at an unfortunate angle. Slippers. She glanced around. Where were her slippers? And she'd had a bonnet on at some point. Her leather pouch with her tools was nearby she hoped. Those were custom made.

She laughed again, a bright burst toward the ceiling. He squinted, gazing at her through a pale silver eye. In appreciation, she took him in, head to toe, lying there like a knock to the head had taken him down. His hair a complete catastrophe, his cravat long gone. Trousers askew. Shirt ruined.

Trailing a finger down his neck, she listened with pure joy as he purred. Stretched his long body and sighed, soul deep.

It was extraordinary to imagine she could do this with him every day. Twice a day maybe if they figured out how to be together. Not marriage, of course, because a rookery brat couldn't be a countess, but there were ways around society's rules if a person was plucky enough to ignore them.

Her list, conjured so long ago, couldn't compare in any manner to real life. A real man. One eventful evening, they'd made it *three* rounds. Bed, floor, desk. That had been the most fun night of her life. Oliver outshone anyone she'd yet to meet or expected to meet. He was a generous lover. Inventive. Playful. But the best thing about him was his kind heart, a heart she wanted for her own.

He scrubbed his fist across his jaw, suppressing a yawn. "We haven't resolved our issues, Sprite. We've just, once again, tupped ourselves silly. Amorous congress, the Duchess Society would rather you call it. Or not speak of it at all, perhaps. I wish I could see you and keep my hands to myself, but I'm pathetically weak. We're left with never settling anything but our thirst for each other."

"I *love* amorous congress. Much more than silly old resolutions." She giggled, covered her mouth in amazement, then did it again.

"Holy hell." He turned his head to stare at her. His dimple flared to life at the edge of his scarred cheek. "Did Necessity Byrne of the Shoreditch Byrnes just giggle? The toughest nut in London to crack? Too much of that, my runaway gardener, and I'll think you're happy."

Her heart sank but not clear to her toes. This was a situation with a solution. Like a plot of earth in need of refurbishment. A lonely garden, a forlorn soul. Ollie was heartbroken beneath the sheen of pleasure, but she was going to repair his injury much as she'd done the wound to his face. With care and determination.

She wasn't going to be reckless with his heart—or hers—ever again.

Yanking her arm free, she rolled to her side, propping her head on her hand. "I have something I want to show you."

He released a wispy breath, his lids fluttering. "Hmm..."

She shoved him, but he only grunted softly. "Don't go to sleep, Ollie. We're in the hallway, where anyone could find us. Quick explorations also involve quick recovery. Isn't that what you told me? Remember how we were nearly caught in the stable by your groom?" Panicked, she shoved to a half sit, glanced down the thankfully deserted passage. Being found in a compromising situation would bungle her plans. Ollie might feel forced to marry her, not what she was going to suggest, and that would be a horrific development for him.

For her, it would be wondrous.

An impossible dream she would subdue for the possible one.

Besides, if she was designing a new life, she wanted it to start *now*.

Impatient, she gave his shoulder a rough shake. How could he sleep like a babe? Like he rested on a feather mattress and not a chilled stone floor? But he could, was gone from consciousness in the blink of an eye. Unaware she was plotting his future. Protecting him from calamitous scandal. Nevertheless, this was an opportunity.

For her viewing pleasure, a satisfied male sprawled across the floor of his kingdom. If she was an artist, she would have sketched this scene in as much detail as talent let her. His hand lay lax on his belly, slim fingers spread. His lips, flushed and swollen, parted enough for her to see the sharp edge of his teeth. His shirt was missing a button, one she hadn't located this time. His trousers hung low on his hips, the close open, and the dark hair around his groin visible between the folds. The pale scar on his cheek, remnants of an incident that had brought them together.

Love was a fist to her chest, a curative to her soul. Tears swam behind her lids and choked in her throat as she sought to contain them. Exhaling sharply with the force of emotion, she straightened her clothing and his with trembling hands, then rested against the wall. She would let him sleep for an hour, two at the most. It would give Jasper time to complete his mission.

Then, she was on *her* mission.

And that, she decided ardently, was that.

Chapter Fifteen

WHERE A PEER OF THE REALM IS
ASTOUNDED BY HIS GOOD FORTUNE

He was unsteady on his feet.

Ollie's brain was sluggish, much more than hers. She looked refreshed and beautiful, marching alongside him, where he felt rumpled around the edges. Burned like toast. Used up and spent. Dazed and confused.

Where did she find the verve, he wondered?

He'd learned two fundamental things about himself since his association with Necessity Byrne. One, he didn't need opium anymore. Two, he *did* need sleep. Years ago, during the troubles, he'd managed on almost none, an hour or two here and there, hollowed-eyed and gaunt. Now with age or contentment, or perhaps proof that love and sex demanded more of a man than any drug, he needed more.

He needed more of a lot of things. And questioned if Nessie's *mission*, as she'd called it when she woke him from his deepest slumber in weeks, was going to bring them.

"Is this yours?" he asked and stepped back, craning his head to study the building she'd dragged him to. A bit of a charade because he knew, from his investigator, exactly which one was hers. There was a cat lounging on the ledge of her window. Delilah, he pulled from memory. Her residence was only minutes from his, in fact. Second floor, above a shop on Bond, a cherry dwelling with navy shutters and a handsome façade. He'd bought someone—the Drury Lane actress or maybe it was the Italian opera singer?—a pair of kidskin gloves there once.

He thought it best not to mention this.

He and Necessity had made it here by way of fog-born backstreets, snaking through the boulevards like ghosts, hats (both his) pulled low on their brows to protect, well, he wasn't sure who she was trying to protect. He worried it was him, when he didn't *need* protection from what he felt for her. Especially with the scent of her clinging to his skin, the taste of her coating his lips. A ripple of irritation fluttered through him, riding on the heels of the tender sentiment filling his heart to bursting. Which happened every time they made love. She was so wrapped up in their damned social standing and difference in upbringing when he could not have cared less.

Still, he was curious and charmed, sneaky responses whittling away at his angst, strong enough that he allowed her to take his hand and guide him through lonesome, misty Mayfair. When he wanted to snatch her back, push her against the rough brick, and kiss her until she was unsteady on *her* feet. Until she could do no more than whisper his name. *Ollie.* He could envision the haze curling around her as he lifted her, wrapped her legs around his waist, and thrust home.

His body, amazingly, absurdly, began to respond to the fantasy, right there in the middle of a London thoroughfare.

The woman unmanned him in ways that stunned.

"There," she said and pointed, unaware of his fantasizing. Hooking her arm through his, she hauled him around the building. "The roof. We'll take the back staircase."

"Roof?" He'd not gone pratting about on rooftops in years. And when he'd done it before, he'd been far from sober. Consorting with a group of young bucks who'd had nothing better to do. Nothing to lose. After he'd returned from war and thought he'd lost everything, so he was equally uncaring. Xander's men had located him on one particularly momentous occasion and carted him home. His brother hadn't shown up that night, however, only protecting from a distance.

He wasn't so fortunate now, Ollie thought with aggrieved affection. The man showed up all the time.

When she reached the building's alley entrance, Necessity released him to search the pocket of her cloak. Fitting the key she extracted into a lock that looked like it had seen better days twenty years prior, she gave the door a grunting push that got them nowhere. "I don't often use this entry," she said, putting her shoulder into the next winded effort. "The building is otherwise very well maintained."

Rolling his eyes, Ollie braced his hand above her head and gave the door a shove, sending them stumbling into the small foyer. Beneath the brim of her hat, he watched her gaze sweep up his arm, linger on his shoulder before hitting his face. Her eyes had gone the misty color of amber lit with sunlight, and he felt the blast like a caress. She enjoyed when he was rough, just a bit, in bed. Enjoyed *being* rough with him when her power wasn't equal physically but, in every other way, outshone his.

Instantly, he knew she'd gone to the intimate place they occupied— as he had moments before. He'd never experienced such unsated hunger for another person. Never completed the act, then wished to dive back into the pond immediately.

And stay there forever.

Ollie supposed he'd never get enough of her, which scared him a little. Or a lot.

She smiled, wickedly confident, sensual certainty on display. "Soon," she said and trailed a finger down his chest. "As often as we'd like. In any locale we'd like. In every *way* we'd like. I mean to erase every trace of disquiet from your eyes, no matter how long it takes me."

Undaunted, a fire roaring through him at her brazen words, he took, backing her into the dwelling and against the staircase railing. Knocking their hats loose, he framed her face in his hands and seized her mouth, his effort to silence a yawning chasm of need. Deeper, tongues, teeth, and lips until there was nowhere else to go. Breathless. Immersed. Captivated. Alone in a universe that was providing the poetry of his life.

She clutched at him, fingertips embedded in the wool of his overcoat. Her faint moan, a sound he knew well, driving him mad.

He meant to have her, Ollie told himself as his heartbeat raced, chest to chest, against hers. As his countess and not one whit less. Pulling away, letting the blood rush back into his head, he pressed his brow to hers and held her close. He'd let her carry out this project, this rooftop presentation, then he was telling her how he felt. Telling her everything. In the morning, picking up the license, one he'd prepared with his solicitor two weeks ago in the event he managed to change her mind about him.

A wedding in his near future, one they'd plan together. An extravagant affair at Westminster Abbey if he could secure the locale or Gretna Green if she preferred. The Duke of Leighton's parlor, Markham's ballroom, Streeter's rooftop. He cared little.

London or Derbyshire or the moon, the choice was hers where they lived. He would be there, by her side. *This* is what he would promise. Although he had a nagging feeling she was set to offer less, imagining it was what he wanted or could accept.

What society would accept when he didn't give a damn about those people.

"Come," she said and grabbed their hats, tugged him up the stairs, the tremor running through her words giving him great satisfaction. If nothing else, he could kiss her until she gave up, confused and flustered, and married him. Make her cry out in pleasure every time she voiced a complaint.

They had that part right in every way. After diligent practice, he knew her well enough to spring her like she'd sprung his townhouse lock.

Up four flights of uneven stairs in the pitch, meager sconce light falling across their feet at each landing, then a return to darkness. The cloying scent of leather from the glove shop stung his nose. He peered down the hallway on the second level, seeing an entrance at the end of the hall that must be hers. He was dying to see her flat and what the space would tell him about her. Maybe that was part of her promise of *soon*. With a cheeky grin, he wondered if they could put her bed to the test as they'd done the one in the coach house.

The door to the roof was ajar when they reached it, a hinge giving boisterous protest as she slapped it open.

A gust of wind tugged at his coattails, sending them flipping about his hips as he stepped out, stared. Without a hat, his hair whipped his face. The night was luminous for London, moonlight awash over the rooftops of the city, dazzling him. He'd missed this during the troubles, the beauty of the view. Being sober provided more clarity.

He crossed the distance to his gift gradually, on leaden legs.

The telescope was magnificent. Brass on an oak tripod. Lustrous, the tawny metal gleaming in the moonlight. The most gorgeous thing on the roof except for Nessie. With a delicate touch, Ollie tilted it up and fit his eye to the lenses. The sky exploded, a thousand stars within reach. He'd only seen such a superb device at an astrological symposium hosted by an Oxford dean. Stepping back, he circled the piece, his gaze shooting to hers. "This is a Negretti and Zambra. They're the appointed opticians to the king. It's worth a fortune. Where in the world did you get it?" He glanced to the sky, his heart giving a solid thump. "And the rooftop is a wonder. I've never tried viewing this high."

Her lips parted as she glanced at the telescope like she'd never seen it and was *definitely* afraid to touch it. "*Oh*... well, um, you see, I have my ways. Best not to ask about them."

"I've only used this model once before, and it was on loan from a museum. I've not known an individual to own one." His lips tilted in a crooked grin. "Unless it's stolen, which of course, this isn't."

"That dirty rascal," he thought she murmured, then decided it was a whisper of the shifting winds. Because her response made no sense unless it *was* stolen.

An idea came to him. "Did Xander have something to do with this? He used to be quite the crook. Could get his hands on anything if he tried hard enough. Including, eventually, a duke's sister. A relationship that's coincidentally led to less criminal activity." Why it annoyed him that Xander might have something to do with her grand gesture, Ollie couldn't say. He guessed because he didn't want his older brother standing alongside him while he figured out his love life.

Necessity tossed out a sly glance, her face glowing. "Believe it or not, he didn't."

He turned to her, ready to know, *needing* to know. He crossed his arms over his chest, vowing not to touch her until they talked. Which included keeping his hands off her gift when he wanted to explore every glorious inch of the telescope. Similar to what he wanted to do to her.

His fascination for both were infuriating and extraordinary. "What is this, Nessie?"

"It's my offer," she said after a helpless pause. "Dreadfully stated but that's my style, isn't it? I'm not traditional, I realize, even so much as to wait on the man to determine what it is he wants." She smoothed her hand down her bodice, chewing on her lip in a move he knew meant she was nervous. "The offer is me. It's that simple." She stepped in until the toes of her slippers bumped the toes of his boots. Digging in her pocket, she came out with a button which she presented to him in the palm of her hand. "It was on the floor of the coach house that last time. Before I left for London. When we argued. Ripped in our haste from your trousers. I thought it was all I was going to have of you, besides my memories. I've decided that's not enough."

His fingertip grazed the button before he pulled his hand back as if scalded. He felt the caress, although there hadn't actually *been* a caress, flow through him.

Reaching into his pocket, he came out with a crumpled sheet, the diagram of his garden that he'd refused to return to her. Her gaze met his, probing and intense, restrained emotion turning her eyes molten amber. Moonlight danced over her, gossamer thin, adding dreamy substance to the moment. The wind whipped past, tossing at her hair. He resisted the urge to tuck a strand behind her ear, twirl one around his finger. *No touching, Ollie.* "I thought the same when I pilfered this from you, Sprite. I knew it wasn't enough."

His heart began to soften, his vexation cool. Miscommunications were likely. They were confused, both of them. Torn over their feelings for each other. Two strong-willed personalities faced with an overwhelming attraction neither had expected. The effort to meld varied lives, a task requiring careful consideration.

She was ready. Willing. *Here.* She wasn't leaving him. Was offering herself.

Their marriage would be a challenge; he didn't doubt it. She was stubborn as all hell. Held a grudge for longer than he thought she should. Was too intelligent for her own good, forget about her feelings regarding her independence. She wanted to manage her own business, and he didn't think being a countess would change her horticultural aspirations one iota. She probably didn't have a clue how to run a home of substantial size, deal with a large staff, which he was coming to find was a monumental task. He loved mornings, she late nights. They rubbed each other the wrong way on quite a few popular topics of conversation. She didn't pretend to agree with him. In truth, she often disagreed on principle.

But other than that...

Decided, he slipped her note back in his pocket. It was simple, as she'd said. He loved her. Her wit, her vitality, her grit. Her beautiful face and delectable figure. Her circuitous charm. The way little traces of cockney slipped into her speech after she'd had a glass of wine. The crinkle that popped between her brows when she stared him down. The freckle above her top lip, the scar on her left hand, both of which he'd run his tongue over on his exploration down her body. She was the only woman he wished to share his life with. The only he'd considered —and he would do anything to make it work. He thought they had an excellent chance of making each other happy if they could find a way to stop arguing for two seconds.

Hence, his blossoming heart.

Then Necessity Byrne of the Shoreditch Byrnes went and ruined his tender feelings.

She cupped his cheek, and he leaned into the caress. Stepped in until her plump breasts bumped his chest. "I'll come to Derbyshire when I can, and you will come here when you can. We'll be discreet but together. The Leighton Cluster will have to know. I'll break it to the Duchess Society that we're"—her hand trembled against his jaw—"decided on this path, and they will have to accept our choice. It isn't as if they aren't scandal-ridden in their own way, the lot of them. Gallons of ink spilt detailing their escapades."

Ollie's lips parted as a thousand responses rushed through his mind, the *least* of which was relief that Necessity seemed to be giving him the easy way out. When he'd chosen the difficult, damn her. He drew a coal-choked breath through his teeth. "What is this you're proposing, Nessie, because it doesn't sound like a proposal? Since you've already stated that you like to step in before the gentleman can decide what he wants, I thought to leave it to you. Although the gentleman in this case *knows* what he wants."

"I'm asking to live my life with you. The telescope is my silly way of asking you to share my life. Bring what's most important from yours and be with me." She shut her mouth so fast her teeth clicked together. Took a protective step back at the look that swept his face. He felt the heat, the temper rising within him.

"Proposal? Of marriage?"

She patted her chest, lost, bewildered. Then patted his, consoling. "Ollie, I can't be your countess."

"Why the hell not?" he snapped, yanking his hand through his hair rather than give her a shake that might not be gentle. "I'm managing the earl thing well enough, and I didn't want that burden heaped on my shoulders, either."

She shook her head, mystified. Curled her fingers around the button and gazed sightlessly at her fist. It made him angrier, no surprise because she was like brandy tossed on his hearth fire most days, that she hadn't even considered it. "I'd never be accepted. It will do you no good to marry me. I have no dowry, only the money I've earned from working. *Working*, Ollie. I'm from Shoreditch, a rookery girl through and through even if I now live on the edges of Mayfair. Above a glove shop. Don't you smell the leather from here? White's would discharge you. Almack's. You wouldn't be invited to musicales or balls or—"

"*Stop*." He grabbed her hand before she had a chance to chew on her nail, another of her nervous tells. "Look at me, Nessie. Look hard and tell me if I care about those things. I'm not the greatest catch. I have issues. Ones you're aware of. I have a meddling family that is growing larger by the day. An earldom that is going to take two to manage. I think I'm getting the better deal in every way."

She followed his order, gazing up at him with the slenderest trace of hope in her brilliant eyes. *So*, he thought. She had considered it. She merely hadn't let herself believe he'd offer.

"I love you with everything I have. There isn't more I can give you because you already have it. My heart, my soul is there for the taking. If only you'd open *your* heart and let me in." He rushed on when he could see her preparing to argue. "I'm not disputing we'd be a scandal the first year, Sprite. Gossiped about all over Town, splashed across the society columns, the chatter rags. My page ripped from *Debrett's* in some households. Well and truly examined, our marriage. Like a bug encased in amber. I don't care. Let them question how we found each other in this mad world. I hope they seethe in envy. And the money isn't an issue and never has been. I'm investing with Xander. I'll be fine. Someday."

"Love. You love me. I thought you did but to hear it..." She exhaled weakly and fluttered her fingers as if she was out of breath. "Countess. Your wife. Josephine Byrne married to an earl. Fifth Earl of Stanford." She backed against a small brick wall near the door and slid to perch her bottom atop the narrow ledge. Dropping her head to her hands, she whispered, "I need a moment. I feel faint."

He grinned, going down on his knee where he should have been from the start. "**Sixth**, but no matter. My father would be insulted, which makes me extremely happy." Taking the hand still clasping his button, he brought it to his lips, pressing a kiss to the taut curve of her knuckles. "I have something else. I've been carrying it around since you left me high and dry in Derbyshire. Wounded heart and all that."

She lifted her head, the first spark of irritation he'd seen in minutes, a new record, lighting her eyes. "I didn't leave you. I would never leave you. I was only doing what I thought was sensible. If I went with my heart, we'd have been married weeks ago. After the first night spent in that blasted coach house. I might have asked then. I was so taken."

Love pierced him, right through his chest. "Taken. Necessity Byrne of the Shoreditch Byrnes taken. I can hardly comprehend."

Finally giving in, she smiled, her lashes fluttering rather shyly. Accepting the opportunity, one of the few tender emotions she allowed, he withdrew the velvet box and cracked it open. The trio of diamonds glittered in the moonlight, turning the band a luminous gold. "The ring was my grandmother's. I've never thought to give it to anyone, Sprite. Never imagined I would, in case you wondered. If I bought one for you, I couldn't pick a ring more... well, right. I've always rather loved it myself. Had it since I was five years old, waiting, I guess. For you."

She held out her hand, spread her fingers. His shook when he slipped it on, his heart racing. The fit was good, not perfect as her fingers were slimmer than his grandmother's, but nothing a jeweler couldn't fix in a jiffy.

Necessity was saying yes, in her way. And that was fine. He'd asked in *his* way. She wasn't trying to change him, nor was he trying to change her. They understood each other, wanted each other. Eccentricities and foibles. Loved each other—

He blinked and rocked back on his heels. "You love me, right? I think you forgot to say it."

She laughed, another sound close to a giggle. A night of astounding events, to be sure. Curling her hand around the nape of his neck, she drew him in for a blistering kiss. "Would I gift a man I didn't love with everything in me a stolen telescope? Bring him home to meet my cat? Offer to restore his gardens in the spring free of charge? Promise to give him children if we're blessed enough? Promise to never, *ever* leave him again? Not for one night if I can help it."

Ollie laid his brow atop hers, happiness catching him like a blow. "Dear God, it *is* stolen. The Metropolitan Police will be pounding on my door tomorrow morning. Everyone in London knows I have an affinity for the stars."

She trailed her finger down his cheek, maneuvering to get her way. He didn't mind being duly persuaded. "Do we have to return it? Since it's already here. I think it would look lovely in the library in Derbyshire, where we shall spend as much time as possible. Well away from London."

He glanced over his shoulder. The telescope was standing proudly against a glorious backdrop, a hundred winking prisms of light tucked into dark velvet folds. It was the most gorgeous piece he'd ever seen. Xander would surely have a way to get it out of town without notice.

Hmm, his brother *and* his future countess were thieves, and he thought he liked it. "I did work hard for it," he murmured.

She huffed a sigh, then laughed. Drew his head around to kiss him again, ending it by biting his lip. Her usual move, one that brought him low. "I'm going to stop expecting everything you say to sit well with me, Oliver."

"If you did, I'd be eternally confused." He pulled her into the protective curve of his body, shooting a glance at the sky. Two hours of darkness left if he judged correctly. At dawn, he was heading home, changing clothes, then going directly to his solicitor's. Followed by a trip to Xander's to tell his brother the news. "How do cats feel about amorous congress, Miss Byrne?"

Necessity bounded to her feet, tugging him across the rooftop toward the door. "They're in favor, my lord earl. Always in favor. Don't you hear them screeching in the alleys? They love it."

Grabbing her around the waist, he swung her over his shoulder, kicked the door open, and took the staircase at a mad dash as she shrieked with laughter. "That's a good thing, then, Sprite. A very good thing."

Epilogue

WHERE AN EARL AND HIS COUNTESS COUNT THEIR BLESSINGS

Derbyshire, Two Years Later

Vines were no longer overtaking the fruit trees. The conservatory windows were no longer shattered. The lawns were neatly trimmed, the side garden filled with flowering shrubs and snaking lines of vegetables. The oak and gum trees the Countess of Stanford had planted along the western edge were thriving, although it would be years before they provided privacy or sufficient shade. The perfume of viburnum and tuberose colored the air, the high chirp of sparrows and the throaty call of finches. Amazingly, Necessity had not known much about birds before coming to live in the country. Now she kept copious lists of what she'd seen each day.

Lifting her hand to shade her eyes, she noted the stream that meandered through the estate's meadow, sparkling in the late summer sun, making for a perfect Sunday afternoon.

The men were on the lawn, gathered round the bowls playing field. Like the vivid splash of sunlight, so much masculine beauty hurt her eyes to witness it. Dash and the Duke of Leighton had gotten into a tussle earlier over a wild pitch the duke said broke an obscure rule no one had ever heard of. They'd gotten in each other's faces, the woman groaning and backing away. Then they were on the ground, grunting and swinging, a tangle of arms and legs, while the others, her husband included, cheered them on. The only man who seemed bored by the bloodshed was the Duke of Markham. He'd wandered off in a quest for tea in the middle of the scuffle, indifferent to the battle. Now, Dash and Leighton were bloodied and bruised, wearing torn clothing and huge smiles.

Oddly, this tribe seemed happier after a beating.

She didn't understand it. Understand *men*, not completely. She'd tried since their marriage to learn everything she could about Ollie. Every. Last. Thing. Her fascination with her husband only increased by the second. There was no one cleverer or more intelligent or kinder. Much like the men he surrounded himself with, she'd come to find.

Therefore, despite her bewilderment regarding the male species, she wanted her children to grow up among this boisterous group. She laid her hand on her belly, her heart giving a fast kick. Especially if the babe she carried was a boy. The Leighton Cluster were loving and loyal, welcoming her with the generosity society had not shown her marriage to the Earl of Stanford. The Country Countess, they called her. Silly, when she wasn't from the country. She tried not to read the society columns, and Ollie did his best to keep them from view.

Not that she cared. Her newfound stature had helped her business, the hypocrites. They wanted the Country Countess to make their estates beautiful. Or they wanted the association, she realized, but she was the best since Capability Brown, so it was no skin off her nose to take their money in exchange for her talent.

Nonetheless, in spite of the gossip and her resentment at a circle he'd been born into and could not remove himself from if he tried, Ollie was happy. His nightmares easing, his headaches almost nonexistent now that he took the prescribed chamomile tea twice a day. He was unjustly handsome standing there, his silver-streaked hair so long it curled over his collar, grazing his shoulders, *oh*, those muscular shoulders of his. Her hands twitched to recall clutching them as they made love this morning, laughing because they'd tried, possibly without success, to be quiet with a full house of visitors.

As if he heard her thoughts, he stilled, glancing her way. Time slowed to the merest faint beating of their hearts. Memory swept his face, darkened his eyes to a gray, near black. He recalled where they'd been two hours ago, lost in each other. He took a step toward her, an unconscious movement, before his brother jabbed him in the ribs bringing him back.

She nodded to his game, then the window of their bedchamber. *Later, my love.* He flushed, a faint tinge in his cheeks, something honest and sweet about him that never failed to make her fall that much harder.

With the men chuckling at his adored display, he returned to the game. Flicked his wrist and tossed the ball, a flawless throw that knocked his brother's outside the boundary. He truly was an athletic man, captivating to watch play any sport. Macauley shot him an incensed look, then he smirked, and bumped Ollie's shoulder hard enough to have him stumbling to the side. Then they were pushing, shouting insults, dancing with fists raised, but thankfully not collapsing to the lawn in a brawling heap. Acting as savior, Tobias Streeter stepped in and shoved them apart.

Though he didn't need to. Xander and Ollie were closer than any siblings she'd ever known. Content to share their businesses and families and aspirations. They holed up in the study here or at the warehouse in London, talking and working into the night. They genuinely seemed to *like* each other. It was as if they were making up for lost time, which she understood. If her family was alive, she'd have brought them to London or Derbyshire and made sure they lived down the street so she could see them every day.

The brothers were building lives together when they'd once been forced to conduct them apart.

She was determined to have two mischievous boys just like them, men who grew up to love each other without reservation. Who had parents who cared enough to protect such a delicate bond rather than seeking to destroy it.

Pippa sidled up alongside her, hooked her arm through Necessity's, and drew her close. "I've missed you, Countess. It has been at least a month since we've seen each other."

"You're busy with preparations for Theo's wedding, playing the part of the devoted sister, which you are. Hildy and Georgie didn't even come this weekend. They're so overwhelmed with planning. I can't believe it's next week! Where does time go, I wonder? I hope the florist I recommended is working out. Macon and Deloitte come highly recommended. I believe they've arranged for a number of the King's events, although one pays dearly for such distinction. Mr. Deloitte was extremely particular about the terrace garden I revamped for his family."

Pippa whistled a sigh and shifted from foot to foot. And in a move utterly unlike her, abruptly changed the subject. "Look at them, the bunch of buffoons. Xander constantly has a bruised face from this group's antics. Aren't they gorgeous, though? Scarred earls and rookery titans and impervious dukes. We have it all, don't we? My goodness, Dash looks like a Greek god with that short haircut. It was getting so you couldn't see his face. I wish I could paint him because he's so pretty, but I can't draw a straight line."

Pippa and her sister-by-marriage, Theo, were the family Necessity had lost to cholera. She adored them. They were hers now, the Leighton Cluster. And she theirs.

"Are you going to tell him? You must let me know when you do," Pippa, the wicked imp, whispered in Necessity's ear. She loved stirring up trouble, adored gossip and shenanigans. "The first baby, oh my, when he finds out, Ollie won't be racing around like this for days. He'll be staring into space. Talking to himself. Stumbling into walls. Be prepared to arrange for his tea and keep him out of harm's way for at least two weeks. Xander almost got run down by a rubbish cart after I told him about Kit. Tobias escorted him everywhere for a time."

Necessity slanted Pippa an amused glance, her lips twitching. "Are you going to tell *your* husband? I will when you do."

Pippa brought her hand to her mouth and chewed on her thumbnail. "Xander's going to faint. Dead away. I'll need salts to revive him. Then laudanum to calm him once he wakes from the blackout, where he'll likely hit his head and knock himself senseless. We'd decided, planned, hoped to wait. Maybe a year, two if possible. Until we have both babies out of nappies and Kit sleeping in the nursery for an entire night instead of with us. What will *three* children bring? I barely have time to breathe as it is. We don't have a bed big enough for five. Of course, we adore the chaos. Drowning in delight, swimming in bliss. But mark my words, enjoy your slumber before the upheaval." She groaned and let her arm drop to her side. "I suppose I'll sleep when they go to university."

"I can't wait. I want scuffles in the parlor and skinned knees and jam smears on my skirts. Stolen biscuits and loose teeth and teaching someone to read. A family so big it's terrifying. I want what I lost. Ollie is..." She swallowed, tears pricking her eyes, salting her throat, amazed still by her luck in finding him. "He'll be thrilled, beyond thrilled. He has so much love to give, Pippa, more than anyone realizes. *He's* only coming to realize. I didn't want to say anything in case... well, you know things can happen. It's safe now, I believe."

Pippa squeezed her hand. "Tell him. But be patient. Because your trips all over London in that snappy little cabriolet Ollie bought you are over. You won't have another business meeting without him in attendance for months. My freedom, as well, will be gone. Done. Finito. My visits to the workhouse and the orphanage I support will resume after the baby is born. Xander gets extremely panicky when I'm carrying. What I'm eating. How I'm feeling. The wind blows, and he's concerned it's hurting me or the baby. I imagine his brother will be much the same. The hardest men to catch are also the hardest to fall. Good luck, is what I'm trying to say. Enjoy the affection he'll shower you with. That part is nice."

Necessity smiled, delighted to imagine Ollie's reaction. He continuously showered her with affection. Nothing would change there. Tonight when they were alone, before bed, she was going to tell him.

Pippa sucked in a sharp breath and pointed, which the Duchess Society had told Necessity one must never do. Evidently, Pippa had handled her lessons with Hildy and Georgie about as smoothly as she had. "What's *he* doing here?"

Necessity circled her velvet bonnet ribbon around her finger and gave it a yank, having expected this question from her inquisitive sister-in-law sooner than this. "Who?"

Pippa snickered and bumped her shoulder, rocking them both.

"Don't jest with me, Countess. Jasper Noble, that's who. He and Xander get along like two cats in a sack as I'm sure you're aware. If they start fighting, it won't be an affable sport. We'll need needle and thread to stitch them up."

Necessity shrugged even as her posture stiffened. Jasper Noble was one of her own. "What can I say? He's lonesome, and I'm persistent. We're Shoreditch chums from way back. He would never tell me he's troubled, but I can tell he is. If I accept the anarchy I've been thrust into with Ollie's friends, he can accept one of my old pals coming to the country for a visit. I'm sorry it's not a society chit who wants to splash watercolors on a canvas and sew a heart on a hankie but instead a scoundrel with a dreadful reputation. *That's* the kind of friends I have, and Ollie knew going in what he was getting."

Pippa grunted, eyeing Jasper like he was an insect that had landed on her piece of cake.

"Be charitable, Pippa. I know you have it in you to be. It's your chosen vocation to help those in need, isn't it? Remember the shape Macauley was in when you met him? The women he was consorting with? The high jinks? Not as bad as Ollie's opium adventure or anything, true. This is close to what Jasper Noble is going through."

"Pathetic shape. I worked for months to turn him around," Pippa grumbled, tilting her head in contemplation. "Noble does have the appearance of a man with secrets. And you know me. I appreciate a mystery. Perhaps you should ask the Duchess Society to get involved. They'll clean him up right and proper. Find someone who wants him that's not a light-skirt. Maybe. He'd be a challenging project."

"I might do that. Actually, he and Macauley have a lot in common if they'd get their heads out of their—"

Pippa sputtered a laugh and grabbed Necessity's hand before she finished the statement. "We're more than friends, darling. We're family. Besides, they'll never get their heads out of there, don't you know? Stuck up their bums for *life*."

They hooted, catching the attention of the men gathered round a mound of balls they were studying as if answers were written on them. Ollie gave her a look of such devotion that her heart skipped, and she drifted toward him as if he held a rope and was guiding her to shore.

Pippa threw up her hands, following along. "Newlyweds."

"You cheated, mate," Necessity heard Macauley say when she arrived. He nudged a red ball with the toe of his boot. "Wasn't in that position when it landed, Noble. I'm not blind. Streeter, was the ball in that position?"

Tobias Streeter frowned, pushing his spectacles down and looking over the frames. "I'm not sure. Good toss if it's legal."

Ollie hauled Necessity against his side, wrapping his arm around her shoulders, pressing a kiss to the crown of her head. They didn't go long without touching when they were together. She wanted this to never, ever change. Even if the Leighton Cluster made fun of them for it. "No one except my wife can best me in bowls, so what's the harm in a spot of cheating, Xan?"

Jasper kicked a ball outside the gaming area. The group watched it roll beneath an azalea shrub Necessity realized needed pruning. "I didn't cheat. Excellent pitch was what it was. I've been playing this game since I was in leading strings, *mate*. You're the notorious swindler, Macauley, not me. I play on the up and up."

Macauley jacked his thumb toward the house. "Up and up? What about that damned telescope in Ollie's study? A piece that should be housed in the British Museum. We all know where *that* came from. Word on the street is, a certain viscount wants it back."

"I'm not returning it," Ollie murmured so low no one heard the comment but his wife.

"Finders keepers, isn't that what they say? Maybe a 'certain viscount' owed a debt, and the looking glass for the stars was payment." Jasper tossed a ball back and forth between his hands, his grin assertively feral. He fit in with this group, though it would have surprised him to recognize it. "Or maybe it is stolen, and the Limehouse King is sorry he didn't make the hit. We Shoreditch men are more dignified in our larceny, so I understand your confusion. Meaning, you shall never know the truth of the matter."

Macauley took a step forward, fists clenched. Then he grinned and glanced at his wife. "You know, Noble, my darling Pip is always telling me to use my intellect before my fists. So I'm thinking, how would a man from the slums be playing bowls as a child? Since leading strings, innit? Most of us rookery lads didn't have those kinds of advantages."

Jasper's ball hit the ground with a thunk. Yet when he rose from picking it up, the color Necessity had seen drain from his cheeks was back. "No idea what you mean, *mate*."

Unable to stand keeping her husband in the dark for another minute now that she'd decided to tell him about the babe, Necessity took Ollie's hand and dragged him from the brawl that was likely to start. He had time to wrestle with the Leighton Cluster any old day. "You can fight with your friends later."

Ollie nuzzled her cheek, slowing his stride to hers as they crossed the lawn. "It's your friend you should stay and protect, perhaps. Probably a good thing Leighton isn't here to see this."

Necessity pressed her nose to his chest and breathed deeply. He smelled like home. Love. The future. "Jasper Noble can hold his own, don't you worry. This crowd may be exactly what he needs."

"What do you need, Sprite? That's what I'm interested in."

Linking their hands together, she brought his fingers to her lips. "I need *you*."

He tipped her chin and kissed her. Lingered until she moaned softly and leaned into him. "You have me, Necessity, Countess Stanford."

I have *everything*, she thought and pulled him inside.

Where she was set to, once again, change his life.

THE END

Thank-you for reading *One Wedding and an Earl*!

Next in line in *The Duchess Society series* is Dash and Theo's story in *Two Scandals and a Scot*. Coming soon!

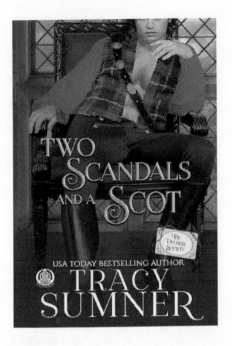

In the meantime, have you read all of the Duchess Society books including the prequel and the newly released Christmas novella *The Governess Gamble*?

THE DUCHESS SOCIETY SERIES

To save her reputation, American heiress Franny Shaw has fled to London in search of a desperate nobleman with a title for sale. An impulsive decision places her in the path of lonely libertine, Chance Allerton. Can a make-believe governess teach a wicked viscount a sizzling lesson in love?

Thank you!

Thank you for reading Ollie and Nessie's love story! This couple was such glorious fun to write! A kind but rough-edged earl and the stubborn, vivacious woman he loves. A scarred stargazer and a rookery chit. What could be better?

Next in line in *The Duchess Society* series is Dash and Theo's story (not spoiling or anything but you knew it was coming) in *Two Scandals and a Scot*. A dull professor is *not* going to be Theo's fate. Then, I'm considering a romp involving Jasper Noble, who stepped OFF the page for me while writing this book, much as Xander Macauley did during the writing of *The Brazen Bluestocking*! *Three Sins and a Scoundrel*, maybe? I can promise second chance, second chance, second chance! My favorite trope, as many of you know. I'd love to hear what you think about Jasper and if he can make a proper hero.

Stephen King says in *On Writing* that we reuse themes as authors. I think this is true. I love writing stories about brothers and male bonding. The Duchess Society is actually a series about the men in the Leighton Cluster as much as anyone. My series, *The Garrett Brothers*, is full of this backslapping and brawling. In fact, if I think about it, the *League of Lords* follows this theme as well. All I can say is, men and their complex relationships is my joy to write!

Little nuggets of gold for those who want to know more about *One Wedding and an Earl*.

1. Capability Brown was a real person, the most famous landscape architect in England in the 18th century! I've mentioned him previously in a couple of books. It must be his name. I just love it.
2. I chose Ollie's title after a favorite character, Stanford Blatch, from *Sex and the City*.
3. As anyone who knows me may recall, I am #teamjess (*Gilmore Girls*) all the way. For life. Remember when Necessity "looks it up"? If you have to ask yourself what that means in the Gilmore world, you aren't at the Rory/Jess level that I am. Which may be a good thing. But I'll share my thinking when I wrote it. As it was for Jess, who didn't want to admit his love either, Necessity's research was an early falling-in-love clue. Who else would take the time to look up Ollie's title in *Debrett's*? Though she continues to confuse if he is the fifth or sixth earl, you gotta love that she put in the effort. How like a rookery girl to fight for what she wants!

Happy reading, as always! Romance is the best.
xoxo
Tracy

Also by Tracy Sumner

The Duchess Society Series

The Ice Duchess *(Prequel)*

The Brazen Bluestocking

The Scandalous Vixen

The Wicked Wallflower

One Wedding and an Earl

Two Scandals and a Scot (coming spring 2023)

Christmas novella: The Governess Gamble

League of Lords Series

The Lady is Trouble

The Rake is Taken

The Duke is Wicked

The Hellion is Tamed

Garrett Brothers Series

Tides of Love

Tides of Passion

Tides of Desire: A Christmas Romance

Southern Heat Series

To Seduce a Rogue

To Desire a Scoundrel: A Christmas Seduction

Standalone Regency romances

Tempting the Scoundrel

Chasing the Duke

About Tracy Sumner

 *USA TODAY* bestselling and award-winning author Tracy Sumner's storytelling career began when she picked up a historical romance on a college beach trip, and she fondly blames LaVyrle Spencer for her obsession with the genre. She's a recipient of the National Reader's Choice, and her novels have been translated into Dutch, German, Portuguese and Spanish. She lived in New York, Paris and Taipei before finding her way back to the Lowcountry of South Carolina.

When not writing sizzling love stories about feisty heroines and their temperamental-but-entirely-lovable heroes, Tracy enjoys reading, snowboarding, college football (Go Tigers!), yoga, and travel. She loves to hear from romance readers!

Connect with Tracy: www.tracy-sumner.com

Acknowledgments

Thanks to my amazing Facebook readers' team, the Contrary Countesses, for proposing writing a scarred hero. I added Ollie's accident during the writing of *The Wicked Wallflower* after a discussion with the Countesses.

Also, kudos to Beth, who suggested I feature a star-gazing hero. (And for her *unwavering* support, which writers need.) The telescope plays a *critical* role in this novel. I love that Ollie looks to the heavens for guidance!

Now, for character names, I incorporated a few into *One Wedding and an Earl* that the Countesses came up with. Michelle, Anne, and Vicki, whose combined efforts helped me create my new hero, Jasper Noble, who is anything but noble. That one line from my group set Jasper up in my mind. (He'll be featured in *Three Sins and a Scoundrel,* so watch out for him. I think he's going to be a confounding presence for a certain feisty woman.) And to Liz, who came up with the lovely name of the widow in the village who keeps our hero, Ollie, um, happy until he meets his match in Necessity Byrne.

Finally, thanks to Chris Hall, editor extraordinaire, who finds things I occasionally still insist upon using. For example, the ghost orchid was not discovered until 1848. Forgive Necessity. Forgive me. My heroine could think of no other flower while looking into Ollie's eyes. And this woman knows her flowers!

Happy reading, always!